Soon, Felicia will be better off dead…

The fog was so thick that morning that Augie was concerned that it might keep Felicia inside. But she didn't disappoint him. Felicia came out for her run…alone.

He followed her invisibly, padding softly in silent sneakers, like a mischievous ghost, shrouded in fog, ready to materialize out of the mist to play his erotic prank.

Augie was the Transmitter of dreams, and Felicia was the Receiver, powerless to disobey his commands.

He led her into the dense fog … deeper … deeper … among ghostly trees and shrubs. Her pretty blonde face wore a vacant expression, blind to everything but her lust.

Augie never removed his mask…

THE ACADEMY

JOHN A. RUSSO

Burning Bulb
PUBLISHING

The Academy
by **John A. Russo**

Burning Bulb Publishing
P.O. Box 4721
Bridgeport, WV 26330-4721
www.BurningBulbPublishing.com

Cover designed by Gary Lee Vincent with the following licensed elements from Fotolia:
– Beautiful robotic woman as a symbol of human development © Arman Zhenikeyev

First Burning Bulb Publishing printing.

Edition ISBN Paperback 978-0692226193

Printed in the United States of America

Library of Congress Control Number: 2014941555

For my daughter, Julia

Special thanks to Andrew M. Schifino and Russell W. Streiner for technical information and to Sean Justice for constructive criticism and creative suggestions.

We have reached a critical turning point in the evolution of man at which the mind can be used to influence its own structure, functions, and purpose, thereby ensuring both the preservation and advance of civilization.

Dr. José Delgato
Yale University

Not only our pleasure, our joy and our laughter, but also our sorrow, pain, grief and tears arise from the brain, and the brain alone. With it we think and understand, see and hear, and we discriminate between the ugly and the beautiful, between what is pleasant and unpleasant and between good and evil.

Hippocrates

In the field of brain physiology, I think it is the most exciting single discovery. I am almost frightened to say what might come of this.

Dr. Robert H. Felix
testifying before the Senate
Appropriations Subcommittee
on Health

PROLOGUE

Behind bulletproof glass, the two chimps were squatting side by side, shelling and eating peanuts from a barrel.

They were observed by two dark-suited men from the Department of Health, Education and Welfare.

Dr. Vincent Parkhurst, a short, bald, lab-coated scientist with a red Vandyke, was chaperoning the two dark-suited men. He told them, "The one on the left, the female, is Coca. The male is Jimbo. They normally get along like that – very compatible."

"Do they ... er ... make love?" one of the dark-suited gentlemen asked.

"They do when Coca is in estrus," said Dr. Parkhurst. "In the normal course of things, about once a year."

"Is there an abnormal 'course of things'?" the other dark-suited man said.

"Well," said Dr. Parkhurst, "we can make Jimbo rape Coca any time we want to. We can make him or her do just about anything."

They were just two ordinary-looking chimps, eating peanuts.

"Make them do something," one of the dark-suited men said.

"In a moment they'll start," Dr. Parkhurst said, glancing at his watch.

Jimbo and Coca had stopped eating peanuts and were taking turns grooming each other.

"Very domestic. Very tranquil. Like an elderly married couple," said one of the dark-suited men from the Department of Health, Education and Welfare.

Suddenly, as if both Coca and Jimbo had been seized by the same idea at the same time, they got up and started strutting around the bulletproof glass cage, one behind the other, arms dangling, paws touching the floor, as if they were performing a simian version of a Sousa march.

One of the dark-suited men broke out singing, "Oh the monkeys chased their tails around the flagpole..." He chuckled, proud of his sense of humor.

Jimbo and Coca stopped marching. They froze in a half-hunkering position, staring straight ahead at the three humans outside the glass. Then they each raised and held their right arms straight out to the side, parallel to the floor. They retained this rigid poses for thirty seconds; then, in perfect unison, they lowered their right arms and extended their left arms.

"Monkey see, monkey do," said one of the dark-suited men.

"Oh, no, they're not *aping* each other," said the other, smiling at his pun. "They're behaving in the same fashion simultaneously, as if on order... on cue."

"Exactly," declared Dr. Parkhurst.

The two chimps lowered their arms and went down on all fours, like a pair of slaves groveling before their masters.

Then Jimbo jumped up. Coca stayed down. Jimbo snarled and spat at her, angrily and ferociously baring his teeth. Then he ran to the peanut barrel and overturned it, madly scooping out the peanuts, sending them flying everywhere. At the bottom of the barrel, he found a pistol —

a .22 revolver. He pointed it at the three humans and squeezed the trigger again and again. Dr. Parkhurst didn't duck, although he may have flinched a bit. The two dark-suited men gasped and scurried... but the loud reports were harmless to them – the .22 slugs were deflected by the bulletproof glass.

Coca wasn't so lucky as the three humans. Screaming and snarling fiercely, Jimbo shot her three times. He kept pulling the trigger even when the pistol was out of ammo...click...click...click...

"My God!" one of the dark-suited men exclaimed.

"Extraordinary!" proclaimed the other.

Suddenly, all of Jimbo's anger left him. His rage simply evaporated, and he was left meek...docile...and apparently remorseful. He crouched, whimpering over Coca's bloody corpse.

"You *made* him do that?" asked one of the dark-suited men.

"My wife did," said Dr. Parkhurst, with a faintly smug and enigmatic smile. "She's in the next room."

"In the next *room* you say?" the dark-suited man said, incredulously.

"Behind that closed door," said Dr. Parkhurst. "Come with me, gentlemen, and we'll show you how we do it. Some of it is training, of course. But not the most important part. The most important part is control."

The two dark-suited men from the Department of Health, Education and Welfare went with Dr. Vincent Parkhurst to be introduced by him to his wife and research partner, Dr. Carol Parkhurst.

THE ACADEMY

In the bulletproof glass cage, Jimbo was still whimpering and mewling over the lifeless body of his mate.

CHAPTER 1

On the day she took her first bad spell, Felicia Patterson rode a bus downtown from Fairchild Academy right after four o'clock dismissal. She was wearing the distinctive plaid skirt, blue blazer and matching blue knee socks that all female Academy students wore, and she had a drugstore purchase to make that would cause her less embarrassment in the bustle of downtown Manhattan, where she wasn't likely to bump into any of her classmates.

She wasn't' an ordinary schoolgirl – she understood that fact without being smug about it. She was more intelligent and prettier than the average fifteen-year-old. But, of course, it was no big deal. All of her classmates were special, too. Only the best and the brightest stood a ghost of a chance of being accepted by Fairchild Academy. Being surrounded by so many high achievers helped keep Felicia humble and motivated.

She had the highest grades in her sophomore class in the most rigorous private school in New York, so she ought to be fairly satisfied with herself. Nothing earth-shattering should be bothering her. Sometimes, when she was alone, she stared at herself in the bedroom mirror, winked mockingly at the ruddy, youthful blonde features that grinned sardonically back at her and realized how absurd it was for anybody who looked so healthy and normal to have any hidden problems. She figured that a lot of teenagers, even some of the ones at Fairchild, would gladly trade places with her. Hell, they'd be on cloud nine if they had her marks. There was no reason for her to believe that anything was drastically wrong with her life just because she felt a little flat when she wasn't in school.

Well, to be quite honest, it was more than a *little* flat; it was an utter lack of enthusiasm. Smoking grass with her boyfriend didn't even help. She didn't seem to get high. Never could. Couldn't get very horny either. She had gone all the way with Ted just to find out if it was all it was cracked up to be, and she had found that for her it wasn't. It was almost amusing to her that she had given up the dubious honor (or at least the uniqueness) of her virginity in return for a smidgen of pleasure, instead of the whopping Big O gloriously celebrated in song and story. Thank God that Ted seemed to enjoy himself well enough and apparently believed that it was all right for her.

She told herself she probably wasn't undersexed; it was just that she was pouring so much energy into more important things. Carrying a heavy scholastic load could be more draining for her than for others. Besides, she was more wrapped up in her studies than anyone else she knew. Later in life, she supposed, she would have time to awaken her sensuality, to get married and have children. But, for right now, being a star student at Fairchild Academy was a lot to handle. Sex simply wasn't one of her priorities for the time being. But she still felt left out when other girls her age giggled and carried on about it and she was unable to share their titillation and verve. Sometimes Felicia wondered if they were all pretending, the way they all pretended to like the same rock stars. So she pretended, too. She didn't let them guess that she could be less turned on in the arms of her boyfriend then in the throes of a particularly engaging computer exercise.

For instance, in school today, she had worked out some complex applications of Mendel's Law, using a computer program designed at the Fairchild Educational and Psychological Research Institute, with which the Fairchild Academy was affiliated. Practically, all of the software, the textbooks and the audio/visual aids used at the Academy were developed by the Institute. It made Felicia proud to be using equipment and methods far in advance of what could be found in most other American schools. They might catch up someday, she thought, once they were shown the way. Her sense of accomplishment was heightened by the notion that she was helping to pioneer dynamic educational techniques.

But why did all of her good, vibrant feelings evaporate at the end of each school day? Today was no exception. She had felt listless from the time her alarm went off. Her morning jog in Central Park hadn't perked her up very much; even the dewy, bird-chirping spring weather was something she could appreciate mentally, but not emotionally. She had little appetite for the hearty breakfast of pancakes and sausage that her mother laid out for her; so she merely nibbled a bit, gulped down her orange juice and made a sneaky getaway, mumbling something about having an upset stomach.

The only reason she was anxious to go to school was that somehow she always felt better once she got there. Thank God, it happened again today, soon as the bell rang and classes got underway. The business of learning made Felicia excited and glad to be alive. It gave her a tingly glow. Energy seemed to flow from her pores and synapses. Nothing meant more to her than what she was doing right now. She became totally absorbed in every lecture and each scholastic activity. She ended the school day on a high note of personal achievement, having successfully worked her way through the difficult computer exercise on predicting the generational patterns of dominant and recessive genetic traits.

Then, soon after the dismissal bell rang, the letdown started. Felicia began feeling empty, directionless, completely unambitious. It was like sliding back into a mundane existence after an interlude of glittering, entertaining adventure. She told herself she must be some kind of weird workaholic, happy only when she was stuffing her brain with knowledge. But, if that was what truly turned her on, why didn't she ever feel like doing any extra studying on her own? Probably because she was already driving herself too hard. The Academy took too much out of her. It provided such a high-intensity "total learning environment" that homework wasn't considered necessary by the staff, was not a policy and was even frowned on, because it could not be properly supervised and was, therefore, more likely to be harmful, instead of beneficial.

When Felicia and Ted were first getting involved with each other, she opened up enough to tell him that school was the best part of her life. She thought he might understand her or even feel a little the same way, since he also was an Academy student and had high grades. But he almost laughed in her face. He thought she was joking. "You're *serious!*" he finally exclaimed in amazement. "You're pretty strange, Felicia, you know it? You're the only kid I know who isn't aching to escape from those slave drivers."

"But they're preparing us so well for college," Felicia defended.

"I'll grant you that," said Ted. "I'll probably go through four years of Harvard like some kind of whiz kid after having my brain force-fed and fine-tuned at Fairchild Academy."

"Don't knock it, then," said Felicia with a lame chuckle. Today, like every other school day, the worst part of her letdown lasted about an hour. By the time she got the bus in Times Square, her mood was on the rebound and she was no longer so completely deflated. The threat of sinking into bottomless despair had given way to a subtle, mild depression. Of late, this was a normal way for her to feel, and she could live with it, counting her hours till tomorrow morning. Then the bell would ring and she would have plenty of things to keep her busy and involved.

The first bad spell hit her in the drugstore. It didn't start out bad, but just strange. In fact, at first she liked it. It gave her hope that a dormant part of her was coming alive, unbidden, on its own, and welcome – although it would have been considerably *more* welcome under slightly different circumstances.

She had come into the store to buy a tube of spermicidal gel, and her intention was to get in, make the transaction and get out as quickly as possible. The prospect of buying birth control stuff had her flustered, not so much because of the nature of the purchase, but because it was connected with an aspect of her life about which she felt inadequate. She quickly selected the product she wanted, glad that no other customers were in the immediate vicinity, and then considered buying a few additional things

11

so the one she had really come in for wouldn't stick out like a sore thumb.

She was shopping her way down between the aisles, her blue Academy blazer slung over her arm so she wouldn't look so much like a schoolgirl – unless the clerk at the cash register glanced down and spotted her knee socks – when a collection of books in one section of the paperback rack caught her eye. They had titles like *Him, Her, You, Me* and *Us*. They were part of a series of erotic novels that many of Felicia's classmates seemed to be hooked on. Ted called them "stroke books." Not exactly what Felicia wanted to plunk down beside the spermicidal gel. But perhaps another kind of novel would do. Her eyes scanned the titles.

Suddenly, almost against her will, she saw her hand reaching for the book entitled *Him*. An extremely lascivious feeling came over her. Her pulse quickened and her fingers trembled. She thumbed open the pages. *I don't want to read this*, a part of her mind cried out, while a contrary urge overwhelmed her.

For a moment she hesitated. She saw that nobody was browsing nearby, except a redheaded, freckle-faced young man in the next` aisle, apparently trying to make up his mind which brand of shaving cream to buy. He wasn't paying the least attention to her. Anyway, she decided not to give a damn if a total stranger saw her reading some pornography In the speed-reading clip she had been taught at Fairchild Academy, she devoured a salacious episode of cunnilingus and fellatio. She felt herself becoming terribly aroused, more so than she had ever been before. Her vagina tingled and moistened. Could a *book* do this to her when Ted couldn't?

Suddenly, all the erotic sensations stopped, like brakes screeching to a halt. Scared by how out of control she had been, she slammed the novel shut and stuffed it back into its slot on the rack. Her face felt hot. She was perspiring. With a jolt, she realized that the redheaded young man in the next aisle was staring at her, giving her the most awful lewd grin. She whirled and practically ran toward the front of the store, his mocking green eyes penetrating her from behind.

God! A long line! Three people ahead of her. She hoped the redhead wouldn't get in line behind her. But, when she glanced back, he was coming down the aisle toward the checkout counter, although he didn't have any drugstore items in his hands. Felicia breathed an inward sigh of relief when he stopped in front of the shelves of cough, cold and allergy remedies. He never once looked at her. His lewd grin was gone. Apparently, he had totally forgotten about her. Why did his nearness make her so uneasy? So what if he had been able to tell she had been turned on by what she'd been reading? It wasn't a crime. Why should she behave as if she'd been caught in an obscene act?

She bit her tongue and forced herself to slowly, silently count to ten. What in the world was happening to her? She had to stop this silliness. She was turning a few minutes of shopping into an emotional crisis. Overreacting. Making a big deal out of nothing. Why couldn't she calm herself down? She preferred her former lackadaisical state to this condition of unfathomable uptightness, but her heart kept racing and she kept feeling panicky. And desperate. But for no reason! *She needed to get out of this store.* But so far only one customer had been helped. Two more to go. And it was taking forever.

Felicia found herself becoming increasingly angry at the cash register clerk, a plump gray-haired woman with a pair of eyeglasses hanging on a chain around her neck. The woman did everything in slow motion. When she had to read price tags she put her glasses on and squinted, and when she worked the register she let the eyeglasses dangle. Instead of hurrying up, she was making chitchat. Didn't she know New Yorkers weren't *supposed* to be friendly? Not paying undue attention to each other allowed everybody to focus maximum energy on the urban survival struggle. Very pragmatic. But this one cash-register clerk was single-handedly trying to sabotage it.

By the time it came Felicia's turn to have her purchase rung up, she was half wild with itching, twitching impatience. She tried to stifle it. It was totally out of character for her. But she couldn't get a grip on herself. Couldn't control her temper. It was as if somebody had her brain in a vise and was turning the handle, slowly tightening . . . tightening . . .

"Hurry up, you slowpoke slob!" she heard herself snapping, her voice louder and shriller than she had ever heard it before. Even to herself she sounded like a crazy woman. A timid, sedate part of her wanted to stuff the ugly words back down her own throat and hide them forever, but a mischievous and gleeful side of her was thrilled at the way they had been spit out.

It was half-comic the way the cash-register clerk's loose jowls flapped open as her wide mouth gaped, showing large yellow teeth. She reminded Felicia of an old, fat cartoon bulldog. "Y-y-you better w-watch y-y-y-your mouth, young lady!" the clerk stammered. "N-next time leave your foul manners at home!"

"Fat-ass!" Felicia barked, "Just waddle over here and give me my change!"

All the customers in the drugstore were staring at Felicia now. Out of the corners of her hot, flashing eyes she caught a glimpse of the redheaded young man. The lewd grin was back on his freckled face.

"What kind of ignorant parents raised a spoiled brat like you?" the clerk blurted. "Here!" She slammed coins and bills on the counter. "*Take* your change and don't you ever set foot in here again!"

Feeling her lips twisting involuntarily into a leering grin, Felicia took her tube of spermicidal gel out of the bag and watched her fingers slowly unscrewing the cap. She squirted the thick, sticky gel into the fat clerk's spluttering face. Then she dropped the tube and ran from the store.

She kept running and running, hanging onto her purse by its shoulder strap, laughing uncontrollably when she bumped into or juked around pedestrians. All of a sudden she noticed her blue Fairchild Academy blazer flapping and dropping from under her arm. She had an urge to keep on running, to let the jacket be taken by the wind and carried along the sidewalk. But instead she stopped and twisted and caught it before it fell. Then she started to come to her senses. My God! She could get expelled for how she had carried on in the drugstore. That one sick thought permeated her as the angry spell started to deflate as abruptly as it had come over her in the first place. Her body was still shivering from the catharsis. The winos, tourists, prostitutes – the dirty, tawdry glitter and grind of Times Square – blurred around her as she walked.

She tried to pull herself together. At first she wasn't able to think rationally about what she had done . . . but, gradually, it began to settle into a shape that didn't give her any comfort. In fact it appalled her. She realized that she had never been in complete control of herself from the time she entered that drugstore. It was as if her mind was possessed by a demon making her do things and feel things contrary to her normal desires. She had taken "a spell." Calling it that made it sound absurdly quaint, archaic, but still frightening. What had brought it on? School pressures? Repressed sexuality? She hated to think she might be that neurotic. None of her classmates seemed to have any such hang-ups. Why was she the only one?

She remembered the tingly erotic sensations that had invaded her when she was reading the pornographic passages. At least now she knew she could *have* those kinds of feelings – deep down inside she wasn't a total iceberg. She only needed to release her inhibitions . . . if she dared.

Maybe it would be better not to risk being dominated by her unbridled passions. She had narrowly stopped short of having an orgasm right there in the store. Why hadn't she ever approached that degree of eroticism before? And why had it ceased so abruptly? As if a switch had been thrown on – and then off – somewhere in her subconscious. The blinding rage that had produced the grotesque incident with the check-out clerk had happened in much the same way.

Was she going insane? Having a nervous breakdown?

She couldn't comprehend how or why these strange forces had been unleashed inside herself, and she was terrified that it might happen again, driving her even farther over the edge.

CHAPTER 2

The redheaded, freckled young man with green eyes purchased a *True Crime* magazine in the drugstore. He got a kick out of the cover photo of a lovely young wench who had been roped to a fence by two tattooed men in leather masks. They had already slit her blouse so that her big tits were hanging out, and were in the act of using their long, sharp knives to slice away her panties. The redheaded young man knew that the articles in the magazine would be just as trashy as the cover. But he couldn't stand to read anything intellectually demanding anymore. His brain had been overloaded for too many years. Now his taste ran to escapism rather than depth. He liked cartoons, computer games, freaked-out rock videos, pornography and practical jokes.

Standing in line at the check-out counter, he got a large charge out of remembering the zany fit thrown a few minutes ago by the pretty little blonde in the blue knee socks. He had ridden with her on the bus, sitting a few seats back, and had followed her into the drugstore. Of course, he had suspected all along that she was a Receiver. And today he had proved it. Now he would be devoting a lot more attention to her.

He almost laughed out loud when he was waited on by the plump cartoon of a check-out clerk, who was still pretty much in a tizzy. She couldn't even count change right — gave him a dollar too much. So he pocketed it. He recalled how ridiculous she had looked with fat greasy worms of

17

spermicidal gel all over her chubby face; spluttering and flailing and turning beet red as if about to keel over from an apoplectic stroke.

He held his chortle in, but once outside the store he let it erupt. In that moment of outrageous hilarity, he decided to call himself "Augie" for the duration of his prankish escapade. He figured he ought to have a code name, since he was in essence a spy and a saboteur. What could be better than "Augie"? It was the perfect *nom de guerre*, fraught with ironic connotations, which heightened his amusement, spicing up his "secret mission."

Every bit of spice he could latch onto had to be savored. He was obliged to be his own entertainment committee, because nobody else could give him what he needed. On an intellectual level, he realized that his life was generally devoid of human warmth and congeniality. But he didn't know how to live in any other way. Romantic love, for instance, was something he considered only in the abstract; he didn't long for it; he couldn't conjure up any impressions of how it might feel, any more than a snail might imagine the sensations of winged flight. He told himself that what he had never felt, he would never miss. In the past his pleasures had mostly been those of the neocortex. But, gradually, even those channels seemed to have narrowed, so that now the kinds of things that stimulated his sense of humor or his sex drive tended to verge toward the unusual or the bizarre.

On the subway, heading back to his Greenwich Village apartment, he thumbed through his *True Crime* magazine, searching out the juiciest articles, scanning photos of mutilated corpses and moldering skeletons, as if they were appetite-stimulating hors d'oeuvres. He was intrigued by crimes of rape, torture and murder, and, at the same time, he was contemptuous of the perpetrators, since they operated on such a banal, lackluster level – far beneath his own capabilities.

He wryly took note of the large number of advertisements slathered between the crime articles – ads slanted toward people with empty lives. The suckers were being offered every kind of rip-off – from dating and mating services to sex potions, astrological charts and easy ways to get rich by doing absurd things like stuffing envelopes or selling elevator shoes. When Augie ran across a full-page ad for an "ESP Manual" that was being sold through the mail, he read the copy for kicks: *You can learn to command, control and completely dominate any beautiful girl you want – by mind power alone! Once you possess this miraculously potent secret, you will make scores of lovely, desirable young women willingly and cheerfully obey your silent, irrefutable commands!* All anyone had to do to receive this life-changing book was send ten bucks and a filled-out coupon to a post office box in Brooklyn.

Augie chuckled, his laughter unheard by anyone but himself in the thunderous, graffiti-emblazoned subway car. He wasn't a sucker. He didn't need any phony-baloney ESP Manual. What he had in his possession didn't depend upon mental telepathy, ESP, hypnotism or any other kind of unverifiable, self-deceptive hocus-pocus. His power was scientifically sound, based upon years of government-backed research and experimentation. Nobody knew that he had stolen the secret. It was fitting and proper for him to have done so, since *he* had helped develop it, against his will.

He had been a human guinea pig. Now he was going to have some little piggies of his own.

CHAPTER 3

Ray Berkshire was in his office at the ad agency, penciling in storyboard changes for some Faraday Family Restaurants spots, when he got the phone call from his distraught wife. He immediately became alarmed: he could hear his daughter crying in the background.

"Shana didn't get accepted by Excel," Linda announced, angry and flustered.

"Thank God – I mean, I'm glad the news isn't worse," Ray stammered. "I can hear her crying. I was afraid she'd been hurt."

"She *is* hurt! *Badly!* She won't even go out and play. She feels rejected and inadequate. She did her best on the enrollment tests and—"

"I feel sorry for her," Ray said. "She's only four years old. It's too much pressure. Why don't we just let her go to the public kindergarten and be done with it?"

"The public schools are abominable. Besides, Shana has to learn to be a fighter. I don't want her to get in the habit of giving up too easily."

There was a long, uncomfortable pause. Ray was at a loss for words. He couldn't believe how obsessed his wife was. She had been bound and determined to enroll their daughter in Excel Child Center, a chic, high-powered day-care facility and nursery school. He had hoped that if she failed, she'd back off. But obviously that wasn't going to be the case.

Shana was still crying, maybe not quite as hard as before. But Ray could clearly hear a few whimpers, even over the phone, and that made him feel terrible.

Linda said, "I put in a call to the enrollment director, Mrs. Emerson, soon as I opened the mail and read the rejection letter. I asked her what was wrong with Shana . . . why she didn't measure up."

"What did she say?"

"Apparently the turndown had nothing to do with Shana as a person. Mrs. Emerson admitted she scored high on all the tests. But Excel is after a certain mix of children as to age, looks and background, and there are only a few slots open. They already have a little girl whose profile is similar to Shana's and whose father is in advertising, like you are."

"Christ!" Ray exploded. "It sounds like a posh dinner party thrown by a clique of arrogant snobs. The kind of people who absolutely *must* invite an author, an architect, a surgeon, a deposed monarch—"

"Well, it's the way they work it," Linda interrupted, entirely unamused by her husband's sarcasm. "It's how *all* the top nursery schools maintain their high- standards. At least Shana didn't fail any of the aptitude tests or personality inventories. I'll have to find another place as good as Excel, if that's possible."

"Why don't we just drop it?" Ray suggested. "It really seems to me we might be pushing Shana too hard. Acting and modeling gigs, gym and swimming lessons, flash card and computer sessions – it's too much stuff for one little brain and one little body to soak up. Instead of trying to a superkid, why don't we just let her be happy and well-adjusted?"

"Because I don't want her to be a happy, well-adjusted failure!" Linda snapped. "I've had enough failure in my life."

Ray knew she meant him. It smarted, even after he got off the phone. It was hard for him to turn his attention back to the Faraday storyboards. His wife had struck a raw nerve. Deep inside, he wasn't entirely resigned to the fact that his career hadn't turned out as brilliantly as he had once wanted it to. But at least he could say he had tried. He had taken his shot at bigger things, but the shot had fallen short; and now he was stuck in a job that was interesting enough to keep him from going crazy, but not challenging enough to truly satisfy him.

He considered whether to tell Linda the tip he had gotten a few days ago from his boss, Walter Patterson. Walter had a fifteen-year-old daughter, Felicia, who was an honor student at Fairchild Academy. He had told Ray Berkshire that the Academy was going to open up a division for preschoolers. There had been no public announcement yet, because the administrators didn't want to be swamped with applications. Enrollment was being filled, as much as possible, through recommendations from insiders. Walter Patterson had offered to put in a good word for Shana, but Ray had staved him off, using the up-in-the-air situation with Excel as his excuse.

Now that Excel Child Center had turned Shana down, Walter's offer could save the day. If Ray told Linda about it, she'd be ecstatic. She'd leap at the opportunity. But Ray decided to keep his mouth shut. He couldn't help hoping that maybe, by the time Linda heard about Fairchild's expansion program from some other source, it would be too late to get Shana enrolled.

***

Shana was breathing softly, sniffling now and then. She had cried herself to sleep on the couch. To her mother she looked like a sad, defeated little angel, curled up on her side, wisps of golden hair wet from tears plastered to her dimpled cheek. Linda touched the blonde hair lightly, ever so lightly and tenderly, so as not to cause Shana to stir; then she touched her own hair, which was dark brown. She wished she knew where her daughter's blonde hair came from. It could have come from the child's maternal grandmother or grandfather: Linda's parents. Nobody in Ray's family was blonde, so the blondeness must have come from Linda's side. But she would never know for sure and would always wonder wistfully about it. She had no idea who her biological parents were. Abandoned by them, she had been adopted at age five right out of the orphanage that had held her since infancy.

Linda's formative years in the hustle and brawl of the orphanage had taught her how to survive by wit, gumption, self-assertiveness and sheer tenacity. After she was adopted, her "new" parents had tried to rule her with an ironclad discipline, instead of guiding her with love and understanding. But she had been resilient enough to withstand their browbeating and mental cruelty till they paid for her college education. She had a master's degree in communications. She was proud of the fact that she wasn't a timid, ordinary housewife. Before giving herself over whole-heartedly to child rearing, Linda Berkshire had been a tough, competitive career woman; and she found that some of the same drives that had served her well in the corporate arena could be applied to being a success at motherhood. She knew that if she wanted something good, she had to go after it, whether it was a job or a promotion or raising a bright, capable child. Because she believed in smart planning, she had waited till rather late in life to have a baby. Instead of getting saddled with a child to raise right off the bat, she had delayed her pregnancy till she and Ray had bought their own home and had money in the bank.

Then, just when she was too far gone to submit to a safe abortion, her married life went sour. Ray's commercial film business started to fail, and a promising career he had launched as an independent director of theatrical features lost its momentum. He scrambled to pull it all together, but his efforts weren't good enough. Not long after Shana was born, Ray declared bankruptcy. Linda had to bail him out by getting him a good job at Wagner, Inc., the ad agency she used to work for. He ought to be glad that his wife still had a few good contacts so he could resume earning a decent living. But, instead of being grateful, he acted downtrodden much of the time, as if his male ego was totally shattered.

Linda constantly worried that Ray's defeatist attitude would rub off on Shana. If he had his way, the child would be a *nobody*. He didn't demand enough of her. Just as he didn't demand enough of himself. That's why the rat race had chewed him up. The same thing wasn't going to happen to Shana. Not if Linda could help it.

She realized that her daughter's future was at stake – a precarious future in a hard, tough world that was becoming harder and tougher with each passing day. Natural resources were being used up. Basic necessities were becoming luxuries. The population was exploding, the job market was shrinking and people were being replaced by

25

robots. In such a mad scramble, only the best-prepared and best-educated people would stand a chance. That's why farsighted parents – like Linda – were fighting to get their children into sophisticated nurseries and preschools geared up to teach modern survival skills, not just fun and games. What chance would an ordinary child, raised in the dull, plodding, old-fashioned way, have against those who were learning not only to read, write and do arithmetic, but to use a computer and speak a foreign language, before they were five years old?

Linda resented any implication from her husband that she might be pushing her daughter too hard. Her fear was exactly the opposite – that maybe she wasn't pushing hard enough. She had learned in the orphanage that no matter how smart and tough you were, there was always somebody tougher and smarter, ready to beat you down and strip you of your possessions, your pride and your dignity. The future that Shana was heading into was in many ways even scarier than the orphanage. More complex. More treacherous. More subject to the whims of sociological and technological upheavals.

In this nebulous, threatening future that she foresaw for her daughter, Linda Berkshire was trying to pave the way for Shana not merely to survive, but to prosper. She was doing her utmost to cause Shana's attributes to blossom and to develop them to their fullest potential. In her mind's eye, she had a vision of what she was striving for. Like an artist's conception, it was pure, idealized, inspirational, but never fully attainable . . . a portrait of extraordinary wit, charm and radiant beauty manifested in one human creation: Shana Berkshire. Linda Berkshire's daughter.

CHAPTER 4

In his two-room apartment in Greenwich Village, Augie worked at his home computer terminal. It was set up on one side of a long folding table scattered with college textbooks, tablets full of scrawled writing and symbols, sheaves of printouts, stacks of girlie and crime magazines and a half eaten peanut butter sandwich. He was wearing only a T-shirt and Jockey shorts, and hadn't shaved, washed or brushed his teeth, because he was so caught up in his work. He was trying to gain deeper access to the data base of Fairchild Academy and the Fairchild Educational and Psychological Research Institute.

Augie was a "hacker" – a computer thief. Now that he knew he had been victimized by the Academy's Ultrachild Project, he intended to undermine it, sabotage it, and turn it to his own purposes, his own gratification.

Computer data pertaining specifically to the Ultrachild Project was protected by NSA – the National Security Agency. The function of the NSA was to constantly monitor the lines, exchanges and terminals of government computer systems processing secret information, as well as private and corporate systems engaged in secret government-backed work. So far, Augie had succeeded in logging onto the more insecure lines used by Fairchild for unclassified communications not protected by NSA and therefore more easily accessible to a skillful hacker like himself. However he could not gain all the information he needed in this way, merely bits and pieces, so that most of his correct deductions had to be made by inference. For instance, zeroing in on Felicia Patterson and pegging her as a Receiver had been a matter of trial and error and educated guesswork, finally confirmed when he tested her in the drugstore.

He chuckled aloud, savoring his remembrance of the prank he had pulled on her. Dwelling upon how he planned to use her in the near future, he began to get an erection. He enjoyed the good tingly feeling in his groin. His eyes fell upon the cover of the *True Crime* magazine he had bought the other day . . . the blonde, big-titted bitch tied up and menaced by two leather-masked rapists. In his mind she was Felicia; the coils of rope around her luscious body were invisible electrical wires, transmitting a magnetic current, binding her to his hidden, pulsating power, making her his love slave.

Sitting before the glowing screen of his computer terminal, he conjured up wild, lusty scenes of sexual domination. As he masturbated with one hand, the fingers of his other hand caressed the plastic buttons of his keyboard. Like the two rapists with the long, sharp knives, he would wear a mask when it was time for him to conquer Felicia Patterson. But he would not need a knife. Nothing so crude, so blatant to make her come to him, trembly, compliant, hot to do his bidding. She would open her creamy thighs and wrap her long legs around him because she *wanted* to. *Needed* to. He would be her master, pleasuring her as she had never been pleasured.

Caught up in visions of eroticism and vengeance, he went off in a sensational climax. Then, after a while, he brought his concentration back to the keyboard. But he kept Felicia Patterson, nude and willing, at the edge of his thoughts, waiting for him, firing his urge to probe and delve into the secrets of Fairchild Academy.

He was hoping to completely break Fairchild's computer code. To do this, he had to find what in hackers' jargon was known as a "node" – a switching junction – where secret and unclassified lines might inadvertently come together, because somewhere in the tangle of systems and cross-systems they were wrongly tied into the same network. He knew that networks and connections between networks were proliferating so fast and in such interwoven complexity nowadays that it was increasingly difficult for anyone, even the experts from NSA, to be exactly sure how everything tied together. So, there could be a security leak from one system to another, and that's what Augie was looking for. He spent hours of spare time at his terminal, just looking.

He dialed a supposedly secret telephone number and got an answering tone that told him he had gotten through to the data bank that he wanted to probe. Then, on his keyboard, he tapped out the letters A-U-G-I-E, spelling the password that he had stolen and taken as his code name.

CHAPTER 5

What if they don't like me, Mommy?" Shana said, biting her lip nervously.

Linda Berkshire glanced lovingly down at her four-year-old daughter, as they walked hand in hand toward the bank of elevators in the huge Manhattan office building. "They're bound to like you, darling," Linda said, "because you're a very pretty and likable little girl. Don't let them scare you. Be brave and confident."

"I'll try, Mommy."

"Just remember, you've got to believe in yourself or nobody else will."

"Not even you and Daddy?"

Linda stopped and looked Shana in the eyes.

"I'll *always* believe in you, sweetie. So will Daddy. Now brighten up and give me smile, okay? Hit me with your terrific dimples."

Beaming transfixed smiles at each other, they got onto an elevator. Linda pressed the button for the fortieth floor, where an audition for a series of Burger World commercials was going to take place. Two weeks ago Shana had passed the casting call. This morning, with the narrowed-down selection of ten little boys and ten little girls, she would go before the ad agency bigwigs who had the final say-so about which of the kids would make it.

If only Shana wouldn't choke up! A lot was on the line. She had done local spots before, but no network stuff. A part in just one Burger World spot could be worth as much as ten thousand dollars – enough to pay a good chunk of tuition at Harvard or Vassar.

Linda was afraid her daughter might get used to thinking of herself as a loser. The turndown from Excel Child Center was still fresh in her mind. It had happened only three days ago. Now, if she didn't score with this audition . . .

Too much early failure could scar a child for life, blunting the drive to compete and get ahead.

The elevator doors opened into the plushly modern reception lounge of Barbour & Lassiter; Inc., the staid and powerful advertising agency that had the Burger World account. Linda glanced at her wristwatch: twenty minutes to ten. Spying a sign that said LADIES ROOM, she tugged Shana off in that direction. She had twenty minutes to make sure that Shana looked tip-top.

Linda wasn't the only one with that idea. The ladies' room was packed with uptight women and keyed-up little girls. The other mothers were just as anxious as Linda to do some last-minute grooming of their daughters – brushing and teasing curls and bangs, straightening and tucking expensive garments, blotting and powdering baby-smooth complexions.

Elbowing for some room at the sink counter, Linda set down Shana's brown leather "audition kit." Then she stooped and squinted at her daughter, trying to assess just what final touches were required. Surreptitiously checking out the other little girls in front of the sinks and mirrors, she felt that none were as pretty as Shana; they were all too primpy and prissy. Smugly, Linda complimented herself on having the intelligence and restraint not to mar her little girl's beauty by trying to augment it artificially. Shana wasn't wearing any rouge, mascara or eye shadow, and her curls were natural. So was her pale golden hair. Her large blue eyes were as bright and clear as only a child's eyes can be. Strangers in supermarkets or shopping malls often came up to Linda to remark how adorable Shana was and to gush over her dimpled cheeks and her long, thick eyelashes. If they could see her now, Linda thought, in her new white satin dress with blue sash and trim, they would think they were seeing the nearest thing to an angel.

She decided that Shana only needed a few loose strands of hair combed into place and her face wiped with Kleenex. No use fussing too much and making the child imagine something drastic was wrong with her. No reason to even open the audition kit. Linda had a comb and some tissue in her purse. When she had finished with Shana, she took time to comb her own hair and powder her nose.

She knew that she wasn't as pretty as her daughter, but she still considered herself attractive. She was thirty-eight and believed she could pass for six years younger. At five feet seven she was lithe and slender with small breasts, narrow hips and cute, firm buttocks. She maintained her youthful figure by working out with Shana at a mother-child exercise center called Childplay. Her dark brown hair wasn't yet showing any gray; she almost wished it would, so she'd have an excuse to lighten it to match her daughter's.

"You look pretty, Mommy," Shana said, gazing up at Linda as she used her powder puff.

"Thank you, honey. So do you."

Linda spoke with the bravado that orphans learn to use in order to assert themselves. She wanted the other mother-daughter teams to hear her and Shana coming on strong.

Exuding confidence. Battles aren't won by destroying the enemies' morale, Linda thought. Feed their self-doubt. Grind them down. Make them feel outshined. Once they lose faith in themselves, they'll be pushovers,

After coming out of the ladies' room and signing in with the receptionist, Linda and Shana Berkshire were directed through a maze of office corridors to a large windowless room where the ten little boys and ten little girls selected from the first casting call would await their turns to audition.

The folding chairs that weren't occupied by kids and their adult mentors were piled with purses, makeup kits and changes of garment. The room was filled with an aura of silent, tense rivalry. Adrenaline-charged looks of appraisal flicked from one person to another.

"Well, hello, Linda! Hi, Shana!"

Linda was startled by the loud, cheery greeting from a tall, lanky, auburn-haired woman who had just come into the audition room and was picking a path for herself and her little boy down an aisle of folding chairs.

"Why . . . hello," Linda murmured, at a loss to recall who the woman was.

Shana came to the rescue by saying, "Hi, Monroe," to the little redheaded boy in a short-trousered navy blue suit. Then Linda realized that it was Vanessa Larson and her son Monroe, who just last week had started coming to the workout sessions at Childplay. "Vanessa," she said when she hit upon the name. But it was about two beats too late.

"You didn't recognize me in my street clothes," Vanessa chuckled. "You're too used to seeing me all sweated up in my jogging outfit with my hair in ponytails." She moved a leather satchel and a garment bag from two folding chairs to a third one, so she and Monroe could sit beside Linda and Shana. In the process she said, "Excuse me, are these yours?" to the mother and daughter who apparently owned the stuff and ignored the dirty looks that were given her in reply. Then she and her little boy sat down, depositing a huge black sack of a purse and a maroon overnight bag on the floor.

Linda said; "I didn't know Monroe was a model. How old is he?"

"I'm three!" Monroe piped up squeakily, his tiny face squinted into a gap-toothed smile.

"I'm four," Shana told him proudly.

"What a doll you are!" Vanessa exclaimed, merrily pinching Shana's cheek.

Vanessa was the picture of health, bluster and good will. She was strappingly tall. She was wearing a pale green pantsuit with a flowery blouse. She had a strong, straight nose and high, prominent cheekbones. Her wide, generous mouth was emphasized by a slash of bright red lipstick.

Surprisingly, Monroe was slightly built, almost girlish. He wasn't a handsome little boy, but he had what some casting directors called an "expressive face." His red hair, green eyes and pointy chin made him look impishly cute. Linda perceived him as a definite threat to Shana as far as the audition was concerned.

"Well at least we don't have to worry that we're competing with each other today," Vanessa said amiably—almost as if she had read Linda's mind. Lowering her voice, she confided, "I happen to know they're going to hire three boys and three girls."

"How did you find out?" Linda whispered.

"Monroe's agent is Tom Trenton," said Vanessa. "He has his ways." She winked an insider's wink.

Linda was stabbed by a pang of envy. The Trenton Talent Agency was possibly the best in the business. Any scoop that came from Tom Trenton himself was good as gold.

"Did he tell you anything else?" Linda asked, her need to know overcoming her fear of being thought pushy.

"Nothing about the concepts. Only that there are going to be three spots, with a boy and a girl in each one. God and the top brass from Barbour & Lassiter are the only ones who know diddly about the concepts, and they're keeping mum. They don't want anything leaking out to TL&C."

"They have the Top Frank account," Linda said knowledgeably.

"Um-hum." Vanessa smiled. "TL&C would do anything to cut Burger World's throat."

"I'd like to get Shana a better agent," Linda ventured.

"Who are you using?"

"Arthur Philips."

"Well, don't be too quick to ditch him, honey. He got you this chance with Burger World."

"I just have the feeling," Linda said, "that he isn't recognizing Shana's true potential. That, and the fact that he never comes up with the sort of inside scoop that I got from you. Your agent certainly seems more on top of it."

"I can get you an appointment with Tom Trenton if you want it," Vanessa offered. "Then, if he likes you, and if you're not tied contractually to Arthur Philips . . ."

"Our contract is due to expire," Linda said quickly. "I can't tell you how much I'd appreciate it. Vanessa, if you'd put in a word for us with Tom."

"I'd be happy to. Shana is a darling." Vanessa glanced at her watch. "Why are they always so late getting started? Some of the children are starting to get fussy."

"You just sit still and behave like a young lady," Linda warned Shana, who hadn't fidgeted at all.

It was a quarter till eleven before a bony young woman in a white blouse and black skirt appeared in the doorway to call the first two children out of the room. She read their names from their resumés – a boy and a girl.

"Thank God, they're ending the suspense," Vanessa said. When the first two kids were escorted back into the room, after a twenty minute absence, two more were called. The adults had to sit and sweat it out; they weren't allowed into the audition room. The kids had to go it alone, as a test of how well they might hold up under hot lights in front of a camera, in a hectic filming session.

"Good luck, darling," Linda whispered, when Shana's name was finally called and she got up to follow the bony woman in the black skirt. Her partner was a tiny tow-headed boy about the same age as Monroe Larson, who was blandly good-looking in an All American way. They were only gone for twelve minutes by Linda's watch, and she wondered if it might be a bad sign that they weren't kept longer.

When all twenty of the candidates had had a first interview, some were called back and tried with different partners. Shana was called back twice; one of the times happened to be with Monroe, and that time they were kept for over twenty minutes.

There was no lunch break. The candy, coffee and soft drink machines out in the hall were used by people who had not packed their own stuff. Linda and Vanessa, experienced auditioners, had both brought sandwiches and thermoses of milk, so their children would have something more nutritious than what came out of a machine. As they were snacking, Vanessa said, "Let's all play the game we learned at Childplay. Shana, you can be first. Name three words that start with the same sound as toy – the 't' sound."

Playing this game helped pass the time, not in a wasteful way, but in a mental exercise that would make the children more proficient in using and recognizing the alphabet sounds. Linda believed implicitly in these types of learning games, and she liked finding out that Vanessa did too.

It was close to four o'clock by the time the casting session was ended. The bony young woman in the black skirt announced that everyone could go home and that the ones who got hired would be notified by next Tuesday. "Do not call anyone at Barbour & Lassiter. If we want you, you will hear from us. If you hear nothing, you haven't gotten a part."

"Whew! I'm glad that's over!" Vanessa Larson said. "I'm dying for a stiff drink. How about it, Linda? Will you and Shana join us? For a nice restaurant dinner?"

"We'd love to," Linda immediately responded, glad of the opportunity to cultivate a new and potentially beneficial relationship.

"Mommy, I thought we were going to stop by and see Daddy," Shana interjected petulantly.

"Daddy's working late today. He won't be able to take a break. He's expecting us to be home when he gets there."

"I want a Top Frank!" Monroe piped and a few of the adults still left in the room turned to stare at him with bemused expressions, while several of the children giggled.

"God! Don't let the Burger World people hear you talk like that!" Vanessa admonished with hearty laughter.

As it turned out, they did end up eating at a Top Frank, partly out of a sense of perverse irony and partly because neither Linda nor Vanessa could hit on a restaurant-cocktail lounge in midtown Manhattan that might be equipped with kiddy seats or that would enjoy catering to a couple of tots during Happy Hour. As they passed under the big red-and-white plastic TOP FRANK sign, Linda said, "My, are we living dangerously – only a block from Barbour & Lassiter! We can forget about landing a part in the Burger World spots if anyone from the agency sees us sneaking in here."

"Oh, they're not *that* narrow-minded," said Vanessa. "The thing that bugs me is I'm not going to get my Bloody Mary."

But service was fast; within a few minutes they were all crammed into a booth, with their audition gear stashed here and there, and they started digging into a tray full of Top Frank hot dogs, Frank Fries and Cokes.

"Don't get ketchup all over you," Linda told Shana.

"I won't, Mommy. Sometimes you treat me just like a little baby," the child replied with a twinge of exasperation.

"She's so quick for her age," Vanessa said to Linda. "I noticed her right away one day at Childplay. So many mothers don't work hard enough with their children, either physically or intellectually. Obviously, you're one of the few who understand how vital it is to get them off to a fast start."

"Why, thank you. I try my best," Linda said, flattered.

"Are you using flash cards and so on? I've been using them with Monroe, and he's already reading at the first grade level."

"Yes, so is Shana," Linda enthused. "I started her out with flash cards, but now she does a lot of work on our home computer. I'm amazed at the terrific software that's available for educational purposes – and most of it is *fun* for her. She loves it."

"Same way with Monroe," said Vanessa. She chewed a bite of her Top Frank, and then washed it down with a sip of Coke. "What about preschool? Which one does Shana attend?"

Linda embarrassedly admitted that Shana wasn't currently enrolled anywhere. "I'm not going to send her to just any old place, that's for sure, and it's so hard to find something desirable. I knocked myself out trying to get her into Excel Child Center, and I was shocked when she didn't get accepted. The reason they gave me was really outlandish. I don't know if sometimes you have to grease someone's palm, or what."

"I wouldn't be surprised," Vanessa commiserated.

"Something seemed fishy," Linda went on, "because they admitted that Shana scored very high marks on their entrance tests. In the same breath they were telling me she didn't fit in with the mix they wanted. They can afford to split hairs, since they only have room for one-tenth of the kids that are scrambling to get in."

"It's a shame," said Vanessa. "I know what you're going through. Monroe has just been accepted into a great new place called Tiny Tot Academy."

"I've never heard of it," Linda said, trying not to sound jealous.

"It's just opening up," Vanessa informed her. "It`s a brand new division of Fairchild Academy. I'm sure you've heard of that. There's no private school with a better reputation. Fairchild only takes kids from age six on up, but now there's going to be the Tiny Tot Academy for preschoolers."

"Do you think I might be able to get Shana in?" Linda blurted. "Or is it already too late?"

"Leave it to me," Vanessa reassured her. "I have an in with the enrollment director. I can give you a good plug. I think Shana's a marvelous child. I'm surprised that Excel didn't snatch her right up – they must not be as classy as they're cracked up to be."

Linda gave Vanessa a warm smile. Her head filled with visions of how wonderful it would be if her new friend could come through with her promises. Tom Trenton as Shana's agent. Plus enrollment in a fine new nursery school. Best of all, once Shana got into Tiny Tot Academy, it would undoubtedly be a perfect springboard into Fairchild, which was exactly where Linda had dreamed of channeling her.

CHAPTER 6

Augie stood on the corner across from Fairchild Academy, waiting for the kids to come pouring out. It was almost time for four o'clock dismissal. Sweet Felicia would soon be prancing across Fairchild Plaza in that sexy long-legged stride of hers, with her pretty little ass pumping and swinging from side to side.

Augie wasn't ready to make his move on her yet. But he wanted to juice her up. Prime her. Test his control by taking her on a trial run. Not really a *run*, a trial *walk*, he corrected himself, smiling faintly. A trial *walk* for one of his human puppets.

He knew that Fairchild Academy was expanding, and the knowledge titillated him, making him feel as near as he could come to actual glee. Soon there would be a Tiny Tot Academy. The sure, silent tentacles of the Ultrachild Project were now stretching and reaching, snatching up the little kiddies. Thus, Augie's nether domain was growing larger. His enemies were unwittingly giving him more human puppets to toy with.

At four on the dot, the doors to the Academy opened; suddenly, the plaza was full of laughing, gabbing, exuberant kids – bursting with the freedom of a bright, crisp spring day. Many of them must be Receivers, although Augie wasn't yet precisely sure of which ones. But to know that they were present in the mob in large numbers helped him sense the scope of his secret power and filled him with near exhilaration.

41

Gloating and licking his lips, he watched Felicia Patterson trotting out to the sidewalk, holding hands with her boyfriend. Ted Meyer, his name was. Sixteen years old. In his junior year. One year ahead of Felicia. Probably getting in her pants. Augie pictured the two of them nude, fornicating, and hated Ted for it, as if it were a crime against a piece of Augie's private property.

Augie followed the young couple as they headed for their bus stop, both of them wearing blue Academy blazers with, in Felicia's case, a plaid skirt and blue knee socks, and, in Ted's case, a pair of plaid trousers. Ted was tall and gangly, with pus-yellow pimples on his chin and forehead; Augie couldn't imagine what Felicia saw in him. Unless he had a cock a yard long. Maybe he did. It was Augie's rueful, envious belief that almost all tall, skinny guys were well hung. He felt ashamed of his own organ, which was too short and slender; and, to make it worse, often he could not maintain a full erection – just as he couldn't maintain a passionate, enthusiastic attitude about most of life's endeavors. But now he was going to change all that. Now he had the *power*. To make people respond to him. Without fear of derision and rejection.

On the noisy, crowded bus, Augie sat about eight seats back from Felicia and Ted, where they wouldn't notice him. He had to be clever and cautious. He didn't want Felicia to remember him from the drugstore. It might foul up the slick, slippery plan he was laying down for her, scheduled to come off a few days from now.

He got himself settled and began to transmit. Even in heavy Manhattan traffic the bus would get to Felicia's place – or Ted's, if that's where they were going – in ten or fifteen

42

minutes. So Augie knew he probably didn't have much time to put the puppet through her paces . . .

Holding hands with Ted, Felicia sidled closer to him, feeling his hard, muscled thigh against hers. Following the advice she had gotten from a sexy bestselling paperback, over the past few weeks she had been trying to think and behave more sensuously in hopes of kindling the hidden fires in herself. Beneath her white blouse she wasn't wearing any bra, and her nipples stiffened as they rubbed against the fabric.

Suddenly, just like that day in the drugstore, she started to get a liquid, tingly feeling between her legs. Looking over at her boyfriend, she squeezed her thighs together, making her moistening panties crease and slip up inside her, teasing her clitoris and arousing a plethora of delicious sensations.

Ted felt her squirming and tried to pull her plaid skirt down, because he saw it riding up, exposing her legs above the knees. Squeezing his hand harder, she pushed it away and moved her thighs in jerky tightening spasms, clenching and unclenching.

"Felicia! What—" Ted whispered, shocked yet aroused by her outrageous behavior.

She gazed at him, her eyes wide and dreamy and full of lust. She wanted him as she had never wanted him before. Even when she tried to calm herself down, the erotic sensations poured into her, as if they were self-generating, flowing unbidden from deep in her brain. She couldn't control herself. The lewdness, the incredible desire for sex, was just *there*. Turned on somehow. Focused on Ted merely because he, his body, was the closest and handiest means of satisfaction. But she knew – much as it scared her to admit it – that if someone else had happened to be sitting beside her – another man – a man other than Ted – it would have made no difference. She would have turned on to him. Anybody. A friend or a perfect stranger. Anybody with a big, fat penis.

"I'm hot," she murmured in a hoarse, trembly whisper. "I'm going to take my blazer off."

She laid the garment across both their laps. Now nobody could really see what they might be doing, even though they might imagine. The elderly couple across the aisle weren't paying attention anyway. The old duffer was reading a newspaper and the old lady was staring blankly out the window. The bus seats had high backs. Nobody ahead or behind could peep at Felicia and Ted. It was almost like being in a private booth.

Under the blazer that blanketed their lower bodies, Felicia lightly tapped her fingertips over the bulge in Ted's trousers. Then she slowly unzipped his fly, the subtle noise of peeling metallic teeth totally masked by the ambiance of bus and traffic sounds. Felicia's fingers caressed the hot, swollen flesh of Ted's sizable penis. She felt his warm, contracting testicles. He stared at her, his face taut, his eyes fiery. She pulled his hand toward her and placed it where she had to have it, and his fingers wormed their way inside her, under her wet panties. His breaths were like hers, ragged and short.

Barely thinking about what they were doing, they turned toward each other and kissed. To the extent that Felicia worried about it at all, she thought, so what if anybody saw – there wasn't anything brazen about a kiss.

No reason for the other people on the bus to get upset over it. But her tongue went into Ted's mouth. All by itself the kiss became deeper and more lascivious than any she had experienced before. Her hand moved rapidly up and down, stroking Ted furiously, wanting him inside her, wanting to feel him spurt . . .

Augie could tell what was going on. His power was *working*. He knew. He could tell by the way Felicia and Ted were French kissing, as if any second they would start tearing each other's clothes off. Then they'd go at it right in front of everybody, the devil be damned.

But Augie didn't want that.

He wanted to be Ted. His own cock was throbbing with the idea.

He had to put a stop to it.

His sweet, sweet power didn't exist for the benefit of someone else.

Angrily, he began to transmit quite different signals to his Receiver.

Putting her through her paces. Making her behave differently. And *feel* differently. Exercising the range of his power a bit more. Testing the puppet. Giving her a good trial. Stopping her from cuckolding him right there on the bus. Causing her to change her thoughts and feelings in a direction that suited him much better, for now . . .

Suddenly Felicia hated Ted. She was *furious* with him. Where did he get off egging her on? She didn't feel at all sexy toward him anymore. She felt spiteful and mean and, on top of it, robbed of an orgasm. He didn't *love* her. For her to ever have believed that was patently absurd. If he truly loved her, how could he leave her unsatisfied so many times?

"Let me alone! I *detest* you!" she spat, smugly watching the look of intense sexual arousal melting from his sick face. At the same time, his penis shriveled in her hand, and she was glad to have made his manhood wither away. She shoved him from her as he zipped himself up. Then she snatched her blazer off of their laps and hastily put it on. It was a crazy, frustrating struggle just getting her arms into the sleeves. She couldn't think straight or do anything right. She was so *blind* with rage!

She heard him spluttering, "Felicia . . . I . . ."

"Shut *up*, you pig!"

She smacked his face. It was a resounding soul-satisfying slap. Loud and clear. She could picture his pimples splattering against her palm.

The bus screeched to a halt. It wasn't even her stop, but she jumped up and ran out. On her way, she almost stumbled over two boys who were in a fistfight, choking and punching each other in the aisle. It didn't even strike her as odd that two other people should be in a rage that apparently matched hers. It seemed only right for the whole *world* to be mad.

After she stormed off the bus, she ran and ran through the crowded New York streets, muttering and crying, hating everybody and everything . . .

And then gradually, and for no apparent reason, her anger wore off . . .

She began to feel sorry for herself and to hate herself for losing her boyfriend and to wonder once again if she might be going insane.

Augie *loved* it. Beautiful! The way the puppet had performed. His secret power had driven her right up the wall, the way he wanted it to. Ted Meyer wasn't going to lay Felicia today. Instead, he was going to go home with a pair of aching, frustrated balls. Augie would take care of Felicia in his own good time. He would soon give her what Ted couldn't give. The fight between him and Felicia had been marvelous . . .

But the big bonus – the thing that *really* made Augie feel pretty good – was the other fight that broke out at the same time.

There could be just one plausible explanation for it, of course: Felicia wasn't the only Receiver on the bus. Another one. Another person picking up on Augie's transmissions. That was what caused the other fight to break out.

One of those two boys trying to kill each other had to be a Receiver. An Ultrachild.

As soon as Augie realized it, he stopped transmitting. He didn't want one of his puppets to get arrested. That would put the puppet out of reach, right after Augie had had the good luck to discover him, by a happy accident.

When Augie stopped transmitting, the fistfight broke up. Some of the other passengers separated the two boys and got them under control. Naturally, the one in the blue blazer was puzzled, ashamed of himself, amazed that he had acted like some kind of savage and wondering why his "fit" had fizzled out as rapidly and mysteriously as it had come over him.

The blue Academy blazer made it easy for Augie. That was the boy whose rage he had inadvertently turned on.

Now that Augie had him singled out, he would have to come up with a devilish good trick to play. Boys didn't excite him. He wasn't a queer. He had no desire to have sex with a boy. But that didn't mean that there weren't other fun-filled ways for his new puppet to help him sabotage the Ultrachild Project.

CHAPTER 7

Foley Ryan had a small fine-boned face, glossy black hair, and strikingly pretty pale blue eyes that moistened and sparkled when she was drinking. Halfway through her second gin and tonic, she gazed at the serious, preoccupied face of the man sitting across from her in the cozily lit cocktail lounge. "Pardon me for mentioning it," she said, "but you've seemed distracted all afternoon, Ray."

"Today my daughter went to try out for a part in those Burger World spots," Ray Berkshire said with a sour grimace. He shook his head disdainfully, cupping his right hand around his chin and stroking his goatee and mustache with his thumb and forefinger.

He aroused in Foley considerable affection and protective instinct, which she strove to keep on a platonic level. She thought of him as a sensitive, artistic person wasting himself by working on television commercials. She had loved his one feature movie, *Dealey Plaza*, about 1970s campus radicals bent on solving the Kennedy assassination conspiracy. She wished he could find a way of freeing himself from the mundane workaday world so he could exercise his creative gifts. After all, he wasn't getting any younger; he was thirty-nine. His hairline was receding, emphasizing his broad, high forehead. His sideburns and beard were flecked with gray. He had a long, slightly hooked nose. His deep-set brown eyes were keenly alert, even when he was troubled.

"You're worried Shana won't do well?" Foley asked.

"Just the opposite." He sipped his martini and rolled the cold liquor his tongue before swallowing.

"You don't *want* her to do well?" Foley said with a touch of amazement, but only a touch; she was well aware that the things that really mattered to most people didn't matter most to Ray.

"I find myself hoping she doesn't make it," he admitted, "so that maybe this nonsense will end. But failing to get her cast this time won't cause Linda to back off, I'm afraid. She'll just drive Shana all the harder."

"I see."

"Foley," Ray rambled on, "you and I have both seen how unscrupulously kids can be used in the marketplace. I don't want my daughter burned out by age nine, or pawed and pampered by the pedophiles who think a baby's ass is just the thing to sell their designer jeans."

"Shana is a little young yet for you to have to worry about that."

"l wonder," Ray said with a sarcastic glint in his eye. "A few years ago I would've thought that nine was too young. But progress marches on. Films like *Taxi Driver* and *Pretty Baby* have paved the way for lots of kids to become porn stars."

"You've got a point," Foley laughed. "Not to change the subject, but I was worried that maybe you were being bugged by some of my arrangements for next week's shoot and didn't want to level with me in front of my boss."

"Oh, no, your arrangements are perfectly fine, as usual," Ray assured her. "Sorry if I didn't seem quite with it at our meeting. Do you think Ken Faraday noticed?"

"Uh-uh. Ken doesn't know you well enough to detect your foul moods. When he and I were out in the hall, he told me he likes the way you have the logistics worked out for the camera crew. You absolutely snowed him. He loves people who display a grasp of detail."

"That's why you've made a hit with him, too," Ray said.

"Well, it's so completely obvious that you and I are both aces in our field," Foley asserted with a flippant, chin-jutting grin.

"I'll drink to that," Ray said, and they clinked their glasses and drank, caught up in the exuberance of being just loaded enough to not mind thinking of themselves as special people.

Foley wished Ray would start thinking of himself that way all the time. Why did he keep his light under a bushel? To her, his talent was awesome. *Dealey Plaza* had gotten rave reviews and had been a hit at the box office, but somehow a sleazy distributor had cheated Ray out of his share of the profits. Then Berkshire Productions had gone broke. To Foley, this was an outrage, a great injustice – the stifling of a man who almost, but not quite, had reached the pinnacle of commercial and artistic success.

She had never tried anything as world-shaking as writing and directing her own movie, but she had once operated her own ad agency. After her husband died six years ago, her little business had supported her and her two children. Her best-paying client had been Faraday Foods, run by Ken Faraday, her present boss. When he had started expanding his chain of family restaurants, he had decided he needed an in-house agency, and he wanted Foley Ryan to head it. So she had hired on at a fat salary with nice fringe benefits, ridding herself of the pitfalls – and pleasures – of being completely on her own. She felt a special kinship with Ray Berkshire, because they were both ex-mavericks, ex-freelancers turned into hired hands.

As he and Foley Ryan enjoyed a dinner of steaks and salad with a carafe of wine, Ray Berkshire mused that it was indeed more satisfying to be with a woman like Foley, who had him on a pedestal, than to be with his own wife, who always had him in the doghouse.

He had met Foley five years ago, when she was still running Ryan Advertising and he was still running Berkshire Productions. Obviously flustered and in awe of him after seeing him on a TV talk show, she had come to him with three spots to produce for Natural Hearth bread. She was embarrassed because they were such "el cheapo" spots; but truth was that any little piece of change was a big deal to Ray at the time, because he was trying desperately to stave off his creditors. The success of *Dealey Plaza* had chased his commercial clients away in droves, because they feared he would no longer knock himself out over their TV spots now that he had had a taste of more heady stuff. He might have been able to rally against their fickleness in good economic times, but this was in the middle of a recession. Not long after he finished the Natural Hearth gig, all the irons he thought he had in the fire stopped glowing and he couldn't keep Berkshire Productions alive any longer.

Foley remained loyal even after he was forced to take his present job in the Broadcast Production department of Wagner, Inc. When she folded her own agency, she had several sizable clients whom she encouraged to transfer to Wagner, setting Ray up as their initial contact. One of these was Ken Faraday, who, at that time, was just getting into franchising.

Today there had been a preproduction meeting concerning a new series of spots for the Faraday Family Restaurants. Ray had brought the third revision of the storyboards to the client's headquarters for discussion and final approval. Then he had asked Foley to dinner, since Linda wasn't expecting him home till much later. He knew that the gossip at Wagner was that both he and Ken Faraday had a thing going with Foley, but it wasn't true in his case, and he suspected it wasn't true for her boss. Why did the thought of Ken and Foley together cause him to fight a pang of jealousy? It was none of his business whom she went to bed with.

He had always liked her first name, Foley. It would be a nice first name for a character in a novel or screenplay, if he was still doing any serious writing. But he wasn't. Wasn't writing anything more serious than storyboard scripts.

Joking about waistlines and diets, they argued themselves into coffee with strawberry cheesecake. Then, when the dessert arrived, the portions were enormous. "Oh-oh," Foley said, her eyes widening. "Maybe we shouldn't have done this, after all. I'm afraid I'm going to need a whole new wardrobe."

"Maybe I'll take up jogging," said Ray. "Linda is always nagging about my lack of exercise."

"But you look trim. Really. You don't seem to gain weight very easily."

"Nevertheless, Linda is convinced that my arteries will clog shut and I'll die of a stroke or a heart attack, unless I get on a physical fitness binge."

"I think that high blood pressure is the result of tension more than diet," said Foley. "And you appear more relaxed these days, Ray."

"Yeah, working for somebody else takes a lot of the pressure off. Right?"

Foley nodded in agreement. But she hoped that Ray wasn't totally resigned to the loss of freedom and independence that had befallen them both. She took a bite of cheesecake and a sip of coffee. Then she said, "Running your own business is tough. But I miss it sometimes. Do you?"

"Oh, yes. But I'm better off now in many ways. I make a lot of money. I can look bill collectors in the face, instead of hiding from them."

"Money isn't everything," Foley said probingly. "Do you think there's any way you can eventually get back to being a serious writer and filmmaker?"

"I don't know. Maybe. Maybe not. I've got a daughter to raise now. And the years keep flying by. Whatever fame and notoriety I got from *Dealey Plaza* is largely forgotten by the fans and by the muckety-mucks in the movie industry."

"I don't think that's true at all," Foley said staunchly. "You're far too modest. Your movie is still written up in the anthologies – it's still called a low-budget classic. Don't sell it short, Ray. You know I'm pulling for you. So are lots of other people who don't even know you – but would pay money to see more of your work."

"I doubt that that's true," Ray said. "Five years ago, I couldn't convince the right people of it, or else I would've gotten financing for another picture."

"Because they sensed that you were desperate," Foley said, getting angry and more fervent. "Now that you're back on your feet, you can come back at them. I'd love to see you do it. Get a project together and shop it around. You don't have to go it alone, you know – you can find a good agent. Why don't you give it a shot, Ray?"

Her earnestness moved him and he cracked a smile. He knew from bitter experience how tough it was to do what she was saying, but he didn't want to dampen her belief in him. "I have a few ideas I've been kicking around," he told her. "I'm going to start putting them on paper."

"Good! I'm glad to hear it!" Foley enthused.

He didn't tell her that his story ideas were so vague and formless at this point that he was highly uncertain as to whether they'd ever shape up into anything significant.

Later that evening, as he was driving home, he wondered why he hadn't made a play to take Foley to bed. It had crossed his mind more than once, but he hadn't done anything about it. As appealing as she was, he had shied away from the danger of deeper involvement. He told himself that he wanted to make his marriage succeed, even though at times it seemed like an uphill struggle. He didn't want to use the fact that he was "misunderstood" as an excuse to start an affair.

Foley saw him as a thwarted genius, and his wife saw him as a failure, and he saw himself as something in between. He wasn't much of a wheeler-dealer, nor did he wish to be. He wasn't cut out for the infighting, ass-kissing and back-stabbing that went on in the agency. Even so, last year three TV spots that he produced for three different clients won Gold Certificates in the New York Commercial Film Festival, This had earned him a raise, but not a promotion. There was no rung for him to step up to except Director of Broadcast Production. But he wasn't playing the right games to get that, even if his boss, Walter Patterson, took a sudden fit and resigned.

Linda wasn't satisfied. To her, he was marking time. She took full credit for "landing him his job," just because she had put in a plug for him. But if he hadn't been overqualified for the position he never would have gotten it. In fact, probably what had really swung it for him was that some of the higher-ups, including Walter Patterson, got off on having the man who made *Dealey Plaza* whoring for them.

Of course, when Linda worked at Wagner she had been a real go-getter. She had started as a lowly copy assistant and had risen to account executive. During that period, Ray was known as a young, dynamic, maverick filmmaker. When *Dealey Plaza* became an instant smash, Linda basked in his notoriety. At their peak they were the "ideal couple," invited to scads of social affairs and given celebrity treatment. Then came the great crash, and Linda never got over it.

Ray knew that his wife's success syndrome went back to her childhood. Her first five years were spent in an orphanage, where she had it really tough. Then she was adopted by Milton McKim, age sixty, and his wife Melva, age fifty-seven, who had been childless through the thirty-two years of their austere, God-fearing marriage. In their golden years, they figured they could store up some treasure for themselves in heaven by giving a proper home

56

to some poor, unfortunate little tyke; they chose Linda, partly because She was old enough not to have to have her diapers changed. From the start, they made it clear that, if she did anything at all to displease them, they were under no obligation to her. They could always send her back to the orphanage.

Linda really believed them and so lived in terror of being sent back. She did everything she could to please her adoptive parents, to make them want to keep her. By the time she graduated from high school, as valedictorian, and from college, magna cum laude, she had long since made the logical realization that Milton and Melva weren't really going to have her locked up again. But, by then, the threat had become a black, formless ogre lodged in her subconscious, feeding off of her tremendous fear of rejection and her deep, desperate need to constantly prove her worth to herself and others.

The ogre was still consuming his wife, Ray Berkshire felt, but now Shana had become Linda's means of appeasing it. The dream of being a successful career woman with a famous husband had been lost. But it had been replaced by the drive to be a perfect mother raising a perfect child.

Before Shana was even born, Linda was making plans for what the experts called "a dynamic interaction" with her offspring. "The old-fashioned way of raising babies is totally wrong," she told Ray. "They're not just helpless lumps of protoplasm. They have perfectly functional brains, and they're struggling to grow up and get smart quickly in order to survive. During the vital period, when they're instinctively trying to learn all they can, most adults treat them like morons."

"You mean it's not enough to say coochy-coo, coochy coo?" Ray joked.

Linda didn't crack a smile. She went on proselytizing.

"Parents have to be teachers, not mere providers of food and shelter. Children need sensory stimulation of all kinds, and, if they don't get it, their brains simply fail to develop. One study showed that deprived kids can have IQs ten to twenty points below average by the time they start school, even if they started out with normal intelligence."

"But you spent your first five years in an orphanage and you're certainly no dummy," Ray said.

"I just happened to push myself hard enough to make up for my disadvantages," Linda argued. "You had better look into some of the points I'm trying to get across to you, Ray. If you don't, you're going to be a lousy father."

"I'll give our child plenty of love," Ray defended.

"That's all well and good, but it's not the whole answer," said Linda.

To please her, he read a manual she had ordered from the Fairchild Educational and Psychological Research Institute. The title was *How to Multiply Your Child's IQ* by Drs. Vincent and Carol Parkhurst, the directors of the Institute. According to the Parkhursts, intelligence was not a genetically determined constant, as had been previously supposed. Sufficient early stimulation could produce greater size and improved electrochemical functioning of the human brain. The limit placed on intelligence by heredity was so flexible, the Parkhursts believed, that probably nobody had ever realized his true potential. They hypothesized that "with comprehensive scientific exposure to sensory experiences" it ought to be feasible to raise any individual's IQ by a substantial margin – perhaps as much as thirty points. But, since the human brain grew at a decelerating rate from birth on, improvement in mental capacity would be less and less attainable as a child got older. By the time he was four years old, half of his adult intelligence was already set. By age eight, regardless of what type of special attention he was given, his intellect could only be improved by about twenty percent.

Ray could understand why these kinds of statistics would make Linda feel pressured. He had to admit that parenthood was a more formidable responsibility than he had realized. But there was no reason to panic. Surely he and his wife were bright and capable enough to make sure that their child would not be intellectually deprived.

At about the time that Shana was born, he was so swamped by the bankruptcy of Berkshire Productions and the pressures of his new position at Wagner, that he had to let his parental obligations slide. But he could count on Linda to focus on the baby's needs, seeing that the child got fed and cuddled and mentally stimulated. In the evenings and on weekends, he helped out with the flash-card lessons in reading, writing and arithmetic, and he played games with Shana that were really learning exercises. All the toys and games that Linda bought had a dual purpose – to teach as well as to entertain. Ray consented to the purchase of a home computer, so Shana could use the educational software. He shelled out money for acting classes, modeling classes and exercise classes. Linda had an absolute zeal for promoting all these activities, and, for a while, Ray thought it was nice of her to take so much of the load off of his shoulders.

He wanted his daughter to do well. To have a head start. To thrive. To develop her innate abilities, so they wouldn't shrivel inside her due to parental shortsightedness or neglect.

But eventually he realized that what Shana was getting from Linda was the diametric opposite of neglect. It was an obsessive-compulsive form of mother love that left the child little room to breathe or to be herself.

Ray could sympathize with the trauma in his wife's background that had made her so insecure. But she had to feed her own ogre. Shana couldn't do it for her. Linda couldn't battle the black, formless shape of her own inferiority complex by turning Shana into an extension of herself, a child without a childhood, programmed to go chasing after a vision of mind-boggling success and happiness that would forever keep fading into an illusion.

CHAPTER 8

Augie had found out that the Fairchild Academy student who had been fighting on the bus was Charles Baich, seventeen years old, a senior. Like Felicia Patterson and the other unwitting guinea pigs of the Ultrachild Project, he was a high achiever with a scholastic record that ranked him near the top of his class. He was tall, well built, dark-haired, with a plain, decent but uninteresting face. He never got in any sort of trouble. He was always well mannered, reserved, soft-spoken, sickeningly *nice*. The brawl on the bus was an aberration. Of his own volition, Charles Baich would have lacked sufficient passion to want to pummel anybody, for any reason whatsoever.

Augie had made him do it, by accident.

Now Augie was going to make him do much worse, on purpose.

On a chilly Friday afternoon in late April, Augie lurked behind a fat, freshly budding weeping willow in a patch of woods on the fringes of a small suburban park. It was a quarter to five. At about this time every Friday, Charles Baich walked his girlfriend along a path past the weeping willow to the Burger World restaurant on the other side of the park, where she worked as a counter girl after school three days a week from five till eight. Charles always escorted her to work and then came back for her at quitting time. Then they would go to a movie, or go bowling, or whatever. The patch of woods wasn't a particularly safe place for a young girl all alone. So it was perfect for what Augie had in mind.

The girlfriend's name was Jane Taft. She wasn't a Fairchild Academy student, so naturally she wasn't a Receiver, like Charles Baich. She was an eleventh grader at a parochial school in Davenport, New Jersey, a suburb of New York City. Charles Baich and his mother and father lived in Davenport, too; in fact, they were neighbors of the Taft family, and that's how Charles had met Jane. She suited him. She wasn't a sexpot by any means. She was bony and flat chested, with a ski nose, thin bloodless lips and dry, brittle-looking straw-colored hair. The main reason that Charles dated Jane was that she seemed to have very little sex drive; like most Receivers, so did he. When he was alone with her, he didn't have to feel pressured to try to seduce her merely to prove something that he had no urge to prove.

Listening keenly, Augie heard faint footsteps and a sporadic, indecipherable babble of conversation in the distance. Ducking behind the fat trunk of the willow tree, he made sure he was well hidden, as Charles and Jane approached, holding hands awkwardly, because they had to walk almost single file on the narrow wooded path. She was wearing a bulky green sweater over her Burger World costume of green slacks, yellow blouse and green bow tie; her green Burger World cap was sticking out of her sweater pocket. Charles was wearing a jacket and slacks of matching dark blue denim, with tan loafers and a tan shirt.

Augie smiled faintly at the thought of what a chilly day it happened to be. Charles and Jane were both going to get a zillion goose bumps on their bare asses. Becoming sexually aroused by the sure knowledge of his power and how he was going to use it, as his prey came closer and closer, Angle began to transmit . . .

***

Although Jane Taft was a virgin, she was certainly no stranger to impure thoughts – thoughts that would have shocked Charles if she hadn't kept them to herself. Around him she was always demure and proper, as a "nice" girl should be. She would never, *ever* let him guess how badly she wanted to do it with him. Maybe her body wasn't as voluptuous as she longed for it to be, but that didn't mean her head couldn't be filled with voluptuous temptations. Sometimes she weakened and masturbated in bed at night, but she knew it was a mortal sin – even if she often tried to convince herself otherwise – because after she gave herself the fleeting pleasure, she always felt mean, guilty and lowdown. She was glad she had such a gentlemanly, respectful, "safe" boyfriend to help her keep her carnal impulses under control. Most of her classmates at St. Agnes High School claimed to be sexually active, and they all seemed to take it for granted that she was making it with Charles. She let them think so. She didn't want to be teased or laughed at for being a serious, committed, old-fashioned Catholic who was trying like heck to hold off and not go all the way till she got married. Every Saturday she went to confession; and at mass on Sundays she always took communion. She would just die if she ever had to tell the priest she was committing the sin of fornication.

Charles was holding Jane's hand, boasting about a chemistry test he had aced at Fairchild Academy, when suddenly, he stopped talking in mid-sentence. A queer look carne over him, as if he had no idea where he was or what he had been saying. His mouth gaped dumbly open. He looked like a retard, a Mongoloid, instead of the unusually bright person Jane knew. Astounded, she watched, rooted on the spot, as he licked his lips slowly, top and bottom, with his wet pink tongue. She blinked, hypnotized by the strange, vacant expression in his brown eyes, the pupils dilated, staring into her and through her at a point somewhere in space.

Suddenly, he pulled her roughly into his embrace and kissed her under the willow tree that she loved because it was so fat and gnarled and rumored to be over two hundred years old. For a fleeting moment it was almost romantic – Charles being uncharacteristically passionate with her. Then something happened: his kiss turned hard, selfish and mean. Jane's lips were being mashed and bitten, his teeth and her own teeth biting the inside and outside of her mouth. At the same time, he was grinding his pelvis into her, bruising her with his boniness, his hard, stiff rod of flesh. "Charles . . . don't . . ." she managed to murmur.

He kicked at the backs of her knees, clipping her, slamming her to the hard ground, right there on the muddy path, under the fat willow tree. Her breath whooshed out of her. Her chest hurt. She couldn't breathe. He was like a madman, his body *crushing* her. She was pinned, flattened, under his horrendous weight and the sucking, suffocating pressure of his mouth on hers. She struggled and tried to throw him off, but she was too weak. He bucked and humped, trying to stab her with his clothed penis, and his hands were all over her, ripping and pawing. He almost strangled her with her knotted bow tie, trying to pull it from under her collar. He clawed at her blouse, the fabric tearing, the buttons popping, his cold hands digging under her bra, his ragged nails slashing into her tender nipples and soft, tiny breasts.

He kept humping and pumping, babbling, muttering obscenities at her, trying to impale her through her clothes. Then he started pulling her slacks off. She got a hand loose and slapped him . . . again and again. As if perplexed as to why she should treat him that way, he froze and stared down at her, breathing hard. She gasped, "Charles! *Stop!* You're hurting me!"

She wanted to believe she could jar him to his senses. She writhed and tried to push him away so she could get up. Too late, she saw the rock clutched in his fist. It crashed down on her head, splintering her skull. She barely got out a scream . . . followed by a weak groan. He hit her with the rock once again with all his strength and she went totally silent and limp . . .

***

Augie was in wondrous awe of what he was witnessing . . . what he had caused. Charles was so utterly dominated by the transmission that he was beyond caring, beyond sense of right and wrong, beyond any fear of danger or the threat of being caught. Continuing to transmit, to keep Charles under his spell, Augie peeked from behind the tree and saw that Jane Taft was unconscious or, more likely, dead. Oblivious to his girlfriend's condition, Charles ripped and ranted and stripped her naked, madly tearing at clothing. Then, fumbling and yanking and breaking his zipper, he pulled down his pants. He had a raging, mean-looking erection.

So did Augie. For him, it was like watching one of the articles in *True Crime* magazine magically brought to life. A story he had "directed" himself. With characters of his own choosing and a script of his own creation in a command performance for an audience of one. The scope and intricacy of his power imbued Augie with a rapturous feeling, as he watched the "story" he had created being acted out.

Charles Baich was having his first real experience of unbridled lust. Augie smirked, watching the boy raping his limp, scrawny girlfriend, more turned on by his own mastery of the situation than by the lewdness of the "crime." In a legal sense, Charles wasn't really guilty of anything, for he had no freedom of choice. He was only doing what any good puppet would have had to do. The *power*, the blessed, sweet power, Augie thought, as Charles let out a savage, orgasmic cry.

Then Augie stopped transmitting, leaving Charles to cope with the aftermath of it all . . .

CHAPTER 9

On the same Friday afternoon that Augie was involved with Jane Taft and Charles Baich, Ray Berkshire and Foley Ryan held a big preproduction meeting of the entire cast and crew of the Faraday Family Restaurants spots. The purpose was to iron out all the logistical details for next week's shooting. They would be on location Monday through Thursday, with the next Friday as a contingency day in case of a rain delay or any other special problem.

The meeting started at two and didn't wrap up till almost seven. Ray had a strong impulse to ask Foley to have dinner with him again, but around noon he had spoken on the phone with his wife and had told her he'd definitely be home no later than eight or nine. He considered making up the excuse that his meeting had gone later than expected, but he had the feeling that, once he started lying to Linda to be with another woman, he would soon find himself on a road leading to the total disintegration of his marriage.

When he arrived home, after the usual long, boring, yet dangerous, drive by way of the Lincoln Tunnel and the New Jersey Turnpike, Linda surprised him with a candlelight dinner for just the two of them. She met him at the front door with a kiss and a warm, welcoming embrace. "Ummmmm . . . what are we celebrating?" he murmured, her arms tight around him, while he tried not to remember how long it had been since he had last gotten this kind of special treatment.

"Vanessa came through!" Linda said, letting her excitement bubble out. "Not only has she talked Tom Trenton into taking Shana on, but she's also gotten us a chance with Tiny Tot Academy, even though they weren't supposed to be accepting any more applicants. Isn't that wonderful?"

Ray put on a smile, but he wasn't happy. Damn it. Even though he'd kept quiet about the tip from his boss, Walter Patterson, this Larson woman had come along and stuck her nose in. Just his dratted luck for Linda to get wind of the Fairchild Academy expansion before it was too late for her to plug away at it. One way or another, it looked as though Shana was going to be sucked in.

"Hard to believe an agent of Trenton's caliber would make a commitment without an interview," Ray said.

"I let Vanessa take him Shana`s audition tape," Linda explained. "Apparently, he liked what he saw, and, of course, Vanessa really talked it up for us. It turns out her husband is Trenton`s attorney."

"Very influential person, this Vanessa Larson. Why is she so willing to help us?"

"She and I just really hit it off, Ray. For heaven's sake, don't look a gift horse in the mouth. You're going to like her as much as I do when you get to meet her. Her little boy is so bright and cute – exactly the kind of little friend Shana should have."

"Sorry, I didn't mean to dampen your enthusiasm," Ray said. "I guess I'm not too accustomed to dealing with lucky breaks."

"Well things are *going* to be breaking our way now. I can feel it," Linda said, pressing her body against his. "We've got to start acting like winners again, and then we'll *be* winners. Nothing can stop us as long as we don't doubt ourselves."

Ray kissed her again. She was almost making a believer of him. It was strange and refreshing to hear himself included in her emotions, an integral part of her pep talk, instead of a mere object of its preachments.

He found that she had really knocked herself out to prepare a sumptuously elegant dinner. Champagne, shrimp cocktail, French onion soup, Chateaubriand and homemade croissants, followed by Ray's favorite dessert: Kahlua Supreme – ice cream, Kahlua, white crème de menthe and cracked ice, whipped in a blender and served in a parfait glass. Now that he fully understood why Linda had phoned him at the ad agency to make sure he'd be home by nine, he was glad he hadn't blown it. Linda had picked a perfect time for them to be mellow together. Shana had been put to bed at eight. Ray left his tie and jacket on during the meal, matching the cozy formality of Linda's clinging satin cocktail dress. At his meeting today, it had struck him that Foley Ryan was prettier than his wife. But now, in the glow of champagne and candles, Linda seemed more beautiful.

As if she had read his mind, she asked, "How is Foley, by the way?"

"She's doing well. Very efficient at her job, as usual. If the shooting next week doesn't go smoothly, it certainly won't be her fault. Ken Faraday considers her indispensable. She asked about you."

"Oh? What did you tell her?"

"That being a parent keeps you constantly on the run. And that you're putting your all into it."

"Did she seem surprised?"

"You mean because she always thought of you as a career woman? I'm sure she understands that mothering can be as challenging a career as any other, if a person is determined to do a proper job of it."

Sipping coffee, Ray thought that maybe he had been too hard on Linda, maybe he wasn't really giving her her due. Lots of guys would just love to have such a competent, hardworking wife. Maybe she only needed a few successes with Shana. Perhaps, once she felt she was going in the right direction, she'd be able to settle down and stop pushing.

"We're going to have to stay on top of it, if we're going to get Shana into the Academy," Linda said. "I have an appointment to take her there for a complete pediatric checkup tomorrow. Would you like to come with us?"

"Sure, if you want me to," said Ray. "But I don't see why we have to go through all that – especially on a Saturday. Dr. Rajendra can simply forward her medical records."

"That's not the way the Academy does things," she informed him. "They won't administer the enrollment exam until Shana passes her physical. They want their experts involved firsthand, so they're not working at cross-purposes with anybody. If Shana gets accepted, Dr. Rajendra can't be her pediatrician any longer. The Academy is set up to take care of the *total child*. That's why it is such a huge complex, with everything tied in together – Fairchild Academy, Tiny Tot Academy, Fairchild Educational and Psychological Research Institute, Fairchild Pediatric Center . . ."

"I expect there's even a Fairchild Fingernail and Toenail Clinic," Ray quipped.

70

But Linda didn't smile. "If you ask me," she said, "it's very reassuring to know that the children's welfare is so comprehensively supervised."

"Except you ought to be able to opt out of specific services," Ray argued. "I've always been extremely happy with Dr. Rajendra."

"Vanessa said that so much of what goes on at the Academy is so experimental that any outside influence could throw a monkey wrench in it. *Anyway*, even though Dr. Rajendra is closer, I'll be glad to get a doctor who speaks English."

"I never thought that was a big problem."

"You're kidding, Ray! I'll never forget the time he was trying to tell me not to give Shana any fried eggs – I thought he was saying I didn't have nice legs!"

Rey chuckled with Linda. But he believed she was suddenly teasing Dr. Rajendra's accent because she was so single-minded about this chance with the Academy. Four years ago, she had been delighted to find such an excellent pediatrician so nearby, thick accent or not. Besides, the misunderstanding over the fried eggs had happened when Shana was only a year and a half old; he was speaking much better English now.

"I just hate to hurt his feelings by dropping him flat," Ray said. "Up till now he's seen Shana through an awful lot."

"Don't worry," Linda replied confidently. "Once we explain things to him in a nice way, he's going to be thrilled that our daughter is getting such a wonderful opportunity."

"If she makes it," Ray said.

"She *will*," Linda intoned with determination.

71

Actually, Ray could see a bright spot for himself in all this. If Shana enrolled in the Academy's "total child concept," a whole lot of monkey business would be taken off his back in one fell swoop. Instead of running around shopping for various child-care services and involving him in each nitpicking decision, Linda would be satisfied that Shana was getting the best of everything from one highly sophisticated setup. Maybe she'd even find some time and energy to devote to aspects of their married life that didn't revolve around their daughter.

Ray reached out and took Linda's hand. She looked more inviting to him tonight than she had for a long time. "Let's blow out the candles," he said with throaty suggestiveness. "Don't bother cleaning off the table. It can wait till the morning."

If she had hesitated or mumbled something about dishes that couldn't stay dirty overnight, it would have shattered his mood. But instead, she smiled in a way that reminded him of the secret smile they used to share when they were both young and in tune, and knew without saying it that they were going to make love.

When they were in bed, naked in each other's arms, he felt accepted and wanted by his wife rather than merely tolerated. Without wanting to acknowledge it, he realized there was a reciprocity to their lovemaking that had been subtly absent for a long while. But tonight it seemed the way it ought to be and could be, all the time from now on, if they could put their lives and their dreams back together.

The mood of hopefulness carried right through to the morning. Linda got up before Ray, washed the dishes from the night before and made breakfast.

"Nothing like the smell of bacon and eggs and strong coffee to get a man's heart started," he said, coming into the kitchen.

Linda smiled. Shana giggled. Like him, they were still in their pajamas. He bent low enough for his daughter to hug and kiss him. She said, "Your heart doesn't get started every morning, Daddy. It has to run all the time or you'd be dead."

"Not mine. Mine rests at night. It has to."

"Oh, Daddy, I know when you're fibbing!" Shana chided.

He sat at the kitchen table, and his wife poured coffee for him. "I was looking out the window at those ugly poplars," she said. "It's going to cost us a fortune to get them taken down."

"Maybe we won't have to," he said, winking. "The best time to do it is before they turn green, and that won't happen for another month or so. By then . . ."

Her eyes sparkled. She had read his thought. "I was going to bring it up," she told him, "but I was afraid you'd get mad. I'm glad . . . if you mean what I think you mean."

"I do."

"I know what you grown-ups are talking about, you can't fool me," Shana said in an accusatory tone, looking up from her bowl of cereal.

"Oh, honey, does it upset you?" Linda asked, putting her hand on her daughter's shoulder and stooping to look her ln the eyes.

"Moving," Shana said triumphantly. "That's what you're talking about, isn't it? I heard Mrs. Larson and you saying it might be better for us to live in New York, if I got accepted by Tiny Tot Academy."

"Would you mind?" Ray asked, holding his breath.

"No. There really aren't many kids for me to play with around here. Most of them are older than me."

"Than I," Linda corrected.

"You mean they're older than you, too?" Ray asked Linda with mock amazement.

She looked at him, and they burst out laughing. So did Shana. A major hurdle had been breached. Now they all knew they were in agreement on moving.

The poplars Linda had mentioned were usually something she liked to throw in his face. When they had first moved to East Stanton, New Jersey, a year before Shana was born, they had discussed putting a high redwood fence around their lot. But then Ray had stumbled upon an ad in *Suburban Magazine* touting the planting of poplar trees as a way of shielding large estates from the prying eyes of strangers. The poplars were for sale cheap-three hundred dollars for a hundred saplings-and the ad claimed they would shoot up faster than bamboo. They did. A third of them were forty feet tall now, but the other two-thirds were rotting and dying, probably because they had lost the competition for sunlight. Ray had gotten bids from a half-dozen pruning and lumbering outfits, and the cheapest price was fifty dollars per tree to saw them down and pull the stumps out of the ground.

Over breakfast, he figured that, since Linda hadn't really jumped on him about the trees this morning, it was a good sign. Maybe she was realizing that they weren't doing badly together, even though all their fondest dreams hadn't panned out yet. As far as material things went, they had it made. They could have a pretty sweet life, if they would work together, instead of fighting each other.

Feeling better about things than he had felt in a long while, Ray told himself he was about ready to trade in some of what he had now – a comfortable ranch-style home, two late model sedans, a backyard swimming pool – all the upper middle-class trappings – in return for a move back to the City. Not only would it eliminate the hassle of getting Shana to and from Tiny Tot Academy, it would put him closer to his job. Ironically, the main reason for fleeing to the suburbs had been to give the child what Linda had called "a more wholesome environment." Ray had grown up in New York and hadn't been so anxious to leave; now he was excited about the prospect of returning. He and Linda had been happier and more successful there. Maybe, if they went back, the magic would return.

CHAPTER 10

Charles Baich couldn't get out of bed. Couldn't face the horror.

What he had done to Jane Taft played over and over through his mind like a repeating nightmare. Guilt. Revulsion. Denial. It just couldn't be true. But it was. He *knew* that it was. He still couldn't believe that there was such a madman locked deep inside himself. And the madman had gotten loose.

Now Jane was dead.

He had dragged her body, her torn clothing, her purse and shoes into a shallow gully back in the woods, perhaps a hundred yards from the fat weeping willow tree. He had covered her with dead branches and leaves. Then he had gone home and managed to sneak in the house and go straight up to his room without being seen by his mom and dad. He hadn't been able to fix the broken zipper on his denim trousers; they were balled up in the bottom of his closet with his bloody underpants. Jane had been a virgin. She had bled all over him.

He cried hot, salty tears, sobbing into his pillow, hoping his mom and dad wouldn't hear. It was Saturday morning. He could smell bacon, eggs and coffee. His parents were downstairs in the kitchen. When the toast popped, he'd be called.

Or maybe they wouldn't call him today. They knew what he was going through. Maybe they'd decide to leave him alone with his grief.

Somehow he'd have to get rid of his muddy, bloody clothing. How? People would be watching him too closely now, more closely than ever before. He could think of no excuse to sneak away from his parents today. They knew Jane was missing. So did the cops. Probably the detectives would come and question Charles again today. They'd probably bring a search warrant. Before he could do anything about it, they'd open his closet and find all the evidence they needed to put him on trial for rape and murder.

Maybe he'd get a chance to burn his balled-up clothes in the fireplace in the family room. If only his parents would both leave the house. Not likely. They were under too much strain to go off on a pleasant shopping excursion.

At half-past five, not long after Charles had gotten home last evening, the manager of the Burger World had phoned. Up in his room the boy had heard the ringing, like his own death knell. Then his mom had called him to come down and get on the line. "It's about Jane," she had said, all nervous and worried. "She hasn't shown up for work."

He had lied to the Burger World manager with a degree of skill and calmness that had momentarily convinced him that he could simply go on lying and lying. "I walked her to the edge of the woods, on your side of the park. All she had to do was walk the last thirty or forty yards to the restaurant."

"Well, she never got here," the manager had said. "I'm stuck for a counter girl. You think she might've stopped to do some shopping or something?"

"That wouldn't be like Jane. She knew she didn't have time."

"You're right. She's conscientious. That's why I like to have her working for me. I tried phoning her parents, but nobody answers. Look – do you think I ought to call the cops?'

"Maybe," Charles had hedged, allowing himself to show concern. "Her mother and father won't be home for a while. They went to some kind of retirement party."

"I'll give it another half hour, then I'll phone the police," the Burger World manager had said. "If you hear anything in the meantime, please let me know."

Charles had promised to do so. Then he had hung up. All the rest of last evening, he had endured the torture of playing out the charade. He had spoken on the phone two more times to the Burger World manager, then to Jane's distraught parents, then to a police detective. Finally, two cops had come to his house to interview him in person. He had managed to get through their interrogation. But he didn't think he could continue to hold up. By the time he went to his room for the final time last night, he thought that not only the cops, but even his mom and dad, were beginning to doubt his story.

Today they'd have a search party out. Today they'd find Jane's body, her thighs bloody, her head bashed in. Today Charles would become the prime suspect.

No longer would he be "that nice, well-mannered boy who's doing so well at Fairchild Academy." He'd be known as a rapist and a killer. People would say that it only went to prove, once again, that the quiet, intelligent ones were the ones you couldn't trust.

At last Charles knew that there was only one reason for him to get out of bed this Saturday. He waited till his mom called him to come downstairs for breakfast. "Just a minute!" he called back to her with feigned cheerfulness.

Then he tiptoed across the hall to his parents' bedroom. He opened the bottom drawer of his dad's dresser and took out the .32 revolver that was kept there to protect the hearth and home.

He tiptoed back to his own room and sat on the edge of the bed. He was in his underwear and he was too shy and modest to want to be found that way. So he put on a pair of clean, crisp blue chinos. Then he sat on the edge of the bed again. He put the cold steel barrel in his mouth. Getting used to the steely coldness, he firmed his lips around it, even licked the tip with his tongue.

Then he pulled the trigger.

CHAPTER 11

Parked in the driveway with the engine running, Ray Berkshire wondered why Linda was taking so long to come out of the house. Shana, already buckled into the middle of the back seat, was fidgety, anxious to get going. "When's Mommy coming?" she asked peevishly.

"She ought to be out any second now," Ray answered. "She waited for *you* to go to the bathroom, so now we have to wait for her."

"But it's taking her so *long*," Shana complained.

"Hush!" Ray told her, annoyed that she was whining at him. She would've behaved better for Linda. Sometimes he thought it was good that he was the more lenient parent, and other times he wondered if he was too much of a pushover. But it would be tough for any father not to be easy on a little girl as smart and pretty as Shana. Linda always bought her such cute outfits, too. Today she was wearing a pleated blue skirt and a white cashmere sweater under her little brown leather coat. Expensive stuff to grow out of. But, of course, she had to dress well to land parts in TV commercials.

Linda always dressed well, too. In black slacks, a green turtleneck and a gray suede jacket, she stepped out onto the front porch and turned her key in the lock; Ray was once more glancing at his watch and thinking that it *couldn't* take so long to go to the bathroom and check the burners on the stove. When she got in the car she said, "Sorry, but the phone rang as I was on my way out the door." She smiled and her voice got more excited. "It was Shirley Sutter, the enrollment director from the Academy. Apparently, Vanessa ran into her last night at a party and hinted that it would be nice if we could be given a tour of the school while we are there for Shana's physical. Mrs. Sutter is going to be finishing up some work in her office today, so she offered to show us around a bit, if we cared to stop by. Naturally, I jumped at the chance. It can't hurt to get acquainted with her before Shana takes her entrance exams."

"Kind of her," Ray acknowledged, pulling out of the driveway. "I would like to get a feel for what the place is all about. It'll probably make today a long day, but it might save us a trip some other time."

"Am I going to have to take all my shots again, Mommy?" Shana asked.

Linda turned toward the back seat. "No, honey, this is just going to be an examination. Dr. Stowe won't hurt you. I'm sure she'll be every bit as nice as Dr. Rajendra."

"A woman doctor?" Shana said with some surprise.

"Yes, of course. Women can be doctors, too. You may decide to be one yourself someday. Always remember, women can do anything men can do."

"Yick!" Shana said. "Sticking needles into people!"

"It's for a good reason, though, Shana. Doctors use vaccinations to help us stay well."

"I know, but I still don't like the needles," Shana said with unwavering conviction.

"I don't like them either," Ray admitted, stealing a peek at his blonde, blue-eyed daughter in the rearview mirror and feeling a surge of affection. He liked it when she showed the same reactions of fear or joy, or whatever, as any normal kid. It reassured him that all the high-powered mothering that Linda was wreaking on her couldn't totally turn her into some kind of efficient, inhibited machine.

Heading for the New Jersey Turnpike, he drove past residential areas similar to the one where he and his family lived. Some of the homes were more ticky-tacky than theirs, and some more ritzy, but they all had the same aura of comfortable complacency. Entirely absent was any of the bustling, friendly good cheer of the small town or any of the roiling, frenetic turmoil of the big city. For somebody raised in Manhattan, as Ray was, this place seemed flat and sterile; a debilitating price to pay for the sake of giving one's child a quiet grassy lawn to be bored in.

Hitting the gas pedal to the floor to merge onto the turnpike, it struck him that the crazy horn-honking stream of rushing traffic was yet another good reason to get away from suburbia. He had to keep darting his eyes in all directions to make sure he and his wife and daughter weren't flattened or sideswiped. Many times he had thought how easily he could get maimed or killed traveling to and from work. It would be absurd to make Shana take the same risk just to go to school. If this Tiny Tot Academy actually came through, back to Manhattan the Berkshire family would go. Before moving to the boondocks Ray hadn't owned a car and hadn't driven much. It would suit him fine to get back to using subways, taxis and buses.

"Let's play a game while we're driving," Linda suggested cheerily. "How about Twenty Questions?"

Half amused and half dismayed, Ray realized that his Wife was about to put his daughter through another disguised learning exercise.

"Oh, good!" Shana cried out. "Give us the first clue, Mommy!"

"Okay . . . I'm thinking of something that starts with the 'b' sound."

"Is it animal, mineral, or vegetable?" Ray chipped in, making his voice light and playful, while inwardly keyed up, driving defensively, barreling toward the Lincoln Tunnel.

Fairchild Plaza occupied a full city block in the West Eighties. There were five buildings of gleaming aluminum and tinted glass surrounding a small urban park. The lamp posts and the leafless trees cast long, black shadows in the late morning sun of an unusually bright April day.

Glancing anxiously at her watch, Linda said, "Let's hurry or we'll be late. Our appointment is for eleven."

"Since when was any doctor ever on schedule?" Ray said, trying to walk hand in hand with Shana and still keep up with Linda's brisk stride. "Even Dr. Rajendra makes us wait all the time."

"But, according to Vanessa, this place prides itself on efficiency and punctuality," said Linda. "I'd hate to do anything to arouse their disfavor our very first time here."

"Which building do we want?" asked Ray. "Slow down – Shana has short legs."

"Over there, I think," said Linda, pointing toward the left of the plaza at a building that looked like all the others. She veered off in that direction, walking just a bit slower, and Ray and Shana followed.

The entrance had a plaque over the double glass doors that said FAIRCHILD #3. Presumably, the other buildings were #1, #2, #4 and #5; their exterior architecture was not differentiated by anything other than the numbers on their plaques, so that one had to simply learn from experience which one held the Academy, the Pediatric Center, the Research Institute and so on. "See if the Fingernail and Toenail Clinic is in this building," Ray joked, as he and Linda scanned the lobby directory.

"Pediatric Center . . . Dr. Stowe . . . Room Four-eighteen," Linda said, ignoring him.

But he was rewarded by a giggle from Shana. "I'm glad you put on your new pinstripe suit," Linda commented as the elevator took them up to the fourth floor. "You look nice, Ray."

"Thanks. So do you." He had trimmed his goatee and mustache in deference to the importance that his wife attached to this appointment. "You look nice too, honey," he told Shana. "If I say so myself, we make an attractive family."

Stepping out of the elevator, they spotted a sign that indicated numbers 410-418 with an arrow that pointed down a corridor to the right. They walked on a gray carpet past a series of gray steel doors till they came to the last one in the hall.

It was five minutes to eleven when Linda signed in with Dr. Stowe's receptionist, a willowy brunette in nurse's whites who looked barely out of her teens. "See, we're on time. No reason to be flustered," Ray said, as his wife sat down next to him and Shana. They were the only ones in the waiting room for a minute or two, till a young woman and a little boy popped out through a door to the right of the receptionist's glassed-in cubicle and grabbed up hats and coats that had been draped over a couple of the orange plastic chairs lining the bare white walls. Ray couldn't help remembering that Dr. Rajendra's waiting room hadn't been so plain and sterile; there had been toys and games scattered about for the kids to amuse themselves.

About half a minute after the woman and the little boy departed, the receptionist came out of her cubicle and said, "Shana Berkshire . . . Mr. and Mrs. Berkshire . . . this way, please."

So Linda had been right. This was indeed a rarity: a doctor's appointment that was going to come off on schedule.

"Have a seat, please," the willowy receptionist said. "Dr. Stowe will be with you in a moment." She backed out of the office after ushering Ray, Linda and Shana in.

They sat on tan armchairs facing the doctor's brown, bulky steel desk. Her office avoided – barely – the totally institutional ambiance of her waiting room by the grace of some fairly decent still lifes adorning the white walls and a tall set of shelves behind the desk, filled mostly with books but with intermittent spaces allotted to colorful ceramic knickknacks and vases of flourishing green plants.

At eleven on the dot, Dr. Stowe came in: a short, stocky middle-aged woman in a white lab coat. Her shoulder-length gray hair was combed back, instead of in bangs, eschewing an opportunity of cosmetically disguising a forehead that was too high and broad. Her face was as flat and moon shaped as a Russian peasant's. "Good morning, Mr. and Mrs. Berkshire," she said with a warm, but thin-lipped, smile, "I'm Dr. Stowe. And, of course, this must be Shana. How are you, darling?"

"Fine," Shana answered, returning the doctor's smile with one of her own. Ray and Linda gave each other

85

glances of relief that their daughter seemed to be responding favorably to the new pediatrician.

Dr. Stowe sat behind her desk, saying, "We'll only need you parents while we're filling out some medical history forms. Then it will take about one hour for Shana's physical exam, including blood tests, urinalysis and so forth." She riffled through a batch of telephone-call memos. "I understand that Shirley Sutter is expecting to meet you today, also. A perfect time for you to see her would be while I'm busy with Shana. Shirley will be expecting you around eleven-thirty in Fairchild #2, on the first floor, where we're establishing our Tiny Tot Academy." She peered sharply at Shana, noticing that the little girl was fidgeting and biting her lip. "Why, what's the matter, darling? Is something troubling you?"

"Did you say 'blood tests'?" Shana piped up, grimacing. "I hate needles," she added, blinking and wincing.

Dr. Stowe smiled ingratiatingly. "Well, you don't have to be afraid of my needle, Shana, because it isn't going to hurt you. It isn't at all like getting a shot, since no serum will be injected and no muscle tissue will be penetrated, and that's what has given you pain in the past. So, now that you understand, you *are* going to be brave for me, aren't you?"

"Well . . . yes," Shana reluctantly promised, her eyes darting toward her parents, wanting to please them, even though she was not entirely convinced that the needle wouldn't hurt.

The nameplate on her door read: DR. SHIRLEY SUTTER, ENROLLMENT DIRECTOR. She was an attractive sandy-haired woman in her late thirties or maybe early forties, wearing a well-tailored mauve suit and a white blouse with ruffled sleeves and collar. It didn't take much chitchat for Ray to decide that he liked her. She seemed effortlessly warm and personable, with a ready smile and a twinkle in her hazel eyes. In keeping with her warmer personality, her office was more expansive and much cozier than Dr. Stowe's. The walls were a soft yellow and the carpet was a dark brown shag. The large desk, bookcases and the cabinets were in rich walnut. On the wall behind the desk were numerous diplomas, plaques and certificates of achievement in her profession. The other walls were hung with oil paintings of sailing and surfing scenes. She made pleasant small talk with Ray and Linda, while they got comfortable in an area of the office that was furnished with a sofa, an easy chair and a round glass coffee table. Dr. Sutter poured fresh, steaming coffee and they each fixed theirs the way they liked it. Then the conversation turned more serious.

"I don't know how much you may already know about our setup here," Dr. Sutter began, "so why don't we just assume that you know very little, and I'll launch into my usual spiel."

She smiled, then took a sip of her coffee. Ray and Linda smiled back, giving her their full attention.

Dr. Sutter went on. "Fairchild is endowed by the National Council for Gifted Children. Our basic concept is to try to do for education what research has already done for fields like engineering and medicine. We believe that a progressive society facing world-wide competition in every area of human endeavor, cannot afford to have an educational system that is primitive, unconnected to any sophisticated scientific base. We are studying how children learn and how to help them learn more and learn quicker. Traditionally, however, the results of such research have taken a long, long time to trickle down to the average classroom. While it can take ten or twenty years for a new and viable idea to reach most children, because of the stifling bureaucracy of the public schools, here at Fairchild we have narrowed that time gap to two years . . . or even less in some circumstances."

"But what if you make a mistake?" Ray asked. "What if you try something before it's proved, and the results are damaging?"

Linda flashed him a distraught, disapproving look, warning him not to make any waves at this early stage, before Shana had even passed her enrollment tests.

But Dr. Sutter seemed unperturbed by his question. With unaltered affableness, she answered, "Nothing we do here is so radical that it could cause permanent harm. And if something isn't working, of course we find out right away, because our results are being closely and constantly monitored. We believe that creativity flourishes best within a framework of solid scientific discipline. Here at Fairchild we know that all of our students are gifted to start with. Our task is to channel their innate abilities, but not to restrict them – to help them achieve and even expand their potential."

"How do you determine which children to accept?" Linda asked nervously. "I mean . . ." She forced a smile, ". . . what chance has Shana got of meeting with your approval?"

"That I can't tell you," replied Dr. Sutter, "until I've examined her. It won't be just her IQ and achievement tests that count; many people with high IQs lack creativity, flexibility and originality. So I utilize special tests developed here at Fairchild. The responses are judged on inventiveness, fluency and attention to meaningful detail. I look for the outstanding cognitive and conceptual abilities that distinguish the truly gifted child."

"Isn't it sort of undemocratic to have all the gifted ones lumped together?" asked Ray. "If they aren't exposed to *all* types of kids, don't they get a distorted view of the real world?"

"We teach them not to be snobbish," Dr. Sutter said. "They are told over and over that they mustn't take pride in any traits that are genetic, rather than learned. And, of course, they have lives outside of Fairchild, where they interact with society's broad spectrum. So they aren't short changed in any way. We would not want it to be otherwise – we who support the type of advanced education that is crucial to this nation's hope of producing more scientists, innovators and extraordinary achievers. Our new generations of leaders will hopefully not only build happy, productive lives for themselves as individuals, but will also help us maintain economic, military and political superiority over countries such as Russia, China, Germany and Japan."

Obviously, it wasn't the first time she had made this speech. But her words still carried such an intense fervor that Ray was impressed, even a bit awed.

Looking at her watch, Linda said, "Gee, it's a quarter to twelve already. I was hoping we'd get to see some of the classrooms."

"Oh, we still have time," Dr. Sutter said, rising. "I won't be able to show you Tiny Tot Academy, since the workmen have everything torn up in that part of the building. But I can show you the first grade, and I think that'll give you an idea as to what Shana might expect here."

"That will be fine," Linda agreed enthusiastically.

She and Ray finished their coffee, and then followed Dr. Sutter. The most remarkable thing about the classrooms they had time to see was that the blackboard exercises in reading, writing, arithmetic and foreign languages, plus the displays of art and science projects, were at such a high level of complexity and sophistication. The teachers' desks and the ten students' desks in each room were about the same as one might expect in any ordinary school – except the kids' desks were too small to fit pupils of the age that might ordinarily be expected to be turning out such advanced work. It was way above the "See Spot Run" and "Fun with Dick and Jane" stuff that Ray Berkshire remembered from his own childhood schooling. He had to keep reminding himself that this was only the first grade. In addition to the standard classroom furniture, each room also contained ten cubicles outfitted with computer keyboards, video-display screens and racks of software programs.

Dr. Sutter said, "As I told you, the Tiny Tot Academy is not operational yet, but it will be in four months. We don't anticipate any problem in meeting our deadline. Then, our ultramodern complex here will cater to the total child – from the nursery on up through high school. The preschoolers get much more than just daycare; they actually begin to read, to write, to do arithmetic, to be exposed to computers and to learn a foreign language. Tiny Tot Academy takes them right through kindergarten – a highly advanced version of it – and then they continue to Fairchild

Academy for the succeeding grade levels. And since we're tied in with all the facilities here at Fairchild Plaza, our students are always under expert supervision in terms of pediatric care, dental care, medical care and even psychiatric counseling."

"I like the pediatrician we already have," said Ray, testing the waters.

Linda flashed him a look of such stern reproachment that he was sure she'd have kicked him if she'd thought she could do it without Dr. Sutter noticing.

"I was wondering if we could retain him," Ray continued.

"There's no reason to," Dr. Sutter said, "since your tuition fee pays for all the services I've mentioned and lots more. Your contract with us would require you to use our programs exclusively, since the Academy *is* set up for experimental and research projects, and we don't want these cultural experiments to be diluted by outside influences. It wouldn't be in keeping with the true scientific method."

"Of course," Linda quickly agreed. "We understand totally."

"We still have time to take a peek at the library," said Dr, Sutter. "Would you like to?"

"Oh, yes," said Linda.

They went down the hall past the first-grade rooms and entered a much larger room; to Ray, it didn't look much different than any other grade-school library, except, once again, the books and other teaching materials on display seemed way ahead of what normally could be expected for the first grade. Dr. Sutter explained that each grade had its own library of not only books, but of microfilms, video and audio tapes, educational slide shows and motion pictures and computer-learning programs. "Also," she mentioned, "we maintain elaborate science facilities and an absolutely wonderful astronomy and space lab that we don't have time to see today – but I'm sure you'll want to take a look at it next time you're here. I should've taken you there first, because I just love showing it off. It's quite impressive."

"Then we'll have it to look forward to," Said Linda. "We can't thank you enough for taking so much trouble."

"No trouble at all," said Dr. Sutter, smiling her warm smile. "I wouldn't worry too much about your daughter's chances, Mr. and Mrs. Berkshire. Vanessa told me she's convinced that Shana is Fairchild material. And she has lots of experience in these matters. She and I used to be colleagues – both practicing child psychologists – but she gave up her profession when she got married."

"My goodness, I didn't know that!" Linda exclaimed, her eyes widening. "She never mentioned it to me. Ray isn't that amazing? I knew there was something special about her. The way she relates to her little boy is a pleasure to watch."

"Yes, she and Monroe get along beautifully," agreed Dr. Sutter.

Crossing the plaza on their way back to Fairchild #3, Linda let loose the anger she had been holding in. She accused Ray of making a bad impression. "You didn't need to come on so strong right off the bat. You could've waited till we're sure we've been accepted. For God's sake, Dr. Sutter is the *enrollment director!* Don't you realize that she's the one who's going to determine Shana's fate?"

"I realize it!" Ray snapped back. "Of course I realize it, Linda, but I also realize something else: I'm going to help determine Shana's fate, too, because she's *my* daughter. And if I can't satisfy myself that this place isn't going to turn her into some kind of fact-stuffed robot, then I won't be in favor of coughing up four thousand a year to send her here."

"If the money is worrying you, I can go back to work and pay her tuition myself," Linda said.

"I'm willing to spend anything we can afford, and then some, to do the right thing for our daughter. But first I have to be convinced it's the right thing. Going by what we've seen here, Fairchild is achieving same marvelous results in terms of the kids' output. But what is the pressure doing to the kids? That's what I wonder."

"I'm surprised at you," Linda taunted. "You used to be the bold adventurer when we were first married. Now you sound like a man who's afraid of the future."

"It's not that," Ray countered. "It's just that I'm not entirely sure yet that some of these so-called dynamic new trends might not turn out to be detriments, rather than improvements."

"Ray," Linda said in a lecturing tone of voice, "you've been in the rat race all your adult life, you know how tough it is to get ahead. And today's kids are growing up in a world much more complicated than anything we used to dream of. The ones who don't learn how to make it in that kind of world are going to be like lost little sheep, incapable of fending for themselves. I pity them. And I can't believe you'd want our daughter to be one of the losers."

When they got back up to Dr. Stowe's waiting room it was ten after twelve. The receptionist was behind her desk in the glass cubicle, and Shana was sitting all by herself on one of the orange plastic chairs in the outer area.

"How did it go, honey?" Linda asked.

"I'm all finished, Mommy. The needle really *didn't* hurt – see?" She showed off the tiny puncture mark in the crook of her arm where the blood sample had been taken. "The nurse lady said for me to tell you that Dr. Stowe is waiting for you so she can talk with you before you leave."

The door to the right of the glass cubicle opened and the receptionist came out. "That's right, Mr. and Mrs. Berkshire. You can go right into Dr. Stowe's office. I'll keep an eye on Shana for you."

No sooner were she and Ray seated in front of Dr. Stowe's brown steel desk when Linda blurted, "Is everything all right, Doctor?"

"Why, yes," Dr. Stowe answered, looking up from the new file folder she had started for Shana. "As far as I can tell, there are no earth-shaking problems. The one thing that bothers me a bit is Shana's red count. It seems a trifle low. Nothing to be alarmed about, but still . . . has she been taking a B-complex supplement?"

"After she was born, I gave her liquid vitamins every day for the first year," said Linda. "But, after that, Dr. Rajendra said they weren't necessary, so I discontinued them."

Dr. Stowe brushed back a strand of gray hair. "Not to criticize a colleague," she said, her moon-shaped peasant's face beaming benignly, "but sometimes it isn't wise to stop the vitamins so soon. Active children burn up an amazing amount of nutrients. Now—" She opened her middle desk drawer and took out a large plastic bottle filled with yellow-and-blue capsules. "This is a special, highly effective supplement developed here at Fairchild. I'm going to give you these and I'd like you to try them for the next three weeks – one a day, with Shana's morning meal. Then we'll see if her red count improves."

"You say it's not anything to be terribly worried about?" asked Ray.

"Not terribly worried, no. She's not truly anemic. It's merely that her red cell count is in the low-normal range. It wouldn't have been wise to let this continue, or else serious difficulties may have resulted. But we should be able to remedy the situation rather easily."

Linda took the bottle of capsules and put them in her purse. "Dr. Stowe," she asked, "does this mean that Shana has failed her physical? Will it cause her not to be accepted by Tiny Tot Academy?"

The doctor emitted a soft, friendly chuckle. "No, Mrs. Berkshire, not at all. As I said before, it really isn't a serious problem – since we did catch it in time."

"Thank God," said Linda, her eyes meeting Ray's for an instant, telling him how right she was to have brought Shana here. "I certainly appreciate the fact that you're much more thorough than the pediatrician were using."

Ray had to grant that his wife might have a good point. Perhaps it was old-fashioned and unwise to cling for the sake of loyalty to someone like Dr. Rajendra. His unsophisticated methods apparently had failed to diagnose what could have become a health hazard for Shana, if it had been left untreated. Why deprive the child of the best that modern medicine had to offer?

For that matter, why not take the plunge and stop balking at the opportunity of getting her into Fairchild?

Maybe the kids were being pushed hard – but look what they were achieving. From what Ray had seen, he would guess that many of the first-graders were operating on about a fourth – or fifth – grade level. He hated to think that some other kids, not any prettier or any brighter than his own daughter, might be able to put her to shame. If he stood in her way.

As much as Ray distrusted the thrust of today's science and technology and despaired of the abuses that had already taken place, he also realized that the hands of time weren't going to be turned backward. The genie was already out of the bottle. Like it or not, huge and highly organized complexes like the one being pioneered here at Fairchild Plaza were probably the wave of the future. Why shouldn't Shana have a slice of the pie? Why should she struggle along in a classroom full of kids with less ability than herself, who would only hold her back and stunt her intellectual development? When it really came down to it, maybe the future actually would belong to those who had the courage to seize it, instead of shrinking from it and retreating into a less complicated world that was doomed to extinction.

CHAPTER 12

On Monday, Felicia Patterson never made it to school.

Her clock radio woke her up at six, as usual, so she would have time to jog three miles and then have breakfast before catching the bus. She dragged herself out of bed, nearly overcome by the lethargy that plagued her every day now, except when she was at the Academy. Somehow, she didn't think of Ted and the way she had lost him, when she was in school.

Listening to the weather report, she found out that it was very cold for late April – in the low thirties – and that Manhattan was enveloped by a dense fog. Anticipation of going out in the lousy weather did not improve her mood. Good thing she had her brother Arnold to jog with, or she would have crapped out. He usually didn't poke around; she had better get moving. She clicked the radio off, tugged a hooded nylon windbreaker on over her jogging clothes, and stepped out into the hall. She noticed a crack of light under the closed bathroom door, heard water running and figured her brother must be in there. It couldn't be her father. He should be gone already. Yesterday evening he had complained about having to get up at four to make a five A.M. location filming of some Faraday Family Restaurants commercials. He was going to put in a surprise appearance to make sure that the producer, Ray Berkshire, had the job running properly.

Felicia wondered why her dad's supposedly big-time job as Director of Broadcast Production for Wagner, Inc., a gigantic advertising agency, produced such a gracious style of living, and a life filled with beautiful things that failed to give her any genuine delight. The luxurious apartment, the plush chairs and sofas upholstered in dark blue crushed velvet, seemed empty, lonely and cold. Her expensive running shoes imprinted their new and perfect tread pattern in the deep pile of the ivory carpet as she went to a ten-foot-wide floor-to-ceiling window, parted the blue velvet draperies and peered out. The fog was so opaque that, instead of a panoramic view of Central Park, she saw nothing but her own reflection. The street lamps five stories below must be on, but, if so, their glow was totally obscured.

Felicia turned when she heard the bathroom door open and soft footsteps coming down the hall. It was her mother, looking pale and unrested, in a pink nightgown and slippers. She said, "Arnold is ill. He can't go jogging. I'm making him stay home from school. He woke me up when I heard him being sick in the bathroom an hour ago. Maybe something he ate after the movie last night didn't agree with him."

Felicia bit her lip, not knowing what to say. Now that she was up and ready, she wanted to go jogging – in fact, she needed to go. She couldn't bear the thought of killing two empty hours waiting for school to begin. It dawned on her that she ought to show some concern for her brother. "You mean he was sick to his stomach? Throwing up? I didn't hear him." It was true. She had slept like a log. Why was it that her sleep did not refresh?

"Thank God, he emptied his stomach," said Mrs. Patterson. "He seemed to feel better afterward. I hope you realize I'm not about to let you go jogging by yourself,

Felicia. You saw the fog out there. I hate the thought of your father being out in it, let alone you. Slogging around Central Park on a morning like this just wouldn't be a wise thing to do. Who knows what kind of maniac will be waiting to jump out at you when you can't see two feet in front of your nose?"

"Ted will be with me, Mother," Felicia lied. "He said he would meet me between six-fifteen and six-thirty, so I'd better get going."

"Buzz the desk man first and make sure Ted is down there."

"He's not going to be in the lobby, Mother. I'm supposed to see him on the corner. If he's not there, I'll come back."

"Even if he shows up, you don't have to jog. The weather is horrible. You can skip it for one day. I'll make the two of you a Western omelet with toast and hot chocolate, and you can stay warm and cozy here watching TV till it's time to catch the bus."

"Thanks a whole bunch, Mother," Felicia told her, giving her a hug, "but I don't want to get in the habit of missing my exercises."

"You bring Ted up here for breakfast anyway, after you're done running."

"I will. Don't worry, he won't need to be asked twice. He loves your omelets."

Getting on the elevator and riding down to the lobby, Felicia was already thinking ahead to the lie she'd need to tell later to explain Ted's absence. She would simply claim that he hadn't shown up, but she'd run into another friend from school – or, better yet, a friend of Arnold's whose name she didn't really remember.

She wasn't usually such an unconscionable liar. But her parents were so used to her being successful at everything, she simply couldn't bring herself to tell them she had blown it with her boyfriend. He was one of the few bright spots in her life, outside of school. She entertained a vague, desperate hope that somehow they'd get back together. Without him, she'd have so many empty hours to fill. She was surprised she'd had to lie to get out of the house to go jogging. Subconsciously, her mind must be telling her to exercise, even though her body might not want to go through with it. Maybe, if she didn't run long and hard today, she would sink into a bottomless depression from which she'd never recover.

Up until roughly a year ago, "slogging through the park" (as her mother called it) had made her feel good about herself. It had given a lift to her spirits that had lasted for as much as several hours after she took her shower and ate breakfast and got into the main part of each day. She hadn't questioned why this was so, but had accepted and valued its contribution to her motivation. Then, one day in biology class, she had seen a movie produced at the Fairchild Educational and Psychological Research Institute dealing with the latest scientific discoveries concerning the electrochemistry of the human brain. She had learned about chemicals called enkephalins and endorphins – natural mood regulators whose function was to counteract severe bouts of pain, disappointment and depression. It was now known that strenuous exercise would influence a greater concentration of endorphins and enkephalins, giving a person an overall sense of well-being – sometimes called "jogger's high." Why, the film's narrator asked, would the human mind be programmed so that strenuous body activity would release "a fix" of pleasure-causing chemicals? Furthermore, why were the same chemicals released in heavy concentrations during meals and during sex?

It seemed obvious that all activities vital to species survival – such as eating, sexual intercourse and physical exercise – had been designed by nature to be physiologically addictive, so that people would be sufficiently motivated to pursue those activities. In other words, it wasn't enough for human beings to be taught that they had to eat, drink, work, play and copulate. They had to *enjoy* doing those things, or they might not do enough, and thus, become extinct.

Mother Nature hadn't left anything to chance.

Then why weren't Felicia's basic drives up to par?

She seemed to have to run longer and harder, week by week, in order to get her fix of enkephalins and endorphins. First, she was jogging one mile, then a mile and a half, two miles, two and a half, then three . . .

Rather than the sense of physical and emotional well-being that she used to enjoy, her satisfaction was becoming more cerebral. Another job well done. A detached feeling of accomplishment. Beneficial, but not the same kick that it used to be. Nevertheless, she was compelled to keep doing it, as if a tiny voice inside her was whispering that something awful would happen if she stopped.

Maybe she would cease caring whether she lived or died.

When the elevator doors opened at ground level, she saw Mr. Brevko, a plump old man in a blue security uniform, sitting at his desk. He was sipping coffee and gazing around the darkly paneled Victorian lobby as if hoping that something, maybe even a ghost, might materialize to relieve his loneliness. His eyes lit up when he spotted Felicia – somebody to talk to on the kind of morning that was so cold and damp and quiet that a person could almost think he was the last human on earth. She gave him a cheery hello – much more cheerful than she felt – which was her habit. Nobody, not even her mother, she thought to herself, could have an inkling that she was anything but a happy, well-adjusted, highly motivated teenager. Mr. Brevko, who reminded her of a Norman Rockwell grandfather, even though she knew he was a childless widower, reacted to her warm and bouncy manner as though she were his favorite granddaughter. It took her a while to tactfully break away from him.

Out on the sidewalk the fog wasn't as soupy as it had appeared from five stories up, but still, visibility wasn't more than twenty feet. Felicia had to listen for footsteps to make sure no one else was close or approaching. There didn't seem to be anyone around. The cold dampness enveloped her, and she watched her white breath adding to the mist. Zipping up her pink nylon windbreaker and pulling the drawstrings to tighten the hood around her face, she started walking. The street lamps that she hadn't been able to see from her apartment window glowed diffusely as she passed them one by one. At the corner of West Seventieth and Central Park West, she looked and listened intently, cocking her head left and right, trying to be alert for any traffic that might screech out of the fog and mow her down before she could cross safely into the park.

Suddenly, eerily familiar sounds were all around her, disembodied by the mist. She felt the presence of about as many joggers and bicyclers as usual, even though she could only see the ones close by. She joined a throng of runners, breaking into a trot, stretching her stride to gradually match the pace. How silly were her mother's fears that somebody might attack her out of the fog, when all she had to do was keep herself surrounded by a crowd. Protected by a cocoon of strangers, the rhythms of her strenuously striving body became automatic and she allowed her mind to wander . . .

The spell she had taken in the drugstore returned, not so much to haunt her, but to puzzle her. She knew that somehow it had been merely a prelude to the crazy episode that had caused her to break up with Ted. Removed from the event by the passage of time, and by the demands of her morning exercise on a day so opaque that it was almost a sensory-deprivation environment, she could now contemplate that earlier "spell" with lessened dread.

What she had done no longer seemed so horrible, after all. With some justification, she had blown her temper at a fat, slow checkout clerk. Obviously, she had been pent up and needed to let off steam, and the dim-witted clerk had tripped her valve. As for the discovery that she could be stimulated by pornography – that certainly didn't make her a freak. In fact, so far, it was almost the only normal thing about her sex drive. It was a move in the right direction. She knew from reading books and articles about sex therapy that one of the ways to work toward a healthy response was to begin by using masturbation or pornography or sexual fantasy – or whatever else could open you up to your blocked feelings.

After school one day last week, in Ted's bedroom before his parents came home from work, she had tried to fill her head with the erotic images that had turned her on in the drugstore. She had even tried doing some of the things she had read about, but had never worked up the nerve to do before. None of it had helped her, although some of it had pleased Ted enormously. Once more she had had to fake her orgasm.

Then, on the bus – what in the world had come over her? It was as if everything had turned loose all at once, in the wrong place, at the wrong time, and with too much of a gush of released pressure – like wanting a trickle of water from a faucet, and getting a torrent.

Funny . . . thinking about it was getting her excited right now. What was wrong with her? Why was she experiencing these moistening and tingling sensations when she was supposed to be concentrating on the pace of her jogging? She tugged at the stretch fabric of her sweat pants, thinking they might be riding up, exerting unwanted pressure on her crotch.

With a sudden jolt, she became aware that one of the male joggers was staring at her. She didn't remember seeing him before. He must have just joined the group. Although it was an admittedly cold morning for this time of year, Felicia thought it was a bit much for him to be wearing a ski mask. He had his arms hugged tightly to his body and his hands tucked inside the pouch of his black jogging jacket, instead of pistoling them as he ran. But he was matching her stride for stride, never taking his eyes from her. Somehow it was like a pursuit – a mating ritual. She was losing control of herself, becoming more and more sexually aroused, despite her efforts to the contrary – and he seemed to know it. All she could see were two green lascivious eyes in the narrow slit of his black ski mask.

Then she saw his hand reaching out to her. She wanted to shrink away from him, but for some reason, she did not.

His warm, slender fingers closed around hers. By some inevitable alchemy, he had become the personification of the passions newly kindled inside her, transmuting sexual apathy into raging desire. The flames were fanned by her sense of danger, mystery and utter helplessness. The erotic force that compelled her was as terrifying as it was alluring.

With reluctance and yet urgency, she shortened her stride and slowed her pace to mesh perfectly with the slackening pace of her seducer, as the rest of the group jogged on ahead, dissolving and disappearing into gray.

Led by the hand of the man with green lecherous eyes, unsure whether she was being pulled into a realm of erotic dream or erotic nightmare, she allowed herself to fade into the fog.

CHAPTER 13

On the same Monday that Felicia Patterson went jogging in the fog, Linda Berkshire was exceedingly anxious over the outcome of the Burger World audition. Would Shana land a role or not? Tuesday was the deadline, according to what they had been told at Barbour & Lassiter. If they didn't hear anything by the end of tomorrow, their hopes would be dashed. A call might even come today. But Linda had no intention of waiting nervously by the phone. She always forced herself to go on with her life as usual, even when something crucial was hanging fire. So, on Monday morning, she trusted that her voice mail would catch any calls coming to the house while she was out and took Shana to Childplay.

The mother-child exercise program was run by a recreation and physical fitness franchise, called Family Spa, in a shopping center fifteen minutes from the Berkshires' home. Linda and Shana drove there in Linda's red Chevy. They were both wearing scruffy white sneakers and purple workout togs faded from wear. Ray had a similar outfit, and much to Linda's chagrin, it still looked brand new. He claimed he was too busy to exercise. He always pointed to his flat stomach as proof that he was still in decent shape and continued to ignore Linda's warnings that his arteries were slowly being clogged with cholesterol. "One of these days" he was going to get around to exercising regularly, just like one of these days he was going to start writing novels and screenplays.

"Take your jacket in with you," Linda told Shana, as she pulled the car into a parking slot. "It's still cold and foggy. We'll be perspiring when we come out, and that's a darn good way of catching the flu."

"Flu!" Shana giggled. "What a funny word!"

"Short for influenza."

"How can wearing a jacket stop you from catching it?"

"Well," Linda explained patiently as they walked, "when you're sweating and a draft or a cold wind hits you, you can get a chill. Then your body heats up too much and incubates certain germs—"

"Where do germs come from?"

"Some are always hiding in our bodies. When we're rundown or we get a chill or something like that, we give them a chance to become more powerful."

"I hate germs!" Shana declared vehemently.

Linda was worried that Shana's low red corpuscle count might make her more susceptible to coming down with something. She had asked Dr. Stowe if it would be all right for Shana to exercise. The pediatrician had said that curtailment of activity shouldn't be necessary, so long as the child was eating a well-balanced diet and was taking her vitamins.

"Mommy," Shana said, "what's that word you used before? Ink . . . you . . . inkyou . . ."

"Incubates."

"Yeah. What's it mean?"

"When you warm something up to make it start growing."

"Will different stuff start growing if you warm it up enough?"

"Only certain stuff. Like when we watched the baby chickens hatching at the pet store. Some stuff can't grow at all. Rocks, for instance."

Linda was glad when they entered the Family Spa building and Shana spotted Monroe Larson in the lobby and ran over to him. Shana had probably been about to ask why rocks couldn't grow even if you warmed them up a lot, and Linda would rather forego trying to come up with an answer.

The lobby was crowded with parents and children in exercise togs, clustering in front of the big brown double doors labeled CHILD PLAY (one word painted in white on each door). Everybody was waiting for the ten o'clock class to end so the eleven o'clock one could begin. Glancing around, Linda was surprised that Vanessa Larson wasn't right beside Monroe. Then she saw her friend coming out of the ladies' room in a red workout suit matching her little boy's.

Vanessa's eyes lit up when she spotted Linda. "Congratulations!" she boomed. "I heard the good news this morning!"

"What good news?" Linda asked, her heart fluttering.

Shana and Monroe stopped chattering and looked up at their mothers.

"You mean Arthur Philips hasn't phoned you?" Vanessa said.

"Why, no. I haven't heard a peep from him. Not since before the audition."

"What time did you leave the house?

"Fifteen minutes ago. Why?"

Vanessa had her auburn hair parted in the middle and tied into two ponytails, the way she always wore it when she came to Childplay, and both ponytails swung from side to side as she shook her head in consternation. "Maybe I should have kept my big mouth shut, Linda, but Tom Trenton sounded so certain that Shana had landed a part in one of the Burger World spots. He phoned to tell us that Monroe made it, so I asked if he knew how you made out, and—"

"Did he say we had made it?" Linda broke in.

"Yes. I presumed Arthur Philips would be letting you know right away, since he's still officially your agent till his contract expires. But he hasn't called you?"

"No. What time did Tom call you?"

"Nine o'clock this morning. The Burger World production schedule has been stepped up for some reason, and they want the entire cast to come to a special meeting at three this afternoon to be measured for costumes."

Linda's heart sank. If Shana had truly gotten cast, Arthur Philips would have gotten in touch with her to make sure she knew about the three o'clock costume call.

"I'm sorry, Linda," Vanessa said. "I shouldn't have been such a blabbermouth – but I was so sure we both had something to celebrate. Maybe Arthur Philips got tied up or something. You may still hear from him. Maybe he's trying to reach you now."

"Maybe," Linda agreed doubtfully. She made an effort to smile – and saw a tear trickling down Shana's cheek. "C'mon, honey, Mommy has to go to the ladies' room," Linda said quickly with artificial brightness, and she guided Shana in that direction, before her tears could turn to sobs. "We'll see you in class – go ahead in without us," she called out to Vanessa and Monroe.

No sooner was Linda's back turned when she heard a lady's voice crooning to Vanessa, "Excuse me, but did I hear you say your son is going to be in a Burger World commercial? How wonderful for you! This is *my* son, Jeffrey. He told me he was sure he recognized your son in a Sugar Duds commercial, but I told him he must be mistaken. But he *is* right, isn't he?"

"Yes, Monroe has been on TV a lot," Linda heard Vanessa boasting, before the ladies' room door shut.

Linda hugged Shana and let her cry for a few minutes without holding back, her tears dampening their purple sweatshirts. Then, using paper towels, she washed and dried her little girl's face. "We didn't lose yet," Linda said. "We won't know for sure till we get home. If there's no message on the machine, I'll phone Arthur Philips and ask him what happened. And even if we didn't make it, there'll be a next time, as long as we don't give up. And we *won't* give up, because we believe in ourselves. You're a little girl yet, Shana, but you're learning some awfully big lessons. Mommy's proud of you, no matter what kind of news we get, good or bad."

The parent-child teams were already into their warm-up exercises when Linda and Shana came into the gymnasium. They circled to the back and found room for themselves next to Vanessa and Monroe. Then they joined in on the Calisthenics, on beat, side by side in their matching workout togs, counting the reps out loud in unison with the rest of the class.

Linda glanced over at Shana. The child appeared to be doing all right. Anyone noticing her slightly reddened face would probably think it was flushed from exercising, rather than from crying. She was caught up in the rhythms of the

110

calisthenics and, hopefully, had pushed the Burger World audition to the back of her mind.

But Linda worried about it all through the exercise routine. She considered taking a break and using her cell phone to try to get in touch with Arthur Philips. But she forced herself not to act rattled and to wait for his call instead of forcing it.

It seemed that the Childplay class was never going to end. After the calisthenics, there were games like Follow the Leader and Mother May I, then tumbling, ladder climbing and log rolling. At last the session was wrapped up with group singing of several nursery rhymes.

"Well, we're going to take off right away so we can make the costume call," Vanessa told Linda. "I hope we'll see you there. Tom Trenton sounded positive that Shana had made it."

"I guess we'll soon know for sure," said Linda, as nonchalantly as she could, while she fiddled with her cell phone and wished it would start ringing.

"See you later, then."

"Okay. Good luck."

"Same to you."

As Vanessa and Monroe departed, Linda looked down at Shana. The child's eyes were dry. The Childplay class must've helped her work off her disappointment. Linda was proud of her. She was behaving quite mature for her age. She was learning, as Linda had learned in the orphanage, that, if she didn't want to have her feelings hurt deeply and often in this world, she had better not go around wearing her heart on her sleeve.

As soon as she got home, Linda checked her answering machine and found there were no messages. She gave in to her urge to phone the Philips Agency and asked for Arthur. He made her wait five minutes, only adding to her anxiety, before he got on the line. "Hello, Linda, what can I help you with?" he said. And she immediately detected a note of snideness in his voice that put her on edge.

"Arthur," she said with forced friendliness, "I suppose I shouldn't have bothered you, but I have to check out a rumor. I bumped into a friend of mine this morning, and she claims her little boy has been cast in the Burger World spots. Her agent is Tom Trenton, and he apparently has a list of all the kids who were cast, and he told her that Shana was on his list. So I'm touching base with you on the chance that you may have been trying to reach me in light of the three o'clock costume call."

Arthur made a clucking sound, which was his way of chortling. "Nothing wrong with Tom Trenton's list," he intoned sarcastically. "Till nine o'clock this morning, it was a fine and dandy list. But then it just happened to get revised, and nobody bothered to consult with Tom."

"Get to the point, Arthur," Linda snapped.

"All right, my dear Linda. You see, if you intend to drop somebody as your agent, after he's sweated blood for you, you really shouldn't let him find out about it before his contract expires. He might not feel deeply inclined to toss you any plums."

"What are you saying?"

"Don't play dumb, darling. Want me to spell it out for you? Shana was cast for the Burger World stuff. But I had her scratched. I informed the folks at Barbour & Lassiter that another client of mine – a little girl who was runner-up would probably perform more capably than Shana when the chips were down."

Linda's blood raced. Her heart pounded. She squeezed the telephone receiver so hard her fingers hurt. "You're a bastard, Arthur, and you always have been," she snarled. "You're not in the same league with Tom Trenton, and this little dirty trick only goes to prove it."

Arthur made his clucking sound. "Be careful, Linda," he warned. "Dear old Torn might change his mind about representing your darling daughter, if I put the bug in the right ears."

"You'd better not spread any lies about us, Arthur."

He Chortled again.

Linda despised him for doing Shana out of a part that she had already landed. He was a nasty low-class man who stooped to taking his revenge on children. But how had word leaked back to him that he was going to be dropped? Somebody must have blabbed.

"Who told you I wasn't going to renew your contract?" Linda asked, even though she was sure he wouldn't tell.

"You really want to know?" he purred. "It was your husband who let the cat out of the bag."

He hung up.

Shocked and enraged, Linda stared at the telephone receiver, then slammed it onto the hook. She didn't know how she could contain her anger till Ray got home.

CHAPTER 14

After the "spell" that she took in the early morning fog at Central Park, Felicia Patterson staggered half-naked into the lobby of Park West Apartments and collapsed onto the cold marble floor before Mr. Brevko, the elderly security guard, could quite get to her. Kneeling arthritically over the sideways-sprawled body of the young girl, he shakily tried to feel for a pulse in her wrist, and couldn't feel one. He liked Felicia, she reminded him of his niece and he hoped she wasn't dead, and, if the elevator doors opened right now and people popped out, there was going to be one hell of an uproar. Mr. Brevko held a trembling index linger under Felicia's nose and was pretty sure he could feel air being exhaled. Then he remembered that proper first aid for persons who might be in shock was to keep them warm, elevate their feet and call a doctor.

There was no doubt in his mind that Felicia had been raped – bits of dirt, grass and old dead leaves were pasted to her wet legs and buttocks – and it made him want to strangle whoever had done it to her. Mr. Brevko was amazed that she had managed to make it back to the apartment building without being arrested or even accosted again – till he remembered the thick fog, the early hour and the probable absence of much traffic, vehicular or pedestrian. Anyway, in New York any sort of "peculiarity" was likely to be ignored, so long as it didn't harm anyone; and a glimpse of a partially nude girl running through the fog would probably strike many onlookers as a pleasant novelty to spice up the day. These thoughts and more jumbled Mr. Brevko's brain while he scurried around, covering Felicia as best he could with his overcoat and his security guard jacket and propping her feet up with his lunch bucket. Then he buzzed like mad on the intercom till Mrs. Patterson answered.

"You better come down to the lobby right away," he blurted. "Something bad has happened to Felicia." The shrill scream that went off in his ear would have stung his eardrum, if he wasn't already hard of hearing.

Hanging up, he almost dropped the receiver when it occurred to him that Felicia's assailant could be coming after her, right through the front door of the building. He whirled and had his hand halfway to his bolstered revolver before he remembered that one of the things he had done while he was scurrying around was lock the door.

Thank God, when the elevator popped open a few minutes later, it was Mrs. Patterson and her son Arnold – both in robes and pajamas. They both froze, staring at Felicia. Then Mrs. Patterson let out a shriek and ran to where her daughter lay so motionless.

"Is she—" Arnold started to say. His eyes were wide and his face pale, seemingly drained of blood, as he stared at Mr. Brevko. He was blonde like his sister, but a year older and not as good-looking; too skinny, too-thick glasses and too much acne.

"She's breathing," Mr. Brevko said. "We'd better call for an ambulance." He lowered his voice to a whisper. "I'm pretty sure she's been raped."

"Damm!" Arnold said, gritting his teeth in anger.

Mrs. Patterson came running over. "We've got to get her upstairs," she wailed, tears streaking her face. "I don't want everybody in the building to see her like this."

"She just staggered in here and fell down," Mr. Brevko said, turning his hands palms up, then helplessly letting them drop to his sides. "I'm sorry, Mrs. Patterson . . . from the waist down she isn't wearing anything."

"Oooh! I *told* her not to go out in that fog alone!" Mrs. Patterson cried. "Where in the world was Ted? She claimed she was supposed to meet him."

"I did the best I could . . . covering her up and all," Mr. Brevko said meekly.

"Well, hurry up – help us get her on the elevator," Mrs. Patterson said. "We're lucky it's so early or this lobby would be filled with gawkers. Why does everything happen when her father isn't here? Once she's resting safely in her room, I'll try to reach him. Thank God, he left a number. I hope he knows how to handle this, because *I* surely don't – I'm no good in an emergency."

"Maybe we should just call the ambulance now and not try to move her," Arnold suggested.

"No, we've got to at least get her to her room so I can put some clothes on her," Mrs. Patterson insisted. "Your father probably won't want to call just any ambulance – you never know which hospital they're tied in with. We don't want them to take her anywhere but Fairchild Hospital for Children. We have faith in the staff there – they'll know exactly what to do."

Mr. Brevko thought it was awfully odd for Mrs. Patterson to ramble on so much and to be so picky about ambulances, when, for all she knew, her daughter could be in a life-threatening condition. Why worry about how

Felicia was dressed or undressed? In this kind of emergency, to hell with propriety. Obviously, Mrs. Patterson wasn't thinking clearly.

"Dear God, I hope she comes to," Mrs. Patterson said, her fingers clasped to her throat as she knelt over her daughter. "It would be best if we didn't need to call an ambulance."

What was she worried about? That the rape would make the newspapers and result in embarrassment? Maybe she was hoping not to have to report it. Mr. Brevko could understand that – it'd be a hell of a weight on a young girl's shoulders for everybody to be looking at her funny, knowing what had happened to her. "Don't worry . . . I'll keep my mouth shut about this," he promised. "Far as I'm concerned, it's nobody else's business."

"Thank you," Mrs. Patterson murmured gratefully, tears glistening on her face as she looked up at him.

Luckily, he carne up with the idea of first moving Felicia onto the big red carpet that he fetched from just inside the foyer. That way, without jostling her very much, he and Arnold and Mrs. Patterson were able to drag her, carpet and all, over to the elevator. Arnold had hit the emergency button, keeping the doors open; that's why none of the tenants had been able to get down to the lobby. Some of them were yelling and pounding now from the upper floors, and the noise was carrying in the elevator shaft.

"God's sake, shut up," Mrs. Patterson muttered under her breath. "This thing is probably going to stop at every floor before we get to five.'"

But it only stopped once, on three, and, when the doors slid open, nobody was there. Whoever had been yelling and pounding had probably taken the stairs.

Arnold hit the emergency button again on the fifth floor, and he and his mother and Mr. Brevko were able to get Felicia off the elevator without anybody seeing them. Using the carpet like a sliding stretcher, they managed to drag Felicia in through the doorway of the apartment and down the hall to her bedroom. They took a short breather. Mrs. Patterson turned on a soft bedside lamp and peeled back the covers. Then they lifted Felicia carefully onto the bed, and stared down at her to see if she was okay. They had bumped her around quite a bit, even though they had tried not to, but it had been tough maneuvering around furniture and things. Through it all, she had never flinched or moaned.

"Is she breathing?" Mrs. Patterson asked, panicky.

Mr. Brevko checked by holding his finger under Felicia's nostrils. "Yes," he whispered, after a moment.

Her breaths kept coming, soft and regular.

But she remained unconscious.

Mrs. Patterson picked up the phone on the nightstand and started dialing the number where Walter said he could be reached on location for the filming of the Faraday Family Restaurants spots.

CHAPTER 15

Working at his computer terminal, Augie chuckled aloud, savoring the delicious prank he had pulled on Felicia Patterson.

He congratulated himself on how clever he had been. He had patiently taken time to learn her habits before he dared to move in. He was a smart saboteur, a clever spy. He had learned that she went jogging every weekday morning in Central Park, always accompanied by her brother, Arnold. He had been the main obstacle that Augie had to remove.

Augie had followed Arnold and his girlfriend to a movie theater on Sunday evening, then to a pizza parlor. His quarry hadn't known him, so he hadn't had to worry about being recognized when he sat at a nearby table. Then, as he was getting ready to leave, he had pretended to accidentally drop his wallet, and, when Arnold and the girl both bent to pick it up for him, he had emptied a vial of chloral hydrate, carefully diluted, into Arnold's soft drink.

Arnold hadn't come out of the apartment building this morning to go jogging with his sister. The knockout drops had apparently done their job of putting him into a deep, groggy sleep that would last till he woke up in a cold sweat, sick to his stomach.

The fog had been so thick this morning that Augie was concerned that it might keep Felicia inside, too, especially without the protection of her brother. But he thought he understood her psychology, since it was similar to his own.

She was exceedingly meticulous, incontrovertibly a creature of habit, driven to do the few things in her life that aroused any shred of genuine emotion. She hadn't disappointed him, of course. She had come out for her run . . . alone.

He had followed her invisibly, padding softly in silent sneakers, like a mischievous ghost, a poltergeist, shrouded in fog, ready to materialize out of the mist to play his erotic prank. His pulse had quickened, as he had fallen in with Felicia and others, who were huffing and puffing over the misty, vaporous trails that were like paths through a cloud.

He was the transmitter of dreams and she the Receiver, powerless to disobey his commands. He had "prepared" her by sending powerfully sensuous signals, as they both jogged along in a matched stride, not unlike a mating rhythm. Soon she had begun jerking her head from side to side, a wanton, lascivious gleam in her eye. He had stepped up the intensity of the signals, and she had wet her tongue and flicked its pinkness over her full lips. His own desire had surged when he thought of how ripe and young and beautiful she was . . . and so totally under his control.

When he had reached out, she had unhesitatingly taken his hand, and they had let the crowd of others go, disappearing far ahead.

He had led her into the dense fog . . . deeper . . . deeper . . . among some ghostly trees and shrubs. On a patch of dewy grass they had "made love," unmindful of the cold and damp. Her pretty blonde face had worn a vacant expression, blind to everything but her lust. He had never removed his mask, but through his eyes slits lit had kept his green eyes boring into her blue ones. For her, he imagined, it must have been almost like having sex with the devil, because she had been under such a strong spell. For him, it had been a wild, fantastically exhilarating experience – blissfully mad and risky and even *funny* – because it was such a perfect joke on those who wanted to have sole power over this innocent young girl. But he and he alone had upset their plans by turning her into a totally uninhibited nymphomaniac, thrashing and moaning and bucking beneath him in the slinky, wet fog, unable to stop driving toward a pure, unadulterated frenzy of sexual release.

Remembering it made Augie almost as excited as he had been during the experience itself. And it made him hunger for even greater triumphs.

CHAPTER 16

Walter and Emily Patterson waited in the emergency room of Fairchild Hospital. Two hours ago, when Felicia was wheeled in on an ambulance gurney, through the gray steel doors of an adjacent corridor, she still had not regained consciousness. Emily had been told this by one of the ambulance attendants, and had told it to Walter when he arrived an hour later. In all this time they had not received any doctor's report, and their anxiety over Felicia's welfare was at a fever pitch.

Walter Patterson, a big fair-complected man with horn-rimmed eyeglasses and a sandy crew cut lightened by streaks of gray, had loosened the knot of his necktie, but had not removed the jacket or vest of his dark, expensive suit. Scowling, he kept chain-smoking cigarettes and drinking cup after cup of foul, rusty-black coffee from a machine in the hall. Having been up since four, he had already gone through a pack of Kools and two large cups of coffee, before getting the emergency phone call from his wife that had sent him speeding back to Manhattan from Ray Berkshire's filming setup at a Faraday Family Restaurant in New Jersey. He hadn't even been able to see Felicia. Over the phone, he had told his wife what to do. Then he had driven like mad to meet her in the emergency room.

He glanced at Emily, who was sitting beside him, thumbing through a ragged magazine, a blank look on her face. Under stress, her mind went numb. It annoyed Walter that she appeared calmer than he did, because she didn't have any bad habits like smoking, pacing or biting her nails. Usually, she wasn't worth two cents in any kind of crisis. It was a miracle that she had been astute enough not to call for an ambulance that might have brought Felicia to some other hospital. To her further credit, she had refrained from notifying the police, and had extracted Mr. Brevko's promise to keep his mouth shut.

It was essential that this incident be hushed up. Felicia mustn't learn about the operation she had had when she was five years old.

"I'm afraid she may have taken a severe blow on the head," Walter said to Emily. "That's why I asked if you had noticed any bruising or swelling under her hair."

"I'm sorry I didn't think to look, Walter," Emily said in her meek way. "My mind was in such a jumble I—"

Walter said, "She may have sunk into a state of catatonia, due to extreme emotional shock. Or . . ." he paused meaningfully, ". . . if she took a hard blow, the device may have been jarred loose. Who knows what kind of damage might result?"

"Dear God . . ." Emily murmured. Her voice trailed quaveringly, as her thoughts slipped backwards in time . . . to the day when Felicia had her first epileptic seizure . . .

It was in the summer, three months before Felicia's sixth birthday. Up till then, it had been a banner year for the Patterson family. Walter had been promoted to Director of Broadcast Production at Wagner, Inc., and both of the children had been accepted by Fairchild Academy. Arnold was going to transfer there from another (almost as good) private school, where he had whizzed through the first grade. Felicia had just graduated from kindergarten and had passed Fairchild's entrance tests with flying colors.

Walter had two weeks' vacation, and one of the producers under him at the agency had loaned him the use of a private beach cottage in Provincetown. It started out as an idyllic summer holiday – lots of fun acquainting little Arnold and Felicia with the sun, sand and surf for the first time and teaching them how to dig for clams and collect shells. When the two kids fell into bed each night they were tuckered out, and Emily and Walter could cozy up by the fireplace and talk and dream the way they seldom found time to talk and dream back in New York. They made love more often and more languorously, too.

One morning at low tide, Walter and Emily went wading with the two children in shallow water, letting them run and splash. Suddenly, Felicia stopped in her tracks and knelt in a few inches of water; a strange look of hilarity came over her, as she dug her fingers into the submerged sand.

Everybody stopped and looked at her.

She started to giggle. Then she began to scoop up fistfuls of wet sand, throwing them into the air like confetti, giggling uncontrollably.

Arnold shrieked like a banshee when a gob pelted him in the face. "'Mommy-y-y-y-y!" he screamed.

Felicia kept scooping as fast as she could, giggling, and showering herself with wet, sandy mud. Her blonde hair was a dark, grainy mess. And she had such an idiotic gleam in her eyes.

"Felicia! Stop!" Emily yelled and grabbed for the child, ready to give her a spanking. Walter came after her, too.

But she let out the shrillest giggle of all and ran from her parents in an all-out sprint.

Scared to leave Arnold by himself so close to the ocean, Emily grabbed his hand, figuring Walter could catch Felicia and discipline her.

Arnold bawled, "Mommy-y-y-y-y! She threw sand in my eyes!"

"Hush . . . we'll wash it out, honey," Emily crooned. "Here! Stop crying – let me see your face." Kneeling beside him, she splashed gently to wash him up.

Out of the corner of her eye, she saw her husband lunge at Felicia and miss. In her giggle tantrum, the misbehaving child somehow managed to juke her father and came running back up the beach, wildly splashing the shallow water, kicking her bony little knees high. Panting behind her, Walter was drenched and pasted with sand.

Felicia stopped so abruptly that Walter nearly ran her down. She went as rigid as a stick figure, her mouth frozen in an O-shape, her legs and arms stiffened in a Frankenstein pose. Walter seized her by the shoulders and spun her around. A peculiar screeching noise came vibrating out of her throat, and she toppled sideways into the ocean.

"Get her, Walter! She'll drown!" Emily cried out, and she dragged Arnold, who was still crying, by the hand to where Felicia had fallen.

Walter pulled Felicia feet first out of the water, her head and shoulders guttering through the sand. Her entire body was as rigid as a manikin – her hands and jaws were clenched tight; her eyes were wide and white, the pupils rolled upwards under the lids.

"Oh, my God, she still can't breathe!" Emily shrieked.

Felicia's face was turning blue, her neck veins standing out like cords. Her tongue protruded sideways, fat and swollen, clamped between her teeth. Blood was running down her face and chin.

"I don't know what to do!" Walter shouted. "She's not drowning, she's taking some kind of fit!"

Emily felt totally helpless and seized by desperate panic.

"Run! Call for an ambulance!" Walter told her. "I'll carry her to the cottage."

Glad that her husband had at least thought of something for her to do so she wouldn't feel so futile, Emily took off running, with Arnold behind her, trying to keep up. Thankfully, he had stopped his crying; the flood of tears must've washed the sand out of his eyes.

By the time she got through to the emergency number and made somebody understand where to send the ambulance, Walter was carrying Felicia sideways through the front door, into the living room of the cottage. Her body was still partially rigid, her bloody tongue still hanging out of her mouth. Walter bumped her head and knees, trying to angle her through the doorway.

"Careful!" Emily gasped.

"I'm doing the best I can!" he snapped. "You're in the way, son," he told Arnold. "Go in the kitchen for a while."

Looking as if he was about to start crying again, Arnold did what he was told.

Felicia kicked out suddenly, slamming her right foot into the jamb, just as Walter had her almost through. He nearly dropped her from the force of her kick. Then she broke into a series of jerky, violent convulsions. Her body was bucking and shaking so hard that he didn't even try to stretch her out on the couch. Instead he put her on the floor. Then he began covering her with the blankets Emily had brought. She knelt to help him, but he shook his head no. "I've got to stop her from biting her tongue," he said. "Bring me something she can bite down on – a comb or a toothbrush maybe."

On the counter by the kitchen sink Emily found the cork from a bottle of wine they had shared the evening before. But when she ran in with it, Walter shook his head disgustedly.

"Too soft – it'll crumble! he snapped, glaring at her as if she had lost her wits. She ran to the bathroom and fetched him a toothbrush. He snatched it from her.

Felicia's convulsions for some reason weren't so violent now, and Walter was able to pry open her mouth and set the handle of the toothbrush between her teeth. The tremors were weakening and weakening . . . and Emily wasn't at all sure whether that was a good sign. She used a damp washcloth to wipe some of the blood from her daughter's face, but more kept coming, though not as fast, She wished the ambulance would come! She kept listening for its siren.

All of a sudden, Felicia's spasms stopped entirely and she went absolutely limp. Red, frothy saliva bubbled between her lips.

Emily let loose a grief-stricken wail, sure that her little daughter was dead.

"Shut up!" Walter told her. "Get yourself under control! I'm trying to hear if she's still breathing!"

Emily heard nothing but the pounding of her own heart, as she watched her husband bending low, putting his ear close to Felicia's face.

"She is," he said. "She's breathing softly, but regularly. I think the attack must be subsiding."

Emily saw the red, frothy saliva continuing to bubble from Felicia's mouth. And in the distance she heard a siren.

The doctor at Provincetown Hospital told Walter and Emily Patterson that they were lucky to have been on hand when Felicia's attack occurred, or else she might not have survived. It was often difficult to diagnose such episodes; but since the parents were present from the onset of this one and could accurately describe all the symptoms, the doctor felt there was little doubt what had caused it. It fit the classic pattern of an epileptic seizure.

From the time Felicia's convulsions ceased and she lapsed into coma, then deep sleep, she had slept for four hours. When she regained consciousness in the hospital, she was totally unaware of what had happened to her. She didn't even remember her giddiness, when she had giggled and thrown sand all over everybody. She wondered why her tongue hurt so much. Emily and Walter hugged and comforted her. They couldn't help crying from relief that she was still alive.

But her future wasn't going to be easy. Before she was released from the hospital, her parents would face the task of gently explaining what had occurred. They'd have to ease her into an understanding of how she was going to be "different" from now on. They'd have to help her accept the sudden blow of learning that she could no longer expect to lead a normal childhood.

"Despite her illness, you should try to make Felicia's life as satisfying as possible," the doctor had said. "She can still attend school – mental exercise does no harm. In fact, she'll need regular physical exercise, too, as long as she gets plenty of sleep; ten hours a night would be desirable. This isn't the Dark Ages. We believe nowadays that improvement in an epileptic condition is less likely to occur if education and socialization are restricted, all forms of pleasure and sports forbidden, and the patient condemned to a gloomy, narrow life, just because she may have a few fits."

Emily and Walter knew that the doctor was mustering as much optimism as could be justified under the circumstances, but no way could he tell them what they desperately needed to hear. They wanted their daughter to "be herself" again. They wanted her to be made whole.

They hated the thought that she would be dependent on barbiturates and anticonvulsant drugs for as long as she lived; if a single dose was omitted, a seizure might occur. The situation wasn't this grievous for all epileptics, but, judging from the severity of Felicia's first seizure, hers was not such a mild case.

She'd be wise to avoid emotional disturbances; she might find herself unable to take part in highly competitive tasks. She'd have to try to go to bed early every day. And she'd have to constantly watch her diet, eating often, but not in large amounts, and not drinking large quantities of fluids. Alcoholic beverages would always be taboo for her.

Water, fire and machinery would present grave dangers. For some reason, bathing could precipitate an attack, and she could be drowned in a few inches of water while swimming or boating. If she wanted to take a bath, she'd have to do it when there was somebody close at hand who understood the risk. She could fall into a fire while having a seizure, so she wouldn't be completely safe joining her friends while they were toasting marshmallows or roasting wieners. There were lots of everyday things she'd have to stay away from: things like working on a ladder, pushing a power mower or driving a car.

The more that Walter Patterson dwelt upon the litany of do's and don'ts that would tyrannize his daughter's life, the more morose he became. He couldn't help wishing that something better could be done for her; he was almost hoping for a miracle. Back in New York, he consulted with Dr. Vincent Parkhurst, a neurophysiologist noted for his explorations of the mechanisms and functions of the human brain and for his considerable success in correcting certain dysfunctions by uncommon surgical methods. If there were any new procedures that might benefit Felicia, presumably Dr. Parkhurst would be the man to know.

At first, Walter was leery of confiding in Dr. Parkhurst; the doctor was connected with Fairchild Academy by virtue of the fact that he was one of the directors of the Fairchild Educational and Psychological Research Institute. But Walter decided that Felicia's illness couldn't be kept a secret from the teachers and administrators, so there was no use worrying whether Parkhurst might tell them. They'd have to be apprised of the special considerations Felicia would require during a normal school day; and, if they chose to renege on enrolling her, so be it. It would be too dangerous to try to hide her problem from them.

Dr. Parkhurst was a short, bald man with a reddish brown Vandyke. His long white lab coat hung so near to his trouser cuffs that it accentuated his shortness. He and

Walter met in his office at Fairchild Plaza, an institutionally bland cubicle, on the twelfth floor of Fairchild #5.

Sitting on an orange molded-plastic chair in front of the doctor's gray steel desk, Walter explained what had happened to his daughter during the Provincetown vacation. "Naturally," he concluded, "her mother and I are anxious that this won't keep her from attending the Academy. Felicia has her sights set on coming here, along with her older brother, and, if she were kept from doing so, it would crush her spirits just when she's trying awfully hard to cope with what I just told you about."

"Yes . . . very unfortunate," Dr. Parkhurst said. "However, I can assure you that we would not turn her out, having once accepted her. Unless . . ."

"Unless what?"

The doctor cleared his throat. "Mr. Patterson . . . in epileptics who are subject to severe or repeated attacks, mental deterioration is apt to occur. This is one of the most distressing aspects of the disease, since once such deterioration takes hold, it is likely to be progressive, and the ultimate outlook can be very bad. Now if, for some reason, Felicia's attacks are not brought under control and, consequently, she would show signs of lessening intellectual ability to the point where she would cease being able to keep up with the rigorous demands of Fairchild Academy, then regrettably we would have little choice but to let her go."

"I see," said Walter. "Quite frankly, this whole thing has me scared. What does my daughter have to look forward to? Even if the seizures can be arrested, she's going to be a slave to drugs all her life. Unless there's a better avenue to pursue."

"You mean an operation?"

"Yes. That's what I came to talk with you about. I keep wishing . . ." With a sigh, Walter discontinued his thought.

"One procedure that stops seizures entirely in most cases," said Dr. Parkhurst, "is to surgically sever the corpus callosum – which is the main neural bridge between the hemispheres of the brain."

"Like a lobotomy?" Walter said, aghast.

The doctor smiled reassuringly. "No, this procedure is not at all comparable to a lobotomy. Severing the corpus callosum leaves normal drives unimpaired and causes no devastating changes in personality or behavior. However, it does result in a 'split' or 'divided' brain. That is, patients who have had this done exhibit certain peculiarities which, while not debilitating, can be rather strange and annoying."

"What sort of peculiarities?"

"Well, the left and right hemispheres of the human brain each seem to have a 'mind of their own' so to speak. There are functions solely controlled by one hemisphere or the other, normally, and yet there are other functions upon which they cooperate, sharing information through the corpus callosum – the neural bridge. When this is severed, the two sides of the brain often don't seem to know what each other is doing. For instance, I have tested split-brain patients by dividing what they can see with their left eye and right eye. By means of split screen, I put a dollar sign on their left and a question mark on their right. When I ask them to draw what they are seeing, they will invariably draw only the question mark; but when I ask them to tell me what they have just drawn, they always claim they have drawn a dollar sign." The doctor smiled. "Man really is of two minds, you see, and these patients of mine have given me an insight into why we sometimes war with ourselves over alternatives."

"Can't make our minds up," Walter said dryly. He wasn't really seeing much humor in this discussion, but he supposed that Parkhurst had to occasionally look on the light side in order to deal with such oppressive matters.

"Exactly," Dr. Parkhurst said. "Each hemisphere appears to have its own separate drives and sensations. I even had one patient who complained of a 'sinister left hand' that untied his shoes while his right hand tied them, or pulled his trousers down as his right hand struggled to pull them on." The doctor stroked his beard, and his smile turned to a chuckle. "Between you and me, I believe that particular patient must've had something else wrong with him besides epilepsy."

"Mental illness?"

"Yes. I don't think the two sides of his brain ever were in sufficient accord, even before his operation."

"Is there anything else you can do besides severing the corpus callosum?" Walter asked. There was a tremor in his voice that he couldn't quite suppress. He tried to forget that his own daughter's future was at stake here. He told himself that he must hear and analyze the facts objectively, stripping away his personal feelings. "I mean," he said, "is there any surgical procedure where the side effects would be less . . . less tricky?"

"Yes. There is one other thing I could do that would leave the entire brain relatively undisturbed," said Dr. Parkhurst.

"What is that?" asked Walter, perking up keenly.

"ESB."

"E-S-B?" asked Walter.

"Yes. ESB. Electrical Stimulation of the Brain. Just as a pacemaker can maintain and regulate the human heartbeat, there is an implantable device which can prevent abnormal and uncontrolled discharges of energy from the cells of the cerebral cortex."

"You don't mean that this would completely cure Felicia's epilepsy," Walter said, not daring to believe.

"That is exactly what I mean," replied Dr. Parkhurst. "The mechanism that triggers her seizures would be permanently inhibited."

"Sounds too good to be true," said Walter.

"But it isn't." Dr. Parkhurst smiled. "I've done this before in several cases similar to Felicia's and, I assure you, the results have been excellent. Now, let me tell you how the operation works."

Walter leaned forward in his chair and gave the neurophysiologist his full attention.

In his friendly and persuasive way, Dr. Parkhurst told Walter Patterson just enough to get him to consent to the operation that he wanted so badly to perform. In the days before the full implementation of the Ultrachild Project, cases like Felicia's were golden opportunities for him to further his research. To expand the practical applications of ESB. To continue developing and improving this marvelous technology that had had such primitive beginnings . . .

In 1786, Italian physicist Luigi Galvani applied a voltaic current to the body of a dead frog and made the animal jerk and twitch as though it were alive. Electrical stimulation of the anatomies of animals and humans

134

immediately became a scientific rage. Probes were even attached to the heads of decapitated criminals in an effort to make them blink and talk.

During the Franco-Prussian War, surgeons operating on soldiers with head wounds used crude electronic probes to try to determine the extent of brain tissue damage. They would remove portions of the skullcap, stick wires into the exposed brain and wait for some response – a twitch of an arm, foot or hand; an erection; excessive salivation; a tongue flick. If no response was forthcoming, the surgeon would assume that the area under stimulation had been afflicted, and would use his scalpel to excise it, often with horrible results.

It wasn't until 1932 that more sophisticated ESB techniques were devised by a Swiss neurophysiologist, Dr. Walter R. Hess. Guiding extremely fine wires through tiny holes drilled in a cat's skull, he delicately inserted the wires into specific brain sites. Then he sent gentle electrical impulses through cables connected to the implanted electrodes. He was startled by the variety and predictability of the sudden changes he could produce in the cat's behavior. A little surge of current to the hypothalamus turned the animal into a hissing and clawing beast; while stimulating other sites caused complete docility. Depending upon where the electricity was applied, the cat would eat, drink, curl up and sleep, blink its eyes, become sexually aroused or simply walk in circles.

Neurosurgeons began using ESB experimentally in the treatment of human brain disorders. They found that their electrodes could provoke in people the same kinds of reactions that had been observed in lab animals. Mild electric currents in the right places could elicit anger, anxiety, euphoria, tranquility or sexual arousal. By stimulating certain areas of the brain, epileptic seizures could be aborted. By stimulating other areas, homicidal tendencies could be curbed. However, the procedures had little practical application, because the patients could hardly go around with wires and batteries sticking out of their skulls.

An important step forward was taken when a Yale University physiologist named Dr. José Delgado invented a brain radio called a stimoceiver that could be worn on top of the head. When it wasn't in use, it could be unplugged from a socket to which implanted electrodes were permanently attached; and it didn't require any external wiring. It picked up transmissions from a remote-control box like the kind used to switch channels on a TV set.

In the 1960s Dr. Vincent Parkhurst set out to achieve even greater miniaturization and portability. He was inspired by his vision of a "genteel society" – a controlled use of neurostimulation to create happier, less destructive, better balanced people. What fascinated Parkhurst the most was the prospect of exploring mental activities and learning processes within the conscious brain. The intellect itself might be not only investigated, but influenced in desirable ways. The brain might even be encouraged to evolve toward greater intelligence!

Parkhurst communicated his enthusiasm to his wife, Dr. Carol Parkhurst, a behavioral psychologist and educational theorist. Together they obtained federal grants for a series of research programs designed to uncover means of educating people more effectively and helping them come closer to reaching their intellectual potential.

The Parkhursts took up where the other ESB pioneers left off. They developed what they called BAS – a Brain Augmentation System based on microchip technology that greatly refined the technique of brain radio-implantation and made it much more practical. The BAS stimoceiver (nicknamed "Augie") was wafer thin, about the size of a man's fingernail, and could be glued under the skin, flat against the surface of the skull. The electrodes used with it were as fine as hairs and were made of platinum insulated with Teflon, biologically inert materials that could be left inside the brain indefinitely without causing infection or pain. The BAS system included a remote-control generator box, so that subjects could be programmed and manipulated at a distance.

Most of the Parkhursts' early experiments were done with BAS-implanted monkeys.

Most, but not all.

Some were done with autistic or epileptic children like Felicia Patterson, whose parents could be convinced that an implantation would help them to lead normal lives.

CHAPTER 17

It was five o'clock Tuesday morning, cold and dark out. Ray Berkshire and the actors and camera crew were in a Faraday Family Restaurant in East Stanton, New Jersey, not far from Ray's home. The cameraman and assistant cameraman were setting up for a dolly shot, while the gaffers were placing lights and stringing cables. The actors were lolling around, sipping coffee and munching doughnuts, trying to start looking wide awake as they waited for their turns with the makeup technician.

Sitting in a booth by himself, Ray was going over the storyboard frames, detailing the action to be covered this morning, when Foley Ryan came in shivering and smiling and saying hello to everyone. She took her coat off and hung it up, then joined Ray in the booth, bringing over a couple of doughnuts and two cups of fresh coffee. She was wearing snug jeans and a rose-colored Western-style blouse. With her petite figure, fine-boned face and bob of glossy black hair, she looked young and pretty. From twenty-five feet away she could almost be taken for a teenager, but up close the maturity that was more appealing to Ray came through.

She asked him if he had learned anything more about the "family emergency" that had forced Walter Patterson to rush away from yesterday's shooting.

"No," he told her. "Later, when I call in to the agency, I might find out something. I don't suppose Walter will show up here again today."

"Too bad it takes something like that to keep him off our backs," Foley said. "He had his nerve showing up here unannounced, even if he is the head of broadcast production."

"My sentiments exactly," said Ray. He knew that another thing that would keep Walter Patterson away today was that Ken Faraday wasn't going to be here on this, the second day of the filming schedule. Walter had shown up mostly to try to ingratiate himself with Foley's boss, because it wasn't deemed good for Wagner, Inc., to have Ray Berkshire as the only TV producer getting close to such a big client. With Foley Ryan already in Ray's hip pocket, if he ever left the agency or got fired, he might be able to pull Faraday Foods with him to his next place of employment.

"The only thing Walter contributed yesterday was confusion," Foley said.

She was referring to Walter's attempt to make himself look good by scrutinizing yesterday's storyboards and redesigning them on the spot. Luckily, Ken Faraday hadn't been snowed by Walter's brilliant ideas. Otherwise the shooting, which had gone on till ten o'clock, wouldn't have wrapped up till well past midnight.

"You look beat," Foley said to Ray. "No sleep?"

"Not much," Ray said, after dunking and swallowing a bite of doughnut. "Not only did I get in late, as you know, but I also had a hell of an argument with my wife last night. She was in a tizzy because Shana didn't get cast in the Burger World spots."

"Which didn't displease *you* too much," Foley said.

"Yes. Well." He sighed. "It'll only be a temporary respite because Linda will not give up. In fact, now that

139

she's been thwarted, she's gone even farther off the deep end. She's decided it must be my fault that Shana didn't land the big role."

"You're kidding!" Foley said, raising her eyebrows m miscomprehension.

"She climbed all over me," Ray said. "Ranting and raving – I've never seen her so flipped out. Just the other day, I thought that things were going better between us, but it must've been the calm before the storm. Yesterday, Linda learned that Shana *did* originally get cast, but her agent, Arthur Philips, had her scratched from the gig, because somehow he found out that Linda isn't renewing his contract. Remember, I told you about the chance of switching to Tom Trenton and how ecstatic Linda was over it?"

"Yes. You told me at our casting session last week." The implications of what she had just said dawned on Foley, and her coffee cup froze in midair as she was about to take a sip. "Oh-oh," she said. "Linda thinks somebody must've overheard you."

Ray nodded, grimacing. "And she's probably right. There were a couple of people auditioning for us who were represented by Arthur Philips, and we didn't cast any of them. I didn't get home till after eleven last night, and I was pooped, and Linda came on very disarmingly, asking if I happened to mention the Tom Trenton thing to anyone. I admitted I had, to you, not realizing I was stepping on dynamite – and Linda exploded. She screamed that I ought to know better than to blab such information – no way that it wasn't going to get back to Arthur Philips through the grapevine."

"I disagree," said Foley. "In fact, I'd plead not guilty. It would be paranoid to go around being afraid of such spiteful people. If they did something underhanded to Shana, I'm sorry, but I don't think you should be blamed."

"I just wanted you to know that Linda might take a notion to call you up and cuss you out," said Ray. "If she does, you can cuss *me* out. I shouldn't have brought your name into it."

"It's not your fault, really. I can't believe Linda is in such an uproar. But if she does get on me, I won't lose my temper. I`ll handle her as tactfully as I can."

"She's pretty tough to handle sometimes," Ray said. "When she's mad and frustrated, she gets totally irrational. She did pay me one compliment though – she said nobody but me could've done such a perfect job of sabotaging my own daughter."

They both laughed a little, even though it wasn't such a laughing matter.

Ray said, "Good thing Linda didn't find out that Walter Patterson offered to try and get Shana into Tiny Tot Academy a month ago, and I didn't let her know. On top of this other grudge, it would probably be enough to get us divorced."

CHAPTER 18

Felicia was still in a coma.

The only good thing about that, Dr. Vincent Parkhurst told himself, was that, as long as she stayed comatose, she would be in no danger of having an epileptic seizure, even though the device he had implanted twelve years ago was no longer working. Somebody – or something – had blown its circuits. The CAT scan had ascertained that much. The device was still firmly anchored inside the skull, but it wasn't emitting any signals.

The problem with the CAT scan was that it could only show Dr. Parkhurst still photos of Felicia's brain in a series of anatomical cross sections, as if he were peering into layer after layer of the organ in wafer-thin slices; it couldn't show the blood and fluids in motion, while they were *performing*. So he had next ordered a more sophisticated diagnostic procedure called a PETT scan. Positron-Emission Transaxial Tomography was still considered largely experimental and was not in use as a diagnostic tool in most hospitals. But Dr. Parkhurst had a PETT machine at Fairchild Hospital, even though it cost four million dollars, took up a space equal to two operating rooms, what with its accessories and computers, and required thirty physicians and technicians to operate it. In fact, it demanded so many operators that Felicia's tests weren't performed until Wednesday evening, when additional personnel from other hospitals could be brought over to help.

By that time, she had been unconscious for three days. Dr. Parkhurst was having a devil of a time calming down her family and stalling any definitive diagnosis.

Since he was the kind of man who had a tendency to be enraptured by any new technology that promised to magnify and enhance his own considerable expertise, the advantage of a PETT scan over a CAT scan made him positively ecstatic. Whereas CAT could give him only stationary, one dimensional images at a rate of just one every five seconds, PETT registered and automatically reassembled 75,000 X-ray pictures of the brain every five seconds, and provided a full-color, three-dimensional panorama of the organ *while it was working.* The pulsations of blood, tissue and fluids were all recorded for delicate and minute analysis.

Dr. Parkhurst's PETT installation was set up in such a way that results could be kept secret, if need be, from the people who had to help run the equipment. In Felicia's case, Dr. Parkhurst made sure that he was the only one watching the scan-outs. They were piped onto a remote screen in a small windowless room, to which the other physicians and technicians were denied access, even though they had to have Top Secret clearances to be taking part in this at all. Dr. Parkhurst communicated with them electronically, coordinating and monitoring their separate functions by means of his remote screen. Thus, he alone actually observed what was inside Felicia's skull.

Outside the screening room, in the main part of the PETT laboratory, the unconscious girl's head was encircled by the huge, revolving, computerized focusing maw of the X-ray scanner – an apparatus that resembled a great metallic truck tire, its outer circumference bristling with one hundred fat, shiny photon detectors interconnected with red and black wires. As the mammoth piece of machinery performed its bulky, but uncannily smooth gyrations, it emitted a soft whir – unbelievably soft in relation to the enormous size and complexity of what was taking place.

Dr. Parkhurst heard nothing but his own breathing; the scan-out room was soundproof. Awed by the flawless perfection of the magnificent device that had been harnessed and put to work for him, like a child fascinated by a kaleidoscope, he studied the resplendent, full-dimensional pictures of the workings – and nonworkings – of Felicia s brain.

In the case of the Baich boy, who had raped and murdered his girlfriend before killing himself with his father's gun, there hadn't been much of the brain left intact for Dr. Parkhurst to examine. The soft-nosed .32 slug had torn upward through Charles Baich's palate, driving splinters of bone in every direction, expanding like a leaden mushroom, mashing cortex and neocortex and cerebellum to a bloody pulp before exiting, blowing half of the skull away.

Luckily, the boy's parents had thought to burn his bloody, incriminating clothing. And to phone Fairchild Hospital for an ambulance.

Dr. Parkhurst had signed the death certificate, stating that Charles Baich didn't die till he got to the operating room. But the only "operation" Parkhurst had performed was to remove all evidence of what was going on at Fairchild Plaza.

The police back in Davenport, New Jersey, might be pretty sure that the boy had raped and murdered Jane Taft before committing suicide. But they couldn't prove it now.

Not beyond a reasonable doubt. Couldn't prove he hadn't done himself in because he was consumed with grief over the disappearance of his girlfriend.

But Dr. Parkhurst knew better. Something terrible had gone wrong. Something inside Charles Baich's brain. The awful question was: had it been a freak accident, or the result of deliberate tampering? Had someone done the unthinkable, the near impossible? Had someone gained access to Charles Baich's mind?

Unfortunately, the doctor wasn't left with enough evidence to find out.

But now, as he studied Felicia Patterson's PETT scans, he was faced with incontrovertible evidence that his worst fear was a reality. He had proof of tampering. Irrefutable proof. He understood clearly what had happened to the poor girl. And the discovery shook him to the core.

He realized that, before he could let Felicia's parents know anything – or, rather, before he could concoct a lie to tell them – he had to report his findings to the Chairman of the Board. There was no other choice in the matter.

Tom Trenton, the Chairman of the Board of Faircild Plaza Corporation, came to Dr. Parkhurst's office at nine o'clock on Thursday morning. With him was Stephen Brownell, the director of the New York office of the Federal Bureau of Investigation.

Trenton was in his early fifties, but could pass for forty, partly because he bleached his hair blonde. There was a youthful sparkle in his blue eyes, and his square, handsome countenance was sun-lamp tanned and unwrinkled – due to a face lift. He was debonairly dressed in a double-breasted gabardine suit of an almost lavender shade, accented by a rose-hued silk tie. Although he fussed over his appearance the way many show-biz types were prone to, Dr. Parkhurst knew him to be serious, intelligent, and utterly dedicated to the success of Fairchild Plaza Corporation and the Ultrachild Project.

Stephen Brownell, the FBI man, was the security chief for the Project. He frightened Parkhurst more than Trenton did. In his late forties, Brownell was tall, lean and dark complected, with straight, slicked-back black hair and a brown mole on the right side of his chin that he kept fingering as if it gave him pain. The physique under his somber three-piece brown suit was as hard and strong as an athlete's, but he lacked an athlete's joviality. Whatever he kept himself in shape for, it wasn't fun and games.

Red-eyed from worry and lack of sleep, Dr. Parkhurst decided not to beat around the bush. "Felicia Patterson's RAS has been broken down – possibly totally burned out," he said. He smacked his desk top with the palm of his hand.

"What's that mean exactly?" asked Brownell in a hard, distrustful tone.

Trenton blinked worriedly.

"R-A-S," Parkhurst spelled out with slow enunciation. "Reticular Activating System. The main bundle of nerves in the brain stem. The so-called 'spark' of the mind. Somehow it's been overloaded. The seat of consciousness has been destroyed – probably permanently."

"She's going to be in a coma forever?" Tom Trenton said incredulously.

"I'm afraid that's the likeliest prognosis. The extent of damage seems well beyond any possible hope for regeneration."

"How did it happen?" Brownell pounced, in an angry, accusatory tone, assuming the role of prime inquisitor. For the next five minutes, Dr. Parkhurst answered his questions, while Tom Trenton sat and listened.

Parkhurst took a deep breath. "Tampering," he said with a despairing sigh. "Somebody *must* be tampering."

"Could something faulty have occurred here?" the FBI man asked. "On these premises?"

"No chance. Our equipment is electronically set and governed to maintain at low output."

"What if something went haywire? Couldn't you get a beefed-up transmission?"

"No. Our circuits would blow first. That's our fail-safe. Whoever did this to Felicia blew *her* circuits . . . by feeding her powerful signals – too much for her brain to handle."

"So this bundle of nerves you're talking about went kaploohy."

"Exactly," said Parkhurst, fidgeting, agreeing with Brownell's thought, but not the crudity of its expression. He glanced over at Tom Trenton, as if asking for help, but none was forthcoming. Feeling increasingly threatened, he went on talking, trying to hide in a cocoon of jargon: "The Reticular Activating System is the watchguard of the human mind. It receives all the messages sent to the cortex from all the body's sensory receptors – one hundred million signals bombarding the brain each and every second. The RAS collects, sorts, filters and discriminates, selecting the vital and deflecting the trivial, so that we are not driven mad by an infinity of choices."

"That's not what happened to Felicia," Stephen Brownell rudely pointed out. "She's comatose. She's not contemplating or acting upon any sensory signals whatsoever."

"That is correct," Dr. Parkhurst admitted, his voice dry and husky.

"So, what could have burned her out? Could it have happened accidentally?" Brownell pressed.

Parkhurst cleared his throat, but it didn't help much. He still sounded raspy and weak, nervously rubbing his reddish beard. "I wanted to believe that the Charles Baich case was a freak accident. Maybe he just happened to go near a too-powerful source coincidentally generating the right frequency – the way a CB radio in a car can accidentally detonate dynamite that's been wired and set, if the car happens to drive through a blasting site. But now we have the Patterson case. *Two* accidents? I can't swallow that premise. Our technology is not that vulnerable. It would be virtually impossible for two stimoceivers to be accessed randomly, because, after all, the right frequency doesn't mean anything without the correct code cues. And besides—"

"And besides," Tom Trenton cut in, "we have to deal with the fact that Felicia was raped. And so was the Taft girl."

"Yes," said Parkhurst. "It can hardly have been coincidental. In Felicia's case, the inescapable conclusion is that the rapist must have somehow accessed her stimoceiver . . ."

"Giving him enough control over her to facilitate the rape," Trenton said, turning toward Brownell.

Parkhurst grimly nodded his head. Brownell sat back, thinking. He had deep-set, black, expressionless eyes. The lack of insight to his thoughts gave Parkhurst the creeps.

The neurophysiologist was afraid of what might happen to him if he got pinned with the blame for this crisis. It shook him when the FBI man said, "You and five other people on your staff are supposed to be the only Fairchild employees who are privy to the intimate details of the Ultrachild Project. How sure are we that all of you can be trusted?"

Parkhurst tried his best not to flinch and to sound fervent.

"I should think that myself and my staff would be above suspicion. We've all passed the most rigorous background and security checks. We'd have nothing to gain and everything to lose by tampering with a government project that we ourselves advocated and helped institute. We're all dedicated scientists with stable, rational personalities. None of us would pervert a sophisticated technology for the mundane, unimaginative purpose of committing a rape."

"I'll go along with that," said Tom Trenton. "I believe that Dr. Parkhurst and his staff are entirely worthy of our trust and respect."

"Till we get to the bottom of this, nobody is above suspicion, as far as I'm concerned," Brownell said, eyeing Trenton coldly. "I don't think rape is the main motive here. I think that somebody who knows exactly what we're engaged in is trying to make it blow up in our faces."

"Foreign operatives?" Trenton ventured.

"Maybe. We know that the Russians have a project similar to ours. If they can derail us by spawning a media scandal, a public outcry, even a Congressional Investigation, we'll be put out of business and they'll get so far ahead of us we'll never catch up."

149

"That's why I was trying to believe it wasn't anything as sinister that," Parkhurst said.

"Even if it's one solitary technological wizard of a rapist, we're in grave jeopardy," said Brownell. "We can't even work through normal law enforcement channels to try and stop him. If he gets arrested by anybody other than us, he's going to blab what he knows. Then our whole ball game goes out the window."

"This free and democratic society has its pitfalls," said Dr. Parkhurst, with a tinge of bitterness. "The Russian leadership doesn't have to worry about what ordinary citizens think. They can rest assured that there's not going to be any public outcry against their vital special projects."

"Not thinking of defecting, are you?" Brownell said sharply, with a thin, cold smile.

Parkhurst squirmed. "I was merely stating a paradox. If fellows like you and Tom and I weren't shrewd and pragmatic enough to cut a few corners and do what needs to be done, this country wouldn't keep its precious freedom for very long. We'd be slaves to our adversaries."

"Every society needs its clandestine operators," agreed Brownell, pretending to be mollified; privately, he made up his mind to put Parkhurst and everyone on the doctor's staff under strict surveillance, in case one of them was a traitor. "Doctor," he asked, "what are you intending to tell Felicia's parents?"

"I'll have to blame everything on the rapist. But I can't claim he hit her over the head. Her father was asking too many questions. I think he found out there wasn't any bruising or bleeding right after the incident took place. I'll have to convince him that her coma is due to psychological trauma. A catatonic reaction."

"You think he'll buy it?"

"Yes. He has no reason not to."

"Unless . . ." said Brownell.

"Unless what?"

"Unless someone tells him different. Someone on the loose out there who knows exactly what we're up to and can tune in to any of our Receivers. He might not keep his little secret to himself. For example, he might decide it would be a real kick to let Felicia's father know that, when you implanted that tiny device in the child's brain twelve years ago, you set it up to perform quite a few other functions besides preventing epileptic seizures."

CHAPTER 19

Ray Berkshire had been on location all week, from five in the morning till ten or eleven each night, with Foley and the actors and film crew. Thursday happened to be rained out, so he went to his office to try to catch up on some things. There he tried to get more information about Walter Patterson's daughter, Felicia, because by now he had learned that she was in the hospital. However, nobody at Wagner, Inc., was clear as to what exactly was the problem. Walter hadn't been coming in all week and nobody knew whether it was an accident or an illness that had befallen Felicia. A collection was taken up for some flowers to be sent to Fairchild Hospital, so Ray pitched in. He knew how proud Walter Patterson was of his daughter and he hoped everything would turn out okay. It gave him a shiver to think of all the scrapes and crises a parent had to be prepared to go through.

On Friday, the rain day was made up, and the Faraday shooting was wrapped. When Ray got home around nine o'clock that night, he found that Linda was magically in a good mood once again. All week long she had barely spoken to him. Now he could tell that she was ready to make up. It was in the way she told him hello. No kiss, no hug – just a hello that wasn't belligerent and wasn't overly amiable.

He decided that he didn't want to prolong hostilities, making the weekend into a bummer for everyone, including Shana. So he said "hi" in a tone friendly enough to signal a thaw. Linda microwaved the supper of pork chops, home fries and green beans that she had been keeping for him. She had already eaten, but she joined him at the kitchen table after pouring herself a cup of coffee. "Good news came today," she announced with restrained joy. "Shana passed her tests. She's been accepted by Tiny Tot Academy."

"Great," Ray said without smiling, without even looking up from the pork chop he was slicing. Now he knew why Linda was ready to climb off her high horse. All of a sudden, all was right with the world.

"You can be proud of your daughter," she told Ray, as he chewed a bite of pork chop. "Shirley Sutter phoned today with an absolutely glowing report. Shana came out beautifully on the intelligence, aptitude and motor coordination tests, as well as the psychological profile and personality inventories."

"That's nice to hear," said Ray. Inwardly, he was wryly amused at the notion that a personality could be "inventoried" – an individual's traits, quirks and idiosyncrasies categorized, counted and stacked like cans of peas and beans on a grocer's shelf. "How's Shana feel about it?" he asked.

"Oh, she's thrilled! So excited and wound up I hated to put her to bed."

"Then this bit of good news makes up for the big disappointment the other day?"

"This is much more important than landing a Burger World spot," Linda said staunchly. "But I would rather have had both, because Shana deserved both. Okay?"

"Just as long as you understand I wasn't to blame," Ray pressed.

"All right. Maybe you weren't. Let's just agree to drop it, okay? Let's not spoil the weekend. Let's show Shana how much we love her and how happy we are for her."

"Suits me," Ray gave in. But he knew that the rift between him and his wife shouldn't end this way, without really being talked over and healed. But it was so hard to talk to Linda anymore.

"We're invited to a party tomorrow night," she said after a while.

Annoyed, he told her, "I plan to use the weekend to unwind. I don't really want to go anywhere."

"If you're too tired to stay late, we can leave as early as you like," Linda cajoled. "But I don't think this is something we should miss. It's a dinner party at Vanessa Larson's home, and Shirley Sutter and some other people from the Academy are going to be there. Drs. Vincent and Carol Parkhurst, for example – remember, we read their book?"

Ray nodded, taking a fork full of green beans.

Linda went on persuading. "It's not as if we'll have to drive the Jersey Turnpike. The Larsons live just outside of East Stanton. Remember, I told you?"

Again Ray nodded.

Encouraged, Linda said, "The Parkhursts are the heads of the Fairchild Educational and Psychological Research Institute. I'd love to meet them. Dr. Stowe is coming to the party, too. *And* Tom Trenton. It can't hurt to get in good with all of them."

"I suppose," said Ray.

"You'll go then?"

"If you really want to."

"I do," she said, brightening. "After all, maybe an evening out is exactly what we both need."

Ray spent a restless night – too keyed up and strung out on the nervous tension of the past five days. While he was tossing and turning, a lot of things kept going through his mind – the unsatisfying resolution of the conflict with Linda; the upcoming hassle of selling the house and moving; the meddling of Walter Patterson into the Faraday Family Restaurant shooting; and the way he kept finding himself being attracted to Foley Ryan, to the point where he was looking forward to working with her on postproduction and wishing they were already into it.

He didn't want to fall out of love with his wife; the complications and the consequences would be devastating, not only for him and Linda, but especially for Shana. He told himself that, although it might be natural for him to be drawn toward another woman when he and his wife weren't getting along, he'd better watch himself and not yield to any crazy impulses. His marriage was bound to get better, if he didn't give up on it. The move back to New York, now that Shana's educational future was settled to Linda's satisfaction, was going to be a brand-new start for the whole family.

Giving up on trying to doze off, he got up around seven and went to the family room, where Shana, in her little fuzzy pink robe and pajamas, was watching a TV program called *Giggleville* on the children's cable channel. The show was a mix of people and puppets, music and mime, that Linda said was "good, intelligent fun." She made sure the right button was pushed on the home video box, so

Shana could watch it by just turning the set on when she woke up early Saturday mornings. Far be it from Linda to give the kid a break and let her watch ordinary cartoons once in a while.

The family room was large yet cozy, decorated in rich earth colors. The wall with the fireplace was finished entirely in reddish brick with a huge, dark wooden slab of a mantel. It was Ray's favorite room in the house. He realized that rooms of this size and style were a suburban luxury, and he doubted that they'd be able to find anything comparable in Manhattan without paying a fortune. He sat on a rust-colored sofa, just behind Shana, who was sitting cross-legged on a Wooly brown throw rug, a few feet from the TV screen. So far, she hadn't reacted to his presence, and he wondered if she had heard him come in.

"Hi, Daddy," she said without turning her head; and suddenly she scooted backwards and leaned partially against the sofa and partially against his pajama-clad leg, her bottom warming his bare foot. "I was sitting too close," she explained. "Too close might make my eyes squinch up."

"Who told you that?" he asked, stroking her blonde head.

"Mommy. Are you and her still fighting?"

The question startled Ray, and he stopped stroking her hair momentarily. When his fingers got working again, he said, "No. We made up."

"I don't like when you and Mommy fight."

"I don't blame you. I'm sorry if we upset you. Sometimes we get mad at each other without knowing why. Grown-up people, and kids too, ought to be able to get along without fighting. But we're only human, and sometimes we don't act as smart as we should."

There was a long interval of silence, during which Ray and his daughter stared at a puppet on the TV. Ray wondered if the things he had just said truly sounded as lame and inadequate as he feared.

"I'm going to the Academy!" Shana announced suddenly, whirling around and giving her father a huge, happy smile.

"I know. I'm very proud of you. Come here and get your reward."

He hugged her, enjoying the warm compactness of her tiny body while he planted several wet kisses on her forehead. When he was younger, he had often said that his life wouldn't be ruined if he never had any children. But now was different; now he couldn't picture himself without Shana. If she should ever be taken from him he supposed he would rally and eventually learn to bury his grief, but he would never be the same man again. A part of his life would remain achingly empty.

Shyly, Shana lowered her eyes. "When you and Mommy were fighting, she said you made me not be in the TV commercial. That's not true, Daddy, is it?"

"No, honey. It's nobody's fault. Especially not yours. When you try out for those kinds of things, you have to realize you may not be picked – for any number of reasons that have nothing to do with how good you are."

"But I tried hard and I didn't get it."

"That's the important thing: *trying* hard. Doing your best. Then if you lose, there's nothing to be sorry about."

"That's what Mommy says. Daddy, are you glad I'm going to the Academy?"

"Yes. Aren't you?"

"I guess so," Shana said softly. "But I'm scared, too. What if I'm not really smart enough?"

"But you *are*, honey," Ray told her. "If you weren't, you wouldn't have been chosen. You're smarter and prettier than any little girl I know."

"Would I be good enough for *you* to put me on TV?"

"You certainly would, honey, except the agency has a rule against the producers casting members of their own families."

"That's a dumb rule."

"Listen," Ray said, "if you don't want to go to Tiny Tot Academy, you can tell us. Mommy and I won't be mad, I promise."

"Maybe you won't, but Mommy will," Shana said, biting her lip. Then her face brightened into a pretty smile. "I'm not going to be scared, Daddy. I just have to believe in myself, like Mommy says."

Holding his daughter in his arms, Ray knew that parental approval was intensely important to her, as it was to any child. He remembered how hard he had tried to please his own parents, who had both died – his father of heart disease and his mother of cancer – several years before Shana was born. He made the Honor Roll all the way through grammar school, and every six weeks when the grades came out, he would *run* all the way home, clutching his report card in his sweaty little hand, because he couldn't wait to show it off to his mother and father. They'd give him a dollar for each A. Getting good marks was one of the few ways he had been able to make them proud.

When he became interested in filmmaking, they told him he was silly. Did he think he was going to land in Hollywood? They wanted him to become a doctor or lawyer – something solid, respectable and lucrative. Going to college to learn how to make films seemed to them as dumb as going there to learn how to bake bread.

After college graduation, when he accepted a job with a small commercial company, his mother and father thought he was foolish for turning down "a better position" with CBS. A few years later, when he launched Berkshire Productions, they considered it a foredoomed effort, and they turned out to be right. The bankruptcy would have shamed them unbearably, had they lived long enough to witness it.

He had loved and respected his parents, even though his relationship with them had always left something to be desired. It was a void that he still felt, coupled with guilt and regret over not trying hard enough to bridge the gap before it became too late.

Now that Ray had his own child to raise, he realized profoundly that being a good parent was not an easy job. He could forgive his mother and father for being too tough on him and for causing him too much anguish and pain. They had only been trying to do what they thought was best for him, according to the limits of their wisdom and understanding.

It was what he and Linda were trying to do for Shana. And many times he had severe doubts as to whether they were equal to the challenge.

CHAPTER 20

In the yellow Mustang that his parents had bought him when he graduated with high honors from Fairchild Academy, Augie took the East Stanton Exit off the New Jersey Turnpike. Slowing down to ramp speed, he thought he heard a *ping* in one of the cylinders, but he decided not to worry about it. The car was almost paid off now, and he wouldn't be keeping it much longer. His mother and father were going to buy him a brand new one for graduating magna cum laude from Manhattan University. Commencement would take place in less than four weeks. He had already told his parents that he wanted a Mercedes this time; a silver one. No problem. He knew he'd get it. They never denied him anything money could buy. The only thing they had ever denied him was the right to be his own person.

He made a right turn one traffic light past the East Stanton Mall, onto a two-lane blacktop that wound through the hoity-toity neighborhood where his parents' friends, Harold and Vanessa Larson, were throwing their fancy-shmancy dinner and cocktail party. Darkness was approaching on a partially moonlit night, and the tree-lined back road was more shadowy than the main highway. Augie switched on his headlights and glanced at his wristwatch; it was damn near seven-thirty, and he was going to be more than fashionably late. So what. He didn't care if he missed out on most of the pre-dinner socializing.

His main reason for making this stuffy gig was that Donna Sutter was supposed to be there.

Beautiful, big-titted Donna. He had a letch for her body. And since he had found out she was a Receiver, he might as well do some reconnaissance and lay a few plans, so he could end up laying *her*.

Of course. his parents had a quite different reason for requesting his presence and they were no doubt already in a tizzy over what could be keeping him. As a sterling example of the efficacy of their educational methods, he was supposed to help shill some people named Ray and Linda Berkshire, whose four-year-old daughter had just been "accepted" into Tiny Tot Academy. The suckers had taken the bait, and now the goal was to make them swallow it hook, line and sinker. Soon their daughter was going to "need" a little brain operation. The parents would be more likely to give their consent once the muckety-mucks of Fairchild Plaza had them seduced and befriended and lulled into docility.

Augie chuckled with malicious glee as he pulled into the Larsons' driveway, which was already full of expensive late model cars. In front of his parents and their clique, he never let on that he was anything other than the polite and personable young genius that they expected him to be. He never allowed them to suspect how much he hated them. But he didn't mind helping them further their aims. Now that he shared their secret, his power would expand with theirs. The Berkshire girl and all the others would belong to him as much as to them.

One nice thing about arriving late was that the Mustang wouldn't be hemmed in. He could leave whenever he chose without having to ask anybody to move a vehicle.

161

Slamming his car door, he noticed that his parents' white MKZ was parked by the stone wall and the steps that led up to the flagstone walkway. He brushed a speck of lint from his white dinner jacket, as he crossed a vast expanse of front lawn toward the Larsons' country manor – yellow brick with white shutters and tall, slender, white pillars – lit up by exterior floodlights, like an antebellum plantation house on a movie lot. With the servants' cottage, which was in the rear, the estate must be worth at least three million dollars. And only three people lived in the main house. Augie snickered at the thought of them rolling around in there like marbles in a boxcar. Talk about decadent rich – the Larsons' little brat, Monroe, who would start attending Tiny Tot Academy when it opened, was going to be driven back and forth by the family chauffeur.

Augie wondered if Monroe would be given an operation. He doubted it. That was mainly for people outside the inner circle. Monroe would probably remain part of control group, unless the Larsons were getting totally carried away with their zeal over the Ultrachild Project – the way the Sutters had obviously gotten carried away, in Donna's case, and the way Augie's father and mother had gotten carried away back in their young and daring days.

Augie rang the doorbell and was admitted by Tucker, the elderly English butler – tall, gaunt and slightly bucktoothed; in a white serving jacket, black trousers and black bow tie. The Larsons not only had a full-time butler, but a chauffeur and a maid who doubled as a nanny – plus, no doubt, a few part-time helpers for tonight's special gathering. One thing they did not have, and ought to have, in order to protect their other wretched excesses, was a cadre of armed security guards. An electrified fence wouldn't be a bad idea either; that is, if they were going to persist in flaunting an aristocratic lifestyle – a lifestyle that was a perfect goad for some brand-new version of the Manson Family to charge up here and butcher everybody.

"Good evening, sir, and welcome," the butler said. "I've been watching for you to arrive. The other guests are in the lounge. Would you like me to show you the way?"

"Thanks, Tucker, but you needn't bother," Augie said. "I remember where it is."

"Very good, sir."

Augie went down a hallway to the left of the foyer past the wide arches of the dining room, where the table was already set with sparkling china, silver and crystal for fourteen people. Then he descended a short flight of stairs carpeted in red shag and detoured into the powder room to relieve his bladder, freshen himself up and make sure he looked perfectly dapper.

The Larsons' "lounge" reminded Ray Berkshire of a pseudo-English pub in a Marriott Hotel. Lots of red leatherette, dark wood, and lithographs of red-coated gentry riding to hounds. The room was large enough and "ambient" enough to do a booming business as a singles bar, if it were located in a commercial zone instead of a private home. Drinks would probably be priced at about six bucks, and there'd be a rock band blasting from the corner where the billiard table was.

Linda had conned Ray by not springing it on him that this was to be a formal affair until Saturday morning, when she also let him know that she'd taken his tux and dinner jacket to the cleaners early on Friday, in anticipation of his agreeing to go. To soften his disgruntlement, she had picked the tux up for him, made arrangements for a baby-sitter, and had pretty much left him alone all day so he could rest.

Sitting at the copper-topped bar with a couple of martinis under his belt, he found himself not regretting being here. The occasion was somewhat strange and therefore stimulating. With the men in white dinner jackets and the ladies in evening gowns, it was almost like a posh meeting – because almost everybody here was connected with Fairchild Academy. Leonard Sutter, Shirley's husband, was an instructor at the Academy. Vanessa Larson's husband, Harold, was chief legal counsel for Fairchild Plaza Corporation. Dr. Marcia Stowe, the pediatrician, was here with her husband, Dr. Peter Stowe, who was a neurosurgeon at Fairchild Hospital. Even Tom Trenton, it turned out, wasn't entirely removed from the world of Academia – he was chairman of the Fairchild board of directors.

The one person present who seemed to have no connection whatsoever with Fairchild Plaza, other than her connection to Tom Trenton, was Tom's date for this evening, a stunning high-fashion model, who called herself Laurel Crown. Tom and Laurel were sitting with Ray and Linda at the bar, along with the Stowes, while the rest of the people were spread around at some of the cocktail tables.

Ray was getting a smattering of ideas about a screenplay that might include scenes like the one he was now part of. It would be a screenplay about the world of TV commercials – something he knew intimately, but had never written about in any incisive way. If he let out all the stops, it could make a good theatrical movie – might even garner some good reviews. Or, if he played it slick and shallow, concentrating on the supposed glamor and glitter of commercial filmmaking, it could still be a decent TV movie.

While Ray's thoughts were meandering, Linda had started recounting the gory details of the Burger World fiasco. He tuned in, on his guard in case she took a notion to heap some more blame on him, in public. But she refrained from doing so.

"So Shana *did* land the part," Linda concluded, "but Arthur Philips pulled the rug out from under her. It proves one thing, Tom – that she definitely has what it takes. And I'm delighted that she'll soon be one of your clients."

"So am I," Trenton said with a gracious smile.

"That Arthur Philips sounds like a real piranha," snapped Marcia Stowe.

"My God, yes," agreed her husband, Peter.

The pediatrician was wearing her shoulder-length gray hair in thç same swept-back style it had been in at her office, emphasizing her high forehead and moon-shaped face. Her short, stocky body was sheathed in a satiny green dress, with girdle lines showing through, and on her flabby right bicep a gold serpent bracelet was entwined. Her thin-lipped mouth was precisely delineated by bright red lipstick, and there were fuzzy red discs of rouge on her cheeks.

Her husband was a bald, mousy little fellow, no taller than she, but much more slender; in fact, so frail that it seemed she would probably beat him up if they ever got into a fight. "I've never understood such backbiting," he commented, shaking his head sadly. "Personally, I've never been cut out for it."

"Me neither," Ray said, for the sake of finding common ground with the timid little guy, even though he didn't really feel he could ever be one-tenth as meek as Peter Stowe looked.

"One doesn't have to be a backbiter," Linda said, with a darting glance at Ray, "but one does have to be self-assured and aggressive enough to avoid being walked on."

Ray let it pass. He was used to her digs.

Peter Stowe said, "Amen."

"One has to be tough, especially in the advertising and entertainment business," Tom Trenton affirmed, smiling a mouthful of capped teeth. Blonde and handsome, he didn't seem to lack any of the aggressiveness and self-assuredness that were being touted. He was the most flashily dressed of all the men at the party, although flashiness had its limits tonight, because of the white dinner jacket requirement. His trousers and bow tie were bright red and his ruffled shirt was trimmed in scarlet. .

"Not to upset you," Laurel Crown said to Ray and Linda with a vivacious smile, "but my daughter landed a part in the Burger World stuff, along with Monroe Larson."

"Melanie was on the original list," Tom Trenton explained. "The list I received before Shana was scratched."

"Oh, Melanie is a *darling*," cooed Marcia Stowe, beaming at Ray and Linda. "Same age as your little girl. She'll be starting at Tiny Tot, too, so maybe they'll become close friends, since they already have so much in common, what with the modeling and all."

So, Ray Berkshire thought, Laurel Crown was connected to Fairchild Plaza through her daughter. That completed the circle. The Academy was like an umbilical cord running through everybody's navel. It might be rash to assume that anybody present tonight could be excluded from the linkup, even the bartender and butler. Maybe they had daytime jobs as janitors in Fairchild #1, 2, 3, 4 or 5.

"Tom," Ray said to Trenton, "it strikes me as a unique thing for a man in your position – head of a prestigious talent agency – to be chairman of an educational concern like Fairchild Plaza Corporation. How did it come about? If you don't mind saying."

"Well," Trenton smiled, "you mentioned the operative word, Ray – talent. That's what fascinates me. I'm in the business of discovering and promoting it. I've had some successes and I've had numerous frustrations. It disturbs me that the truly gifted and talented people aren't always recognized and rewarded. This holds true in all walks of life, not just acting and modeling. In America there's enormous pressure on everybody to be merely *average*, as if that's what democracy and equality are supposed to mean: for nobody to stand out above the rest. Our brightest and most capable kids – the ones who could be the future scientists, innovators and leaders that we desperately need – don't receive much special attention in the public schools for fear that the teachers and administrators might be accused of elitism. Fairchild Plaza Corporation is a small light in the wilderness, attempting to put a stop to this shameful waste of American brainpower, and that's why I became a supporter."

After about half a beat, Linda Berkshire and Laurel Crown both applauded. Marcia Stowe joined in.

"Well put, old man," said Peter Stowe.

"Yes," agreed Ray Berkshire. He hadn't expected an explanation so lengthy or so altruistic. Could it be that most of the people here regarded themselves as patriots?

Augie, having come out of the powder room, had been about to enter the lounge, but stayed in the hallway for the climax of Tom Trenton's diatribe. That way he didn't have to pretend to be enraptured, when he had heard the same snow job many times before. He made his entrance just as the applause was fading. Spotting Donna Sutter with her parents, he decided to first say his hellos at the bar, then work his way back to join his mother and father who, as good luck would have it, were sitting one table away from the Sutters.

"Well, hello David. Traffic hold you up?" Marcia Stowe called out pleasantly as Augie approached.

"A little, but mostly I just got a late start," he said, smiling socially. "I was working out a computer log system and got a bit carried away." His smile broadened, but they couldn't know the true reason for his amusement: the log system he had been working on was that of Fairchild Plaza Corporation. He had found a node and was now probing it, hoping to gain deeper access to the Ultrachild Project.

"We're glad you're here, your parents were worried about you," said Marcia Stowe. "David Parkhurst, meet Ray and Linda Berkshire and Laurel Crown. You know everybody else, David."

As if standing outside himself, Augie – the spy in enemy territory – watched himself being David Parkhurst at his polite and affable best, exchanging handshakes and how-do-you-dos with the folks at the bar.

"David," said Tom Trenton, "I was just telling everybody why I'm so gung ho for Fairchild Plaza Corporation. And I'd be remiss if I didn't say that, when I decided to become heavily involved fifteen years ago, it was mostly because of your father and mother. Ray and Linda, I don't know if you two realize that Drs. Vincent and Carol Parkhurst, David's parents, are the pioneering force behind our drive for educational excellence in this country."

"Yes, Ray and I have read their books," said Linda. "We've tried to follow their theories in bringing up our daughter, so we were especially thrilled at the opportunity of enrolling her at the Academy."

"I'll drink to that," Peter Stowe piped up, sounding a bit slurred. "What are you having, David? Join me in a Manhattan?"

"No, thanks, better go back and say hello to Mom and Dad," said Augie.

"Nice meeting you," said Laurel Crown.

"Same to you," Augie said, smiling ingratiatingly. She was a real knockout. He was sure he had seen her face on some magazine covers. He'd love to have control over those slender, shapely legs of hers, making them wrap around his naked buttocks, drawing him in deep.

But, if he couldn't have Laurel Crown, he could instead have Donna Sutter – big-titted, long-legged and sweet sixteen. He scoped her out as he approached his parents' table, smirking to himself, contemplating the streamlined efficiency of his newfangled courtship process. He didn't have to waste time wooing and dallying with sexy, but intellectually vapid, young creatures, feeding them some kind of phony line in order to get what he really wanted.

Shaking hands with his father and embracing his mother, he secretly gloated over the power that he had usurped from them. Whereas once he had held them in awe and fear, now they seemed old, frail and ineffectual – Dr. Vincent Parkhurst, short and bald and pale, his reddish beard twitching from a nervous tic at the corner of his mouth; and Dr. Carol Parkhurst, dumpy and gray in a strapless black tube of an evening gown that revealed the heavy sprinkling of freckles on her shoulders. From his mother, Augie had inherited the freckles on his face, and from his father, he had gotten his red hair and green eyes – and he wasn't proud of the evidence of kinship. His father's handshake, his mother's skin and even the peck she gave him on his cheek were as dry as . . . as what? Parchment. Onionskin. Computer printout. If they had any love in them, it was for the Ultrachild Project. Not for David/Augie. Little did they suspect the "sibling rivalry" that was going on right under their noses. Their flesh-and-blood son, who had once been totally under their control, subject to their designs and whims, was going to sabotage their precious "brainchildren" one by one.

Linda Berkshire loved the elegance of Vanessa Larson's party. Glancing at Ray, she told herself that he was probably making plans to satirize the occasion and the guests in some comedy-of manners – a novel or a screenplay – that he would never write. To him, excessive wealth and social position were gauche. That's why he would never attain either.

At the lace-covered dining table, this evening's fourteen guests dined in relaxed splendor beneath a huge crystal chandelier, whose beaded sparkles were accentuated by tall white candles in cut-glass holders spaced evenly between the place settings. About the table and on the sideboards were low, unobtrusive arrangements of daisies, rosebuds and asters. The serving bowls and platters were of ornate, highly polished silver. The cuisine was Cantonese: bird's nest soup, Peking duck, shrimp with lobster sauce and sweet and sour pork, all prepared with the subtle artistry that one expected only from the finest Chinese restaurants in Manhattan.

Over coffee and after-dinner drinks, the conversation turned once more to the current state of American education. Peter Stowe slurringly quoted the Education Commission report, which stated that, if some foreign power had wreaked the havoc on our school children that we ourselves had wreaked, it would have been considered an act of war.

"Well, the public schools have such an utter lack of discipline," said Leonard Sutter, a sandy-haired, craggy-faced man with thick glasses. "Nobody forces the children to pay attention."

"They don't see that illiteracy is any particular handicap," Shirley Sutter chipped in. "Why should they bother to read when they can watch television?"

"I read something the other day," purred Laurel Crown, "about how TV is robbing children of their childhood. They soak up the soap operas, while their mothers and fathers are out making a living, and they see sex, violence, injustice, marital infidelity, political corruption – all the dirty side of the adult world. It makes growing up seem threatening instead of safe."

171

"That's right," Shirley Sutter agreed. "At Fairchild, we allow kids to develop emotionally at a reasonable pace. In some ways, we don't want them to grow up too fast – for instance, sexually. It's best to gently repress their sexuality by divulging information gradually and emphasizing proper moral standards."

"We're not prudes," Leonard Sutter hastily interjected, with a sideways glance at his voluptuous sixteen-year-old daughter. "But we do realize that young people whose innocence is prolonged will devote sufficient time and energy to their studies and to the kind of healthy, creative play that builds a sense of achievement and self-esteem."

Sex and discipline. Augie looked across the table at his mother and father, wondering if they might be sharing similar thoughts. He knew as well as they how much the stimulation of pleasure-punishment centers was used by the Brain Augmentation System at Fairchild. He had been his parents' first human guinea pig.

Like one of their lab monkeys, he had been implanted with a BAS stimoceiver when he was five years old. He had grown up with precious few thoughts or feelings of his own. By remote control, his parents had been able to elicit from him any emotion they desired; they had been able to manufacture each and every basic impulse. Love. Hate. Sexual desire. Fear. Pain. Anger. Curiosity. Dread. Cowardice. Bravery. All these passions and drives, and combinations thereof, had been at the beck and call of their Transmitter.

They hadn't been parents to him, but puppet masters. Pushing buttons. Putting him through his paces. Making him do what they wanted. Entertaining themselves by the intricacy and cleverness of their control over him.

Now *he* was at the controls. *He* was the Transmitter. The electronic master of human puppets. Lord of the Ultrachildren.

Not only did he enjoy the satisfaction of revenge, he enjoyed the diversion. The mental challenge. The signals had to be transmitted in the right sequences, combinations and intensities; also, one had to set the situation up properly, paying attention to the subject's established drives, whims and predispositions in order to have subtle, rather than blatant, control over an Ultrachild.

For example, to make a child kill his mother, one might have to stimulate feelings of love, dependency, hatred and rage – all at the same time – and in a proper mix – so as to produce the desired result. And *timing* would be a factor. The child would be less able to resist the murderous impulse, if something had already happened in his immediate or his subconscious past to predispose him toward matricide.

For the purpose of "accelerated education," select students at Fairchild were implanted with a sufficient number of electrodes to subtly control their drives, ambitions and orientations, and also to stimulate the pleasure-punishment centers of their brains. Being good little children and devoting themselves wholeheartedly to their schoolwork resulted in a glow of pleasure and well-being that was almost like a total body massage – a subtle tingle just below the threshold of sexual arousal. On the other hand, misbehaving and neglecting their lessons caused a pervasive static-like anxiety tinged with nausea. No wonder the Ultrastudents were such darlings. Nothing could make them feel so good as doing exactly what was expected of them; while doing the opposite made them feel terrible. Just a little "buzz" of electricity kept them functioning "perfectly."

But what would happen when the microchip circuitry and the electrode filaments in their brains were removed or switched off? Could they ever be what one might call "normal"?

Or would they be like Augie?

Cold. Analytical. Calculatingly intelligent. Amoral. Unable to feel ordinary emotions. Literally turned off . . . like an unplugged robot.

Sometimes, on a vague, intellectual level, he wondered if maybe the BAS technology might have been refined in recent years, so that without the artificial drive provided by the system, the Ultrastudents wouldn't need to feel the same deep malaise that overtook him once his circuits had stopped functioning. But he did not waste much time wondering. Because nothing could inspire him to truly care.

Very few things motivated him very profoundly these days. The best thing was revenge mixed with wild, freakish sex.

At the dining table, he was seated next to Donna Sutter – a bit of matchmaking by Vanessa Larson, who liked to have all the males and females paired off. Donna certainly looked fetching, despite being rather demurely dressed in a ruffled high-necked dress of pink organdy. Her large breasts jutted out proudly against the soft fabric, more tantalizing than if they were nude. She had luxuriant curls of light brown hair, dark brown eyes, dimples at the corners of her full-lipped mouth, and a slight cleft in her well-formed chin.

Augie had tried striking up a conversation with her in the lounge and had found her unresponsive, even churlish. He had tried putting his arm around her waist to escort her upstairs for dinner, and she had flinched as if she'd been touched by something slimy.

He started picturing all the interesting things he could make Donna do if he had his BAS control box with him. He could get her hot and bothered enough to masterbate under the table. If he turned up the juice, she'd probably rip her clothes off and try to screw everybody. Better yet, he could make her pick up a knife and start butchering the charming guests. Then he could jump on her and fuck her, slipping and sliding in goblets of fresh blood.

The fantasy had Augie so titillated that he had to force himself to keep a straight face. He was reminded of his earlier vision of a neo-Manson Family coming up here to wallow in gore. He didn't want everyone at the dinner table to think he was going feebleminded all of a sudden, smiling at nothing. Luckily, Laurel Crown made one of her inane comments just then – something about a wholesome childhood and a happy adulthood – and he was able to pretend to be laughing at what she said, instead of his own wild idea – which was too far-out to be truly feasible.

But it made him think of something just a bit less freaky that he was sure he could pull off.

CHAPTER 21

On a Wednesday in the second week of May, four days after Vanessa Larson's dinner party, Ray Berkshire came home at two in the morning, exhausted, anxious to tumble into bed after an eighteen-hour marathon session of rough-cutting the Faraday Family Restaurant spots. He was surprised to see a light on in the kitchen and to smell freshly brewed coffee, as he let himself in by the front door. It was unlike Linda to wait up so late for him. She came into the living room as he hung his jacket in the foyer closet, and he turned to see a tense, distraught look on her face.

"Is Shana sick?" were the first words out of his mouth. But, because of the look on his wife's face, he fought a rising panic that the trouble might be something worse than sickness. Fears of accidents and other nameless calamities tumbled through his mind.

Linda took two steps toward him and stopped five feet away, pulling her robe tight and cinching it, and hugging her arms around her breasts. "It's not Shana," she said with a slight quaver.

Ray felt relief, and also perplexity. Then who could it be? Had something happened to one of their friends? Someone from the party the other night? Foley?

Linda said. "Ray, I might as well not beat around the bush. What I have to say can't be said very tactfully. I don't mean to deal you any kind of shocking blow, but I don't know how to avoid it. I want us to get a divorce."

176

"What?" he said. Although he had heard her words clearly, they produced a certain numbness in his mind that was a defense against a painful comprehension – against the sudden feeling of his life starting to pull apart at the seams.

"I said I want a divorce. I tried to think of a good time to tell you, but there's no good time. Now, please don't start yelling and wake up Shana. If we're both as considerate and cooperative as we can be under the circumstances, we can break it to her gently."

"What about *me*!" Ray exploded. "What about breaking it gently to me!"

"Shhhh!" Linda cautioned, with a glance down the hall toward Shana's bedroom. "I know you're upset, but I was hoping you'd exercise your usual self-control." She came closer to Ray, and kept her voice low and well-modulated. "Come into the kitchen and have some coffee. I made some." She actually reached out and took his hand. "It's awful to have to lay this out on the table all of a sudden, but I think we both realize it's something that's been festering for a long time. I'm willing to talk about it, if you are."

Her poise infuriated him. He thought it wasn't fair for her to be more controlled than he. But, of course, she had planned this and prepared herself for it, while he was being hit over the head cold. "I don't *want* any coffee," he said, flinging her hand away. "I can't believe you're serious, Linda. You talk so matter-of-factly about ending our life together – and Shana's life with *us*. She needs *both* her parents. How does raising her in a broken home fit in with all your fancy theories of child rearing? Is Super Mom so super that she thinks she can handle it all alone?"

"Please Ray," Linda pleaded. "Don't start hurling insults. Don't make this harder – on me than it already is. Believe me, it's tearing me up, but I'm trying to be brave." She didn't sob, but tears started to roll down her cheeks. "I'm sorry to have to say it . . . but I don't love you anymore . . . and l don't think you truly love me. We've both been clinging to . . . to what we have . . . for fear of letting go and stepping into the unknown. This hasn't been a spur of the moment decision on my part, but I think it's an honest and courageous one. After I finally came to grips with my own feelings, I kept worrying and worrying about what a divorce would do to our daughter. So I tried to hang in and make things better. But it's no use. You know it as well as I, don't you? Deep down, our marriage has been dead for five years. It's time we buried it."

"Think about this some more, Linda. Maybe we can try a temporary separation . . . or marriage counseling . . . something. The house is up for sale now. When we move back to Manhattan it's going to change our whole outlook and the way we feel about each other. We're going to be sorry if we throw everything on the scrap heap just when we have so much to look forward to."

"I agree that it's going to be a fresh start," Linda said, wiping her eyes with a balled-up tissue. "But I think it needs to be a fresh start all the way. When the chemistry stops working between two people, a change of scenery can only be a short term cure. It can't make them fall deeply in love all over again. It can't permanently rekindle what needs to be there in order to sustain a meaningful relationship."

"Well, look, you're not a child! You know that romantic love doesn't last forever – sooner or later the glow has to wear off." Ray stopped talking and stared at his wife, stunned by the banality of his own words. "Chrissakes, Linda, we're arguing in platitudes! I never thought it would come to this. All I'm trying to say is I never expected our marriage – or any marriage – to be perfect. Maybe we don't have everything we always wanted out of life . . . but we've made some damned good compromises and adjustments."

"That's just it!" said Linda. "You've always been willing to settle for less, but I really haven't – it's not my style. That's the basic difference between us that makes us incompatible."

Ray grimaced and shook his head sadly from side to side. "I'm going to bed," he said tiredly and defeatedly. "I hope that by morning you'll change your mind."

"I won't," Linda insisted. "I've already seen a lawyer and filed the papers. This morning." She gave a thin, rueful smile. "Actually, I've been telling myself this whole mess might work out well for you in a certain sense. The way will be clear now for you and Foley."

"There's *nothing* between me and her!" Ray snapped. "If female jealousy is behind this—"

"It isn't," Linda squelched. "For a long time I've felt that you two had a thing going and . . . well . . . maybe I've been wrong. I'd assumed you'd been sleeping with her, but maybe it hasn't actually happened yet. In any case, I believed it to be so, and the fact that it didn't bother me so awfully much is even more evidence that I've stopped caring about you in that way. Foley *has* always wanted you, Ray. You're suited for each other, and you're going to need somebody new. I wish both of you the best. I say that in all sincerity."

"My, how magnanimous of you!" Ray scoffed. "Can't you see what a domineering bitch you are, Linda? You not only want to divorce me – you want to storyboard the next chapter of my life. Well, you're not going to do it. If you go through with this, I'm going to fight you for custody of Shana. You'll end up a sad, pathetic woman without either of us around to boss or manipulate."

Linda's face flushed and her lips curled into an ugly sneer. "You can't *win* custody!" she spat. "You would have to prove I'm an unfit mother! And how would you hope to do *that?*"

"I'm not entirely unclever. I'll think of a way."

"No, you won't. You're a *loser*, Ray. You'll only make it more agonizing for Shana if you force her to choose between us. I thought you'd at least have sense enough to spare her an ugly court battle."

"Sure, Linda," Ray said with weary sarcasm. "You want *me* to be the sensible one – which means I'm supposed to take this lying down. But you miscalculated this time. I'm not going to let you have your way." He turned his back on her and walked down the hall toward the bathroom.

"I *hate* you!" Linda shrieked. "I hate you and I'm *glad* the divorce papers are filed!"

Ray stopped in his tracks and faced her with as much deliberate restraint as he could muster. "Please keep your voice down, Linda," he said mockingly. "Anyone would think you're an unfit mother, waking your little daughter by screaming at the top of your lungs in the middle of the night."

CHAPTER 22

The divorce papers were served to him by registered mail at his office at Wagner, Inc., on Thursday morning. "That figures," he muttered angrily, when he saw that the lawyer who had filed the action was Harold Larson. At the dinner party last week, Larson had reminded Ray of a suave, charming snake in the grass, reeking of too much money and the sly, unscrupulous determination to acquire still more. Apparently, this was the sort of person Linda cottoned to these days.

Ray phoned his lawyer, Andrew Berman, who had seen him through the embarrassments and entanglements of the Berkshire Productions bankruptcy. Berman was heavily booked today, but he agreed to a one o'clock meeting, after Ray told him why he was calling.

He tossed the thick sheaf of divorce papers into his briefcase, along with the scripts and notes he was taking to VidPro, a postproduction house, where he was meeting Foley Ryan at eleven for a screening of the Faraday rough cut. Then he attended a meeting called by his boss, Walter Patterson, which had been his main reason for stopping by at the agency this morning. It was supposed to be a brain-storming gig. He and Walter and a copywriter and account man were trying to come up with a TV/radio campaign for a new line of weight-loss products.

Walter was useless at the meeting. He didn't even talk much, just sat there and chain-smoked. Ever since his daughter landed in the hospital, he had been listless, apathetic, tired of life and ready to give up. Felicia still hadn't come out of her coma, and rumor had it that she never would. The other producers at the agency were like barracudas, taking advantage of Walter Patterson's depressed state to try to knock him out of his job. Ray was the only one who wasn't ganging up, and that was probably why he was the only producer Walter had asked to this idea session. But he wasn't worth any more than Walter. He couldn't focus his thoughts this morning on appetite-suppressant pills, vitamin supplements and low-calorie frozen dinners. He contributed next to nothing, and hoped nobody noticed.

He took a taxi to VidPro, on West Forty-sixth Street, where, in a small private screening room, he and Foley looked at all the Faraday picture and sound takes that had been cut together in sync and in rough sequence yesterday. From these takes they were trying to select the ones that would end up in a final edit.

Ray couldn't forget about the divorce papers nestled in the bottom of his briefcase. The commercials were obviously going to cut together beautifully, but when Foley got ecstatic over this or that, he had to force himself to exhibit enthusiasm. After one of the run-throughs, when the screening-room lights came up and the tracks were being rewound, Foley snapped at Ray that if there was something about the takes that was bothering him, he should feel free to come right out and say so. He was stung by the tone of her voice, more like client-to-supplier than friend-to-friend. He should have known better than to try to fake it with her.

"I'm sorry," he said. "It's no use pretending I'm not preoccupied. I might as well tell you why. Linda has filed for a divorce. I just got the papers this morning, and I have to see my attorney today, when we take our break."

Foley stared at Ray, her eyes wide. "How serious is Linda about this?" she asked. "I don't mean to pry, but is there any chance she'll change her mind?"

"I doubt it," said Ray. "She interprets my efforts at saving the marriage as a kind of weakness. So I'm not going to give her the satisfaction of rebuffing me anymore. I'm going to fight her for custody of our daughter."

"That's going to be tough," said Foley. "The court usually rules in favor of the mother, no matter what."

Andrew Berman was several years older than Ray, but the lawyer enjoyed his work so much that he seemed young and buoyant, despite his potbelly and the flecks of gray in his sideburns and mustache. Sitting behind his huge mahogany desk, he read over the divorce papers, while Ray sipped coffee from a Styrofoam cup. "Okay," he said with a cheerful smile. "We're being hit with the standard counts. She wants custody, child support payments, alimony, a fifty-fifty property distribution. She's asking you to pay her attorney's fees and court costs."

"Shit," Ray said. "*She* should pay. She's the one who's filing."

"Is she employed?"

"I assume she'll go back to work in advertising," Ray said. "She was an account executive when she resigned to have Shana. She's capable of earning a fat salary – eighty or ninety thousand – as much as I make."

"But she might be intending to sit home and be a full-time mother now," said Berman. "We'll have to find out.

183

For now, since your wife has marketable job skills, we`ll allege that she's fully able to pay her own legal costs. By the way, I 'm assuming that you don't want to contest the divorce."

"Do I have that option?"

"As a practical matter, no. We could buy time with it and that's all. Unless your wife is legally incompetent – deranged, senile, something of that nature."

"I assure you, she seems deranged to me."

Berman chuckled. "I'm afraid your testimony would be ruled prejudicial. We'd need psychiatrists . . . expert witnesses."

"I don't want to contest the divorce," Ray said. "But I do want custody of my daughter."

"The best we can probably achieve is joint custody," said Berman. "No judge is going to separate a four-year-old from her mother, unless she's totally unfit – an alcoholic, a drug addict, a prostitute – and even then we'd have a tough time winning full custody. But, Ray, you might truly be better off under a joint-custody arrangement. You work long hours and travel to all parts of the country filming on location. Having you absent so much of the time would be hard on Shana . . . and you'd wind up feeling very guilty."

"Chrissakes, you sound like Linda's lawyer, not mine," Ray snapped.

"Take it easy," Berman said. "Part of my job is to try to think like our opposition. I have no objection to filing a counter petition for custody for you, but it's my duty to advise you that in the long run it'll probably be futile, and you should prepare yourself for that."

"I really hate to give up living in the same house with my daughter just because my *wife* doesn't want me around anymore," Ray said bitterly.

"Joint custody really isn't so bad," Berman asserted. "You would be able to see Shana on weekends and holidays. And you'd have equal say-so with Linda as to what doctor Shana sees, where she attends school and so on."

He took a cab back to VidPro, where he and Foley finished selecting takes, then started working with an editor, honing down the rough-cut into a more polished form. He could barely concentrate. It seemed weird to him to be sitting there figuring out how to edit pieces of take together into nice coherent patterns, while the pieces of his life were fragmenting and falling apart. Yet, what he was doing was enough of a buffer against his emotions that he wished he could keep at it. But he and Foley had to knock off at five. They had been unable to schedule editing time for this evening; VidPro was booked up on somebody else's rush job, so they couldn't hit on the Faraday stuff again till tomorrow morning.

"I'm not going home tonight," he told Foley. "I don't live there anymore. I'm going to treat myself to a good, expensive dinner, then get good and soused. What the hell, I'm a free man now."

"I'll tag along for the dinner part," Foley said. "If you want company, that is."

"Sure," Ray said.

Foley phoned her baby-sitter and told her she wouldn't be home till eight or nine. Then Ray made reservations for two people at Wharf Ten, an excellent seafood restaurant.

185

His main course was baked Imperial Crab and hers was Lobster Newburg. They shared a bottle of champagne. "Since this is my divorce party," he told Foley, "I'll make a toast." Grinning woodenly, he touched his glass to hers. "Here's to the future," was all he could think of to say.

"Cheers," she said, winking, and they both sipped.

Even after a long day's work, she didn't look as tired as he felt. Her black hair still appeared soft and clean and her pale blue eyes still sparkled. He wondered for the first time if she might be too young for him, even though he only had her beat by six years. She could pass for twenty-five, and right now he felt more than twice that old.

"This is nice," she said. "I mean, under the circumstances."

"Very nice," he agreed.

They ate and drank in silence. Despite his wish not to be morose, he couldn't stop feeling the agonies of his failed marriage. He worried about what he was going to say to Shana, and what Linda might already be telling her about him, and how he was going to get along when the divorce became final. He was embarrassed when he finally broke out of his reverie. "Sorry, Foley," he said. "I don't mean to be ignoring you. I guess I'm just not the fun guy I was trying to be."

"That's perfectly understandable," she said, reaching out and touching his hand.

Her touch warmed him and made him feel sad. Looking across the table at each other, they both smiled tight, rueful smiles. He knew that they weren't going to sleep together tonight. It would be wrong to press it right now. It was enough to just be friends. He was glad that he wasn't too drunk and hurt and angry to realize this.

They finished their dinner, and he escorted Foley outside to a warm, balmy spring night. He hailed a taxi for her. She gave him a light kiss on the cheek before getting in. When the cab pulled away, he felt utterly alone. Out of years of habitual love for his wife and daughter and the sense of belonging to a family, he wanted to go home.

He checked into the Montclair Plaza on Forty-Ninth Street. He bought toilet articles and underwear and socks in the little store opposite the registration desk. He took the bag of stuff up to his room and tossed it onto the strange bed. Then he rode the elevator back down to the lobby and went into the hotel cocktail lounge, where a rock band was blasting and where he intended to get drunk enough to fall asleep.

CHAPTER 23

At the Long Island home that she shared with her parents, Donna Sutter was lying down in her bedroom, listening to an album entitled *The Devil's Workshop* by a new punk rock group called The Idol Minds. The pun on the word "idle" was intentional, not just a spelling mistake, because, according to the blurb on the back of the album jacket, the members of the group were into devil worship. Satan was their idol. A wild, scary portrait of him was on the album cover.

Donna had found the CD in the mailbox when she got home from school. It was in a plain brown wrapper with no stamps and no postal marks, just a hand-printed note saying: FROM A SECRET ADMIRER. PLEASE LISTEN TONIGHT AT SEVEN. MAKE SURE YOU ARE ALONE. Just before seven, she had gotten a phone call, and a whispery voice had reminded her to play the record, alone, in her room. "Who is this?" she had asked, giggling, but the secret admirer wouldn't tell. "All will be revealed after you play the record," he promised. She thought it was fun, and was excited about who it could be and whether he'd end up asking her for a date, so she went along with the gag.

She already had heard from some of the kids at the Academy that the strange background sounds used extensively on *The Devil's Workshop* were human voices transcribed backwards with eerie reverb, and if you listened to them the right way, they were saying blasphemous things like "Satan is God" and "Death to Mommy," and "Death to Daddy." To hear the voices talking forward, you had to have the songs on tape and play them on a tape player that could go in reverse – which Donna didn't have. But still, in a crazy song about human sacrifices, she thought she made out something that sounded like "eemoM oT theD." Pretty weird! Unless it was her imagination.

About fifteen minutes after she got done listening to both sides the mysterious caller phoned her again. "Did you listen?" the whispery voice wanted to know.

"Yes – who *is* this?" she said, smiling and trying not to laugh.

"Patience," admonished the whisper. "All will be revealed in good time. But first you must promise me to listen to the record as you fall asleep tonight."

"I'm not sure I can fall asleep to it. It's too scary."

"Promise," insisted the voice.

"Okay, I'll do it," she said. "But this is the last time."

"You won't be sorry." The phone clicked and went dead.

"Mmmmm . . . Lenny . . . Donna will hear us," Shirley Sutter murmured under the covers.

They were both lying on their sides. Leonard had his body folded against hers from behind, his chest against her back, the fronts of his thighs against the backs of hers. He had warmed his hands by hugging her to him, then had worked them under her pajama tops to cup and fondle her breasts. Her nipples were hardening, and his erection was nuzzling her; she felt its throbbing warmth even through the fabric of her pajamas.

189

"Donna won't hear a thing," he whispered huskily. "She's got her radio going."

"It's just that . . ." '

"I know," Leonard said testily. "I know, Shirley – but that was ten years ago."

Shirley Sutter could only make love in an *almost* uninhibited way when she was absolutely sure that she and Leonard were alone in the house. The phobia went back to the day Donna had walked in on them when she was six years old. They had been in the throes of a wild, noisy climax when Shirley opened her eyes and saw the child with her teddy bear standing in frozen terror at the side of the bed. Shirley had screamed – a bloodcurdling scream that mustn't have sounded to the child any different than her mother's orgasmic cries – and Donna had run shrieking and bawling from the room. Later, when she recovered her composure, Shirley had tried to explain that Daddy hadn't been hurting Mommy, but had been doing something that all daddies do to mommies to make them feel good and to start babies growing inside them.

"Then am I going to have a sister?" Donna had asked warily, seeming to be desperately hoping for at least this minimal compensation for the extreme fear she had felt when she saw her father "torturing" her mother.

"Well, it doesn't always work," Shirley dissembled. "So I don't think we started a baby this time."

"Because of me. *I* stopped the baby," Donna said, covering her face with her hands, tears leaking through her fingers.

"No, it's not your fault, it just wasn't the right time, honey," Shirley tried to explain.

"Then why were you doing it?" Donna wailed.

190

"This time we were doing it to make each other feel good," Shirley explained. "You'll understand when you grow up and fall in love and marry someone."

"I won't want to do *that!*" Donna bawled. "I hate it! It's an *ugly* thing to do!"

The incident wasn't brought up between parents and daughter after that. Shirley and Leonard wondered whether to engage professional counseling for the child, but they were bound by their contract with Fairchild Plaza Corporation to use the psychiatric services available there, and they found themselves reluctant to air such a personal problem in front of their colleagues. So they convinced themselves that, at Donna's tender age, what she had seen was not going to make a lasting impression. She would outgrow the negative feelings she was expressing, the way she usually outgrew a dislike of a strange person or a new and temporarily frightening toy.

Leonard was tormented by the cruel irony that had given him a wife so beautiful and youthful that other men envied him, while not guessing that his sex life could be less than satisfying. He ached to have Shirley back in his arms in mind and soul and body, as lustful and wanton as she had been ten years ago. But she was deathly afraid of letting loose again. She kept her passions tightly reined.

Tonight, as on other nights, he settled for the thing she could do for him that would not involve her enough to provoke her subconscious fears to cry out. She peeled back the covers and bent over him. He lay back in the circle of her warm lips, hearing faintly the throb of some crazy music through the closed bedroom door and the closed door of Donna's room across the hall.

Donna saw the silhouette of her six-year-old self backlit by the brightness of her bedroom as she stepped out. The shadow of herself and Sally, her teddy bear, folded almost in two where the green carpet met the baseboard, then the shadow cast itself at a sharp angle up the white wall. When she moved two steps sideways, the shadow was bisected by the crack of light under Mommy and Daddy's bedroom door. She juggled Sally into her other arm and reached up and turned the doorknob. The door opened without making any noise that could be heard above the other, more awful sounds.

They were naked, and Mommy was screaming and fighting to not be hurt anymore. At first, they didn't see Donna and Sally. They came closer, wanting to yell Daddy-y-y-y . . . Daddy-y-y-y . . . stop . . . don't hurt Mommyyyyyy! Their bodies slurped and pounded . . . like a big four-legged monster heaving and smacking in the orange glow of the bedside lamp. Daddy doing the ugly thing to Mommy, hurting her real bad, not stopping but doing it, doing it, even when she kept yelling and trying all her might to throw him off. He had a fat red snake between his legs that kept stabbing into her again and again, coming out all wet and slimy.

And then Mommy's eyes opened wide and white, looking scared to death. And she screamed louder and uglier than before.

Daddy turned and saw Donna.

She tried to run but couldn't. *Couldn't.* Neither could Sally. They were frozen solid. Couldn't move or breathe or anything. They were both scared Daddy was going to do the ugly thing to them.

Music from somewhere kept saying "Kill Mommy, Kill Mommy . . ."

Sally the teddy bear jumped out of Donna's arms and ran away.

Daddy got up and came toward Donna with his big red wet and snaky thing.

All of a sudden she *wanted* him to do it to her. Wanted him with all her might. She was lying naked on a big white table that was a kind of altar with tall white candles, gleaming silver and sparkling goblets of blood. She wasn't little girl Donna anymore. Her breasts were milky white globes with long erect nipples and the pink slit in the fur between her legs was open and moist. Around the table were gathered sneering, drooling people in tuxedos and evening gowns of flashy colors that were unearthly bright. Her father and mother were watching her with all their friends. They wanted what she wanted so desperately and frantically. They wanted her to have sex. The music kept wailing, "Kill Mommy, Kill Daddy."

She recognized the whispery voice on the phone. David Parkhurst, her secret admirer, was at the head of the table, staring scornfully and lecherously down between her legs. He licked his tongue over his lips. His green eyes flashed evilly and greedily, and he whispered, "Kill Mommy, Kill Daddy." The freckles on his face merged until he became red and grew horns. Then he lowered his face to her pink slit. His tongue was fat and long as it penetrated her. Somehow it could thrust in and out and lick her all at the same time. She arched and bucked against his puffy lips. "Kill Mommy, Kill Daddy," the music wailed – while David fucked her with his penis tongue and the Larsons, the Stowes, and all the others did every conceivable obscene thing. To her and to each other. She had penises, tits and vaginas in and on every part of her, filling her mouth, her ears, her arms, her hands, her legs, her anus.

"Kill Mommy, Kill Daddy," they all chanted as they fucked in every imaginable and unimaginable way.

She felt good and mean at the same time. Waves of pleasure crashed over her body as the tongue slurped in and out . . . and she laughed and laughed at the top of her lungs.

She picked up a long, sharp silver knife that was lying with the other silver and crystal articles on the altar. She laughed harder when she realized there were no idle hands or mind or bodies in the devil's workshop.

A child again, she pushed open the door.

The long black shadow that preceded her was not of herself and Sally the teddy bear, but of herself and the long, sharp knife. Her mother and father were still worshipping Satan of the flesh. She knew how good it felt now, for there was still a delicious tingly glow between her legs thanks to the serpent's sly, clever tongue.

"Kill Mommy, Kill Daddy, Satan is God," the music said.

Daddy's eyes were closed, squinted tight. He panted and moaned like a madman as his naked bony hips pushed in and out.

Then Mommy's eyes opened wide and white. But Daddy was the one who yelled first as gobs of white splashed Mommy's screaming lips.

Then the knife came down into Daddy's belly button. Then it kept coming, some more and some more . . .

CHAPTER 24

On Friday morning, in his New York FBI office, Stephen Brownell got a frantic phone call from Dr. Vincent Parkhurst. The neurophysiologist was rattled because Leonard and Shirley Sutter hadn't reported for work at the Academy, and their daughter Donna hadn't shown up for class. "Their home phone seems to be out of order," Dr. Parkhurst said in a nervous, ominous tone. "No matter how many times I try dialing, all I get is a busy signal."

"Now look, calm yourself down," snapped Brownell. "Don't get all upset when there might not be a good reason. Have the Sutters ever taken a long weekend before?"

"Not without going through proper channels. I just *know* something terrible is wrong. You do realize that Donna is a Receiver, don't you?"

"Yes, of course. I have the files."

"Well, what if—"

"Easy, Doctor. Don't let your imagination run away with you. You did the right thing by notifying me immediately. My responsibility is to take care of these potentially disastrous situations so that no one is compromised."

"You see what I'm worried about then. If something *has* happened to them—"

"I understand the ramifications perfectly. The Bureau will handle all the details so that no other law enforcement agency needs to be involved."

"If we're not already too late," said Parkhurst.

"Relax, Doctor. I'll attend to this immediately. It might turn out to be the break I've been hoping for. If our adversary has struck again, this time he may have made a mistake. Each time he moves against us, he risks leaving clues that could give away his identity."

"I'm not cynical enough to be cheered by that possibility," said Parkhurst. "I'll continue to hope that my colleagues and their daughter will turn up safe and—"

Brownell broke the connection. Parkhurst realized in mid-sentence that he was talking to the dial tone. Angrily, he slammed down the phone. "That man is insufferable," he said to his wife, who was sitting in front of his desk, nervously smoking her umpteenth cigarette, ash dribbling down the front of her white lab coat.

"What is he going to do?" she asked apprehensively.

"He says not to worry, he'll take care of it," Vincent Parkhurst said with an indignant wave of his hand. "I can't understand the hateful, irrational lack of respect he's always shown us. Yet he pretends to be supportive of what we're doing here. I think he's jealous. He knows we're the driving force behind the Ultrachild Project, and, when it comes right down to it, he's nothing but a glorified security cop."

"Vincent," Carol Parkhurst cautioned in a tense whisper, leaning forward to be heard. "This room is probably not safe."

"If he's got us bugged, he's going to hear what I would've told him, if he hadn't rudely hung up on me," Vincent said out loud. "It's not *our* fault the Project is in jeopardy. You and I have done *our* job. If there has been a security breach, then Brownell is to blame, not us. He's the fellow who gets paid to prevent such mishaps."

196

Carol didn't say anything, merely lit another cigarette and tried to keep her hands from shaking.

"Give me one of those," Vincent demanded. He had quit smoking four months ago. But he needed one right now.

She meekly handed him the pack of cigarettes and a book of matches, and he lit up frantically, taking a deep drag and exhaling, watching the smoke waft toward the ceiling, dreading the idea that a tiny microphone could be hiding behind any of the fluorescent light panels. His fear of Stephen Brownell and the FBI was the atavistic fear of intellectual versus brute.

He and his wife sat and smoked, grimacing and glancing woefully at each other, both finding it difficult to be brave under a threat of doom. The Ultrachild Project was the culmination of their life's work. Now they had to pray that its sanctity could be shielded by an insensitive federal agent who didn't truly understand its technological virtuosity or its conceptual brilliance. The Parkhursts felt that they were sharing the unfair plight of other visionaries and geniuses like Michelangelo, Leonardo da Vinci, Galileo and Einstein – who had had to depend upon the patronage and protection of mediocre, but powerful, people in order to survive and create great triumphs of science and art. They believed that if it weren't for the clandestine nature of the Ultrachild Project, they would be in the running for the Nobel Prize. Someday, when they could reveal their accomplishments to a more enlightened world, they would bask in the recognition that they weren't getting now.

They had come a long way from the days of their first ESB-BAS experiments with monkeys, when they had

197

confirmed their ability to turn aggressive lab animals into pacifists, meek ones into aggressors, sexually passive ones into satyrs and nymphomaniacs and apathetic ones into avid food gatherers and pack leaders. They would never forget the first thrills of pushing buttons on a BAS remote-control box and watching normal-appearing live subjects go through an astonishing sequence of responses – salivating, lifting their legs, snarling, whimpering, and stiffening their tails – as if they were electronic toys under human control. Over the years, building on what they had learned with animals, the Parkhursts had been able to help people with various brain dysfunctions, such as epilepsy, suicidal depression and severe psychosis. They had unlocked many of the secrets of intelligence and emotion. Their mission was to harness brainpower and expand it to its fullest potential for peace, progress and prosperity. They believed with all their hearts that they were destined to discover, reshape and redefine the mechanisms of thought, feeling and creativity, thereby enabling mankind to attain a higher level of culture and a more harmonious civilization.

At nine o'clock that Friday morning, David Parkhurst drove his yellow Mustang into the Sutters' sedate Long Island neighborhood. He parked across the street from their split-entry brick and cedar home. There did not seem to be any more lights on than had been on late last night when he had left, after hiding in the darkness of the backyard pressing the buttons of his BAS box in a carefully timed and orchestrated sequence. He had heard muffled screams and sobs mingled with the songs of *The Devil's Workshop*.

Then all noises inside the house had stopped, even the music.

David had resisted the strong temptation to have a look right then – out of fear of getting caught. Instead, he had driven back to his apartment in Greenwich Village, entertaining himself with imaginary visions of what must have happened in order to keep alive the vicarious thrills. But imagining just wasn't good enough for him. He had lain awake all night, aching to actually see how his prank had turned out.

Sitting in the Mustang, he watched the Sutters' house, mustering his courage. The sun had come up on a beautiful spring day. Birds were chirping. A couple of rabbits chased each other in the lawn, under a maple tree that was just beginning to grow new leaves. There were no sirens or cop cars or any other signs of danger. No indications of people moving around inside the house. Normally, the Sutters would have been gone by now. They would already be at Fairchild Academy.

The thing that was making David hesitate was that he had taken the precaution of placing a call to the Sutters from a payphone at a nearby Park-N-Go grocery store and he had gotten a busy signal. This had almost stopped him from driving over here. But, gradually, he convinced himself not to be so skittish. It was probable that a phone had been knocked off the hook during last evening's wig-out. The thought increased his joy of anticipation. Nobody able to put the phone back on the hook was a wild, freaky sign.

He already knew where he was going to break in: the sliding glass door leading in from the patio at the rear of the house. Once he got inside the high redwood fence encircling the yard and the pool, he could use his crowbar with no fear of being seen. He got out of the Mustang, carrying the crowbar in a long, narrow cardboard box of the sort that florists use to wrap flowers. He went up onto the front porch and rang the doorbell. He rang it again. And again. As he expected, no one came to the door.

He went around the side of the house and unlatched the gate. He was wearing gloves. No fingerprints. He re-latched the gate from inside and felt reasonably secure. The morning was reassuringly peaceful. It was the kind of upper middle class neighborhood where most people went to work or school or whatever without hobnobbing with each other or prying too much into each other's business. Definitely not a Crime Watch neighborhood.

There was no dead bolt or steel bar in the inner trough of the sliding glass door. The flimsy lock jimmied open with ridiculous ease. David let himself into the semi-dark family room, holding his crowbar in his gloved hand, ready to hit somebody with it if he had to. But he felt a quietness beyond ordinary quiet that soon made him believe that nobody was going to attack him.

From being here with his parents on social occasions, he knew his way around the house. Padding softly through the family room with its fireplace, sofa and television set, he crept up two short flights of carpeted stairs. Then he prowled through the living room, dining room and kitchen. No lights were on in any of those rooms, and there was no sign of life or of recent death. Neatness abounded. No dirty ashtrays, no mussed-up furniture, no unwashed dishes.

He went down a hall, toward some light that was spilling from a doorway. On his way he passed the bathroom and noticed a crack of light under the closed door. He stopped. Listened. Rapped softly on the door. No one responded.

The first bedroom he entered was Donna's. The messy, empty bed smelled like sex. There were stains on the wrinkled sheets. The ceiling light was on and so was a small lamp on a long, low combination book-case-and-record-cabinet, where a CD player was situated. With satisfaction, David noted that the CD that had played last was *The Devil's Workshop*. The player was still on, but the disc wasn't spinning.

Tsk-tsk, David thought to himself. Lots of electricity being wasted in this house. CD player and lights on for people who can't see or hear anymore. Then, with a burst of panic, he realized he should have turned on the light in the hall so he could look where he was walking. But it was too late now. He had stepped in blood. His sneakers had made smudgy jogger-grip patterns on Donna's pale blue bedroom carpet. He wiped his shoes as much as he could, trying to get them perfectly clean, scraping them against the carpet as he retreated from the room.

Angrily, he hit the hall light-switch and froze for a moment, collecting his wits. He decided he had nothing to worry about; he could get his sneakers nice and clean before leaving the house.

He didn't go barging into the next bedroom, since it was from there that most of the blood seemed to have been tracked. A bloody hand print was on the white wall near the door jamb. The doorknob was smeary also. David pulled a fistful of Kleenex from a box on Donna's nightstand and, using the tissue so he wouldn't get his glove bloody, he twisted the knob and pushed the door open. He stood in the doorway and looked in.

The ceiling light was on, very bright. A table lamp was broken on the floor, its bulb smashed. The bedside phone had been knocked off the nightstand and was making a rhythmic electronic burping signal . . .

Stephen Brownell and Tom Trenton drove to Long Island in Brownell's tan Chevrolet. The regional FBI director was one of the few people who knew that Trenton was a CIA operative. He had been "planted" in his role as a prominent talent agent. Under that cover, he was able to channel children of outstanding potential into the Ultrachild Project; and, as Chairman of the Board of Fairchild Plaza Corporation, he was in an "insider's position" when it came to overseeing the Project's internal integrity and secrecy.

The CIA had a stake in the international ramifications of the Ultrachild Project: the development of "intellectually enhanced assets" would enable the United States to compete on all levels with foreign powers employing similar methods of military and political electronic mind control. The FBI was charged with enforcing domestic security, which technically was outside of CIA jurisdiction. So it was vital for Brownell and Trenton to work together against the present dire threat to the Project that must be ferreted out and eliminated.

Neither Trenton nor Brownell wanted to involve any other CIA or FBI agents at this moment. Even within their own organizations, secrecy was paramount. Only a handful of high-level intelligence officers were privileged to know the full details of what was going on at Fairchild Plaza. The fewer people who had the "need to know," the better.

Perhaps the lid could be clamped on this thing, before it got too much further out of hand.

As he drove the tan Chevrolet into the Sutters' neighborhood, Brownell said, "If we find what we think we're going to find, it may be a break for us. Our adversary may have tripped himself up this time. I said as much to Parkhurst and he damn near shit a brick."

"Well," said Trenton, "naturally he's deeply concerned about the Sutter family. He`s been friends with them for fifteen years."

"I appreciate that. Still, it's an ill wind that blows no good. I'll take any break I can get."

Like Dr. Parkhurst, Tom Tremon privately disliked Stephen Brownell's coarseness and distrusted the FBI man's ability to handle a difficult situation with subtlety and tact. "I hope you realize," Benton said, "that if our adversary *has* struck again, we've not only got to find a way to track him down, we've also got to cover his action."

"I realize it better than you do, Tom."

The suave "talent agent" ignored the scornfulness in Brownell's voice. He went on pressing his point. "It's imperative that we keep civilian law enforcement out of this, or, if they do tumble to it, we've got to make them think it's something else. We don't want any autopsies performed on the victims, unless we order them ourselves from our own forensic specialists."

David Parkhurst dropped the fistful of Kleenex he had used to open the doors of Leonard and Shirley Sutter's bedroom and the adjacent bathroom. He wanted to get away from the sickly sweet stench. Wanted to get the hell out of there, even though he was so pleased that his power had been wielded with such terrible effectiveness. Reveling in the aftermath of it all had suffused him with an erotic amazement and awe.

But he couldn't resist one final touch.

Picking up the toilet brush, he dipped it in the half-congealed paste in the bathtub. On the white tile he wrote: AUGIE WAS HERE. Then he dropped the brush. His gloved hands were clean. He was much smarter than the Manson Family. They had written slogans in their victims' blood, using their bare hands, thereby leaving bloody fingerprints that caused them to get caught.

David/Augie went to the kitchen, washed the soles of his sneakers in the sink and dried them with paper towels. Then he went downstairs to the family room and out through the sliding glass door.

He got in his yellow Mustang and drove away.

Brownell and Trenton got there a few minutes later, parking the tan Chevrolet in roughly the same spot that the yellow Mustang had just vacated. Trying to give the impression that they might be a couple of salesmen, they both carried briefcases, as they crossed the street and mounted the Sutters' front porch. A lady down the street sweeping her sidewalk gave them barely a glance. After ringing the doorbell a few times, they let themselves in, Trenton screening Brownell as he used his lock pick.

Once inside, they drew their .45 automatics. At first they split up, quickly moving through the whole house, an area at a time, vaguely hoping to catch someone red-handed. Brownell took the upstairs and Trenton took the downstairs. The FBI man was the first to see the carnage and the CIA man found the busted lock on the sliding glass door. After they realized with bitter disappointment that they were too late to apprehend anyone, they holstered their .45s and began to inspect the scene.

Neither man was easily shocked, yet they were both numbed by thc grisliness of what had occurred.

Leonard and Shirley Sutter were sprawled across their bed in opposite directions, their legs entangled. Both had been stabbed numerous times. Leonard was nearly decapitated, his head hanging by what was left of a gaping blood-caked neck, his hair almost touching the floor. Shirley's public area looked like raw, chopped meat. Leonard's amputated genitals were strewn on the mirrored dressing table.

Donna was naked in the bathtub, disemboweled, keeled forward in a three-inch-deep, drying, stinking puddle. The toilet brush had been dropped into the tub, the handle touching one of her calves.

Brownell and Trenton stood looking at what had been written in a paste of blood and visceral fluid on the bathroom tile.

"Butchered her parents, then committed hara-kiri," Brownell said. "I hope we catch the freako who made her do it. It wasn't enough for him to engineer this. He had to come in after it was over and gloat over his victims."

"Augie was here all right," said Tom Trenton, looking at the dark, smeary scrawl on the bathroom tile. "He's taunting us, showing off that he knows all about the Brain Augmentation System."

Brownell said, "I don't think we can keep civilian law enforcement out of this entirely. But we can reconstruct the situation cosmetically so they'll arrive at a scenario that won't hurt us."

"One way or another, we've got to get Donna out of here," said Tom Trenton. "We don't want anybody doing an autopsy on her. We can call for an ambulance from Fairchild Hospital."

Brownell rummaged in the cabinet under the bathroom sink. "There's some cleanser here," he said. "I'm going to use it to scrub that mess off the tile. You can take the knife out of the girl's hand and stash it in your briefcase. Better stash the toilet brush, too. Then make the ambulance arrangements."

They decided that Brownell would place a call to the New York Police Department only after the ambulance had departed, carrying Tom Trenton away from the scene of the crime, along with Donna Sutter's dead body. The ambulance would perform its mission with lights flashing, siren wailing. Brownell's story would be that he and "another FBI agent" had found the girl barely alive. That way, she could "die" at Fairchild Hospital, where no civilian pathologist would meddle with her body.

The NYPD would be told that the FBI agents had arrived at the murder scene, as the result of a phone call from the perpetrator, bragging about what he had done and even giving his name: Charles Stasiak. Brownell had suggested blaming the killings on Stasiak, since he was a kidnapper and murderer already wanted by the FBI. It would do no harm for the NYPD to believe they were helping to hunt him down; and it would give Brownell a perfect excuse to "work hand and hand" with the New York police and to be privy to any useful information they might uncover. With the bathroom tile scrubbed clean, the NYPD would never have to know that AUGIE WAS HERE.

CHAPTER 25

Ray Berkshire timed his arrival at the house in East Stanton for eleven o'clock Saturday morning, when Linda and Shana ought to be at Childplay. He was terribly hungover from his second night in a row of solitary drinking in the Montclair Plaza cocktail lounge. He had asked Foley Ryan to join him, but she had declined without giving him a reason, making him feel totally alone and unwanted. Now he was feeling so bad physically that his mental and emotional pain was partially numbed out. So the binge had been therapeutic to that extent.

Linda's red car wasn't in the driveway. He peeked through the grimy windows of the garage, and her car wasn't in there either. Good. He could pack some of his clothes and other necessities before his wife and daughter came home. He wanted to talk with Shana before he left, but he preferred to do the other stuff while Linda wasn't around adding to the awkwardness and perhaps picking an argument. By hustling around and ignoring the misery of his hangover, he got it all done by noon. Then he made himself a pot of coffee and sat in the kitchen, waiting. Fifteen minutes later, he heard tires on gravel and car doors slamming.

When Linda and Shana came into the house, they were both crying. Ray's heart sank. He assumed that Linda must have chosen this particular moment to tell Shana about the divorce – on their way back from a session of mother-daughter "interaction" in their matching purple workout togs.

"Oh, Ray – have you heard terrible news?" Linda said, tears streaming down her cheeks.

"News? What news?" he mumbled, looking at Shana, whose eyes weren't as wet as her mother's.

Linda said, "We just heard it while we were driving home. Leonard and Shirley Sutter and their daughter Donna – some maniac attacked them in their home. They're all dead! Murdered! It's so hard to believe!" She grabbed some Kleenex from a box on the kitchen counter and wiped her eyes. Then, saying, "Here, honey," she knelt and did the same for Shana.

"Did the cops catch the guy?" Ray asked.

"No. They know who did it, but they haven't caught him. Apparently, it's somebody who's been on the loose for a long time. He's killed people in other states. The FBI is working on the case."

"They'll get him," Ray said.

Shana had stopped crying. "Hi, Daddy," she said, more subdued than usual, and came over and hugged and kissed him.

"I can't get over it," said Linda. "You realize these things happen, but you don't expect them to happen to people you know."

"We didn't know them very well," said Ray. He refrained from pointing out that she could save some of her grief for a situation more near at hand; specifically, the one right here in this house.

"But they were good people," she said. "Shirley was so nice about helping Shana get into Tiny Tot Academy."

"Is that still on?" Ray asked.

"Of course." Linda turned to Shana. "Go and start getting ready for your bath, honey. I'll be there in a few minutes. Your daddy and l have some things to talk about."

Shana obeyed promptly, and it almost annoyed Ray that Linda had such good control over her.

Linda sat at the kitchen table with Ray. She didn't pour any coffee for herself, and he didn't refill his empty cup. "I had hoped you'd at least be in touch the last two days," she said. "Where were you? With Foley?"

"What do you care?" he snapped.

"Shhhh," she whispered, with a glance in the direction of their daughter's bedroom. "Shana doesn't know exactly what's happening yet. I wanted to discuss it with you, if you would have at least phoned me, and then both explain the situation to her in the most sensitive and caring way we could devise."

"No other way would do," Ray said sarcastically.

"I don't think I could do a good job of talking to her at the moment," said Linda. "I'm too upset about the Sutters. It's enough to deal with for one day – for me and Shana both."

"Well I intend to talk with her before I leave," said Ray. "You can have your mother-daughter powwow whenever you please. I'm not playing your game of being 'civilized' about this, Linda. It's not the way I feel."

"You still intend to fight me over custody?"

"You'll find out when you hear from my lawyer."

"Well you can't win," said Linda. "I have it sewed up. You'll see when you hear from *my* lawyer. I didn't want this to be a bitter divorce, Ray, but you're turning it into one."

"Look, I want to get out of here. I came to pack a few things and talk to my daughter. I'm going to do it right now. I don't want to wait till she's finished with her bath."

"Fine with me," Linda said.

"I didn't ask your permission."

"Please be gentle with her."

"You started this, Linda. Stop kidding yourself that there's going to be any way to make it mildly unpleasant instead of terribly painful and traumatic."

He talked with Shana in her room with the door closed. They sat on the bed together, surrounded by shelves full of toys, storybooks and stuffed animals.

He said he wasn't going to be living with Mommy anymore, because Mommy no longer loved him. Shana knew what a divorce was, so he told her that's what was going to happen. "Mommy and I both want you to live with us," he said, "so you may have to tell us which one you'd like to live with day to day . . . and the other one would come and see you as often as possible. We both love you very much and we don't mean for our grown-up troubles to cause you so much hurt."

He and Shana were both crying by the time he got done saying it all. Hugging her tight, he waited for her to say something. Finally, in a trembly, tearful whisper, she asked, "Why doesn't Mommy love you anymore?"

He told her that he didn't know. She pushed him away and threw herself down, sobbing into her pillow. He caressed her hair and cheek, wet from tears.

Blotting his own face with his handkerchief, he backed out of the room. "I'll come back and see you soon," he said. "I'm sorry, Shana. Please remember that I'll always love you. So will Mommy."

He almost bumped into Linda in the hallway. "I did the best I could," he told her. Then he walked straight out of the house, got into his car, and drove. The roads, the signs, the traffic and the direction of his life were a half-sick, half-numb blur as he made his way back to the city.

On Monday afternoon in Andrew Berman's office, Ray was told that he had to relinquish his last shred of hope of winning full custody of his daughter. "I spoke with Harold Larson at length," Berman said. "He told me that your wife will shortly be going to work for the Trenton Talent Agency at a salary of eighty thousand annually. Also, Tom Trenton has arranged a scholarship for Shana to attend Tiny Tot Academy. It won't be difficult for Linda to work during the day and still give the child all the parental attention the court would require."

"What it boils down to," Ray said bitterly, "is that her friends from Fairchild Plaza are helping her to get rid of me. What about *joint* custody?"

"I'm afraid I have bad news on that score, too. Harold Larson is advising your wife against it, and he tells me flatly they won't agree to it. They claim joint custody isn't feasible and would be detrimental to your daughter's well-being, because it would be impractical to consult with you regularly, and in an emergency situation you might not be reachable at all."

"Can they make a judge buy this crap?" Ray said, angrily pounding his fist in his hand.

"They'd stand a damned good chance of it," Berman told him. "But I wouldn't just knuckle under, if I were you. I'd try to hang onto joint custody. You might even consider changing jobs, if you have to, so you're not out of town on location so much of the time."

"Suppose I give in and let Linda have full custody," Ray said. "What would l be left with?"

"Weekend and holiday visitation. Summer vacation with Shana. It would be worked out on a schedule that'd alternate between you and Linda."

"All right. That's what I'll go for. How soon can it be wrapped up?"

"Maybe as soon as three days from now . . . if Larson can draft the agreement right away and you and Linda will immediately sign it. That will finalize the custody and support arrangements – the basic divorce. But a formal decree will take about ninety days."

"No way of speeding that up?"

"No. Not really."

"Let's get it started," said Ray.

"You don't want to agree to alimony, do you? I don't believe you should, since your wife has admitted she's going to be employed at a substantial wage."

"Okay. No alimony."

"I advise you to take some time to think all this over, said Andrew Berman. "Don't plunge ahead in the screwed up emotional state you're in now and regret it the rest of your life."

"I know exactly what I'm doing," Ray told him. "My mind is made up."

He meant that his mind was made up to take Shana away from Linda for good. Without any help from the lawyers or the courts.

CHAPTER 26

One of the nice things about working at the Trenton Talent Agency was that Linda got the inside track on roles that Shana might be able to land and even got to escort her to auditions during work hours, as a normal part of a talent agent's job. This morning, with Tom Trenton's permission, she didn't have to report to the Agency, because she was taking Shana directly to an audition that was set for nine o'clock.

Linda was happy with her new life. It was amazing how many things had come together for her in such a short time and how well it suited her to be a free woman! She felt good about having important, influential friends like Tom Trenton, the Larsons and the Stowes to help her get such a wonderful new start; it was nice to be valued by people of that caliber.

In another two months her divorce would be formally decreed, but it was already signed and settled. Linda and Shana were a team now, and Ray had apparently had a change of heart and accepted that as the way it should be. It proved how weak he really was; when push had come to shove, he had given up without much of a fight. He even seemed to be deteriorating, losing a grip on himself, in the month or so since the divorce agreement was signed. He had taken his share of the profit from the sale of the house and had quit his job at Wagner, Inc., ostensibly to start being a writer and filmmaker again. Linda would bet that he wasn't touching pen to paper. During one of the visitation days, when he had come to her new apartment to pick up Shana, she had asked him how his writing was coming along, and he hadn't had much to say.

It was all panning out the way Linda had expected. The divorce had freed her to be a success and had freed Ray to be a failure. But at least he wasn't dragging a wife and daughter down with him. He was living in a cheap hotel on Ninth Avenue – no place to bring Shana to. He claimed he was trying to make his money last till he could get a book published or raise money for an independent movie. Linda almost didn't trust him to take proper care of Shana when the two of them spent time together. He didn't seem to have his wits about him anymore. He used to be a reasonable man, if not an ambitious one. Maybe he just couldn't get over the shock of the divorce.

The audition this morning was at an advertising agency called Brent Strang Associates. They were producing a series of television commercials for a new candy bar, called Lucky Break, to be launched with a heavy media blitz. Because of the huge number of time buys on the important networks, if Shana got cast she could pull down more money than she would have gotten if she had landed a part in the Burger World spots.

Monroe Larson was auditioning, too. So Linda and Shana had breakfast with Vanessa and Monroe in a restaurant on the first floor of the Seymour Building on Madison Avenue, where Brent Strang Associates was headquartered. The kids had rehearsal scripts this time, so, after they had eaten, they practiced delivering the lines, while their mothers coached them. There were three scripts, each for a thirty-second spot featuring a little boy and a little girl. Monroe and Shana gave such cute, funny line readings that Linda and Vanessa laughed. The adult approval made the kids relax, have fun and perform better. They both looked like shoo-ins as far as Linda was concerned, and she hoped the casting director wouldn't be too much of a jerk to see it. Monroe was impishly handsome in a little blue blazer and checked trousers, and Shana was a blonde, blue-eyed angel in a pink frilly dress. "Wouldn't it be great if they both got cast in the same spot?" Linda said; but in her heart she was mainly pulling for her own child and knew that Vanessa was, too. It would be hard to take if Monroe won out and Shana got passed over again.

Wrapped up in rehearsing the scripts, Linda almost forgot to give Shana her vitamin pill. In fact, she didn't think of it till just before nine, when they were all gathering up their audition gear, ready to head out to the elevators. She had to ask a waitress who was busy with another table to bring a glass of water so Shana could swallow the capsule. "Don't wait for us. Go on up. You'll be late," Linda told Vanessa.

"That's okay. I'll be at the cash register. Here . . . give me your check."

"I'll pay you my half upstairs," said Linda. "Thanks."

"That's okay," Vanessa smiled.

The waitress finally brought some water, and Shana took her vitamins. Dr. Stowe had said just last week that the child's red count was almost back to normal, and Linda didn't want to undo her progress. It was a relief that she was doing so well, despite the strain of seeing her parents split up. Thank God, she seemed to be getting over it and adjusting quite nicely to her present circumstances. Linda thought that it had helped to leave the old, bad memories

216

behind in East Stanton and to plunge her daughter into lots of entertaining, interesting activities connected with their new lifestyle in New York.

Linda was sitting in a waiting room crowded with the usual array of parents, agents and child actors. Shana had been called away to be "read" for the third time with a freckled, frizzy-haired urchin named Jason Vanderburg. Linda was upset because she felt that Jason didn't go at all well with Shana. He didn't look like he stood a chance of getting cast, and Linda hated for her daughter to be lumped along with him. How could it bode well? Unless, by some miracle, they actually *wanted* such contrasting types. Maybe they did, or they wouldn't have called them in to read together so many times. But it was only three times, and, of course, there were three scripts; one time per script was probably all it meant.

Mrs. Vanderburg, as freckled and frizzy-haired as her son, was thrilled about it all. Who could blame her? From her standpoint, it must be terrific to see little ugly Jason paired up with a child as beautiful as Shana. Maybe it helped her imagine that her little boy was as handsome in the eyes of others as he was in her own eyes. It was Linda's bad luck to be sitting right next to her. It was impossible to carry on any conversation with Vanessa Larson without Mrs. Vanderburg batting in, chirping inane things like how nice it was to have children who were special.

Despite her worries and her wish not to be bugged by Jason's mother, Linda flashed an encouraging smile at Shana when she and Jason appeared in the doorway of the waiting room.

The smile froze on her face.

Jason was heading back to his seat, but Shana had stopped in her tracks, a giddy, idiotic look on her face. She was tearing her Lucky Break scripts into little pieces and showering them like confetti all over herself. She didn't look angelic anymore – instead, she looked demented, as if an evil spirit possessed her.

"Shana! Stop that immediately!" Linda yelled. She got halfway out of her chair.

Shana started walking across the room, directly in front of everybody, her arms and legs jerking spastically – like a windup toy with all its mechanisms out of whack. A strange, ululating cry was coming from her mouth, and, at the same time, she was chewing frantically, in exaggerated jaw-clenching movements, as if trying to grind her teeth to stumps.

Linda was rooted, unable to believe what she saw.

Mrs. Vanderburg screamed. Jason clutched her skirt and started to giggle.

Angry, embarrassed and scared, Linda charged after her daughter down an aisle of folding chairs, stumbling over an audition kit someone had left on the floor. Grabbing onto the back of a chair to stop herself from falling, she caught a glimpse of Vanessa Larson running out of the door with Monroe in tow.

Shana was still walking like a human robot gone haywire, her tongue drooling out of her mouth. When her mother got to within two feet of her, the screeching sound she was making abruptly stopped. She spun around and faced Linda with a dead, vacant stare. Then she began to laugh, not like a child, but like an old, malevolent crow – emitting hiccups, barks and rasps of raucously insane laughter.

Linda's mouth gaped open. Her heart thumped wildly as adrenaline coursed through her, urging her to action, but not helping her to think or understand. She was dimly aware of the giggles and titters coming from many of the children in the room, who could not fathom Shana's outrageous behavior, except in terms of an amusingly childish tantrum that they'd like to throw themselves. Some of the adults were gasping and muttering in shock and indignation. Linda wondered why Vanessa Larson had fled. She'd never forgive her for running out on her.

Just as Linda reached for Shana, she noticed that the child's complexion was an odd color – dusky, almost bluish. Shana's knees buckled and Linda barely caught her in time to ease her collapse to the hard tile floor. Her body was perfectly rigid, her little hands clenched into tight, white-knuckled fists, her jaw clamped so hard that the muscles stood out in lumps. Her eyeballs were as white as chalk, the blue irises dilated and riveted on something distant and unattainable.

"Mommy! Mommy! Is she sick?" somebody wailed.

Linda's head swam. Her pulse raced. She could hear the pounding of her own heart, but the flurry of sounds around her was a meaningless blur. The gawkers and gapers were a faceless, amorphous mob, like leering onlookers in a nightmare. She fought for self-control, presence of mind. She wanted to behave bravely, to do the right thing in a crisis, to live up to her self-image as a cool, collected, levelheaded woman. But all she could think of was: *Please, God, please help my little girl* . . .

Shana's face had gone from faintly bluish to icy blue. A froth of reddish saliva bubbled from her lips. Her neck veins swelled and throbbed, as if they would burst.

Suddenly she broke into a series of jerky shudders, like waves crashing and rippling through her whole body, over and over again.

Linda was truly afraid that these might be her daughter's final spasms and she couldn't bear to look. She covered her face with her hands and knelt there crying, hearing her own sobs, as if she were watching some lesser person, a diminished effigy of herself, less capable and less competent than she had always imagined herself to be. She became aware of a hand on her shoulder, pulled her hands away from her tearful eyes and looked up. It was Vanessa Larson. She and Monroe had come back into the room. "I've phoned the emergency room at Fairchild Hospital." Vanessa said. "They're sending an ambulance and a doctor. They'll be here soon."

Linda was astonished and ashamed to have not even thought of calling an ambulance herself when her cell phone was right there in her purse. "Thank you," she managed to croak. Watching the convulsions wracking Shana's tiny body, she had no idea what to do to help. It was the sickest, most futile and panicky feeling a mother could have. She smelled feces and urine, and realized that Shana's bowels and bladder had emptied, staining her frilly pink dress and making a foul puddle all around her on the tile floor.

The frothy red saliva was now bright red blood running down Shana's chin and neck. When each spasm hit her, she jerked and bucked so violently that it seemed she would break all the bones in her body.

Linda was hoping desperately for the ambulance to get there. But she couldn't fight off a horrible premonition that it would be too late.

CHAPTER 27

Ray Berkshire hadn't told Linda that he was going out of town. He hadn't told anybody, because he wanted nobody to know. He didn't want to use his own car either, since he was traveling under an assumed name and his New York driver's license and vehicle registration could give him away. He went to Philadelphia by Greyhound bus, paying cash for his ticket, so there would be no record of the trip on a canceled check or a credit card receipt.

The name he was traveling under was James William Perry. As he had found out from researching newspaper files in the Public Library of Philadelphia, on the first of two previous trips to that city, the real James William Perry had been killed in an automobile crash in 1978 when he was two years old; both of his parents had been killed with him. It was a perfect new identity for Ray to assume, since nobody was likely to associate it any longer with the infant who had died thirty-six years ago. If James William Perry hadn't died, he'd have been thirty-eight. Ray was thirty-nine. The close age match was good, because, of course, he did not want to have to pass for too much older or younger than he actually looked.

Having found what he was after on that first trip to Philadelphia, Ray had then rented a room in a cheap hotel under the name of James W. Perry. He had paid two months' rent in advance, explaining that he wanted to ensure the availability of the room, even though his job as a sales rep for a shoe factory might keep him away from it for unpredictable stretches. Obviously interested in little besides the cash he was paid, the registration clerk had barely listened to the explanation. Ray's true purpose for renting the room had been to establish a "permanent" place of residence, while he took necessary steps to affirm his new identity.

Enclosing a money order for ten dollars to cover bureaucratic costs and using his address at the hotel, Ray had sent a letter to the State Registrar of Vital Statistics in Harrisburg, Pennsylvania, requesting a copy of his – James William Perry's – birth certificate, which regrettably had been "recently lost in a fire." He had supplied the parents' names and their dates of birth, which he had obtained from the newspaper file in the library.

On his second trip to Philadelphia, Ray had picked up the birth certificate, which had been mailed to him at the hotel. Using the document as identification, he had then applied for a Social Security card and a Pennsylvania driver's permit under the name of James W. Perry. That had been four weeks ago. Before making this third trip, he had phoned the hotel, and the registration clerk had told him that two pieces of mail were waiting for him, one from the Social Security Administration and one from the Pennsylvania Department of Transportation.

When Berkshire Productions was still in business, Ray Berkshire had worked on a documentary entitled *Parents Who Kidnap Children*. The movie told of the thousands of kids who are "stolen" each year by their fathers or mothers. At the time, Ray never thought that one day he'd be employing the same tactic to make a custody decision wind up in his own favor. But here he was, plotting a kidnapping. From making the movie and researching the narration, he

222

had learned that the odds of getting away with it were in his favor. Law enforcement agencies weren't inclined to treat what he was doing as a "crime." To them, it was just a domestic dispute, and they had more terrible things to worry about. Even the FBI didn't usually get involved in these cases, because they weren't "true" kidnappings in the sense that they didn't involve demands for ransom and threats to the children's health and safety. Ray figured that Linda would be stuck hiring a private detective to come after him. But, from one of the particularly clever and resourceful fathers he had interviewed for *Parents Who Kidnap Children*, he had learned enough tricks to probably never get caught. If he could hang on for about ten years, as that father had done, till his child got to be about fourteen or fifteen years old, then she'd be so set in her new life that no court would take her away.

When Ray was younger, he would've thought that ten years of such intrigue and evasive action would be more than he could take. But now he knew how fast the years fly. Now he thought he could pull it off and still lead a pretty good life. He felt that he deserved to have his daughter living with him. He felt justified in defying the laws and the lawyers who had stacked things in his wife's favor. He believed that Linda's way of raising Shana had less to do with the *child's* needs than with his ex-wife's needs and neuroses. Before the divorce, he had been partially denying his perception that Linda was treating their daughter like a possession instead of a person. But now the blinders were off. And he was convinced that he had to save his daughter from his ex-wife and her cronies at Fairchild Plaza.

Ray's plan was for this trip to Philadelphia to be his next to last. He intended to stay for about two weeks,

223

maybe three. His driver's permit was only temporary, and he'd have to take a test for a permanent license; he'd need a licensed driver to accompany him on the test, so he figured on going to a driving school and paying for a few "brush-up" lessons just to get cooperation from one of the instructors. While this was in the works, Ray wanted to use his new Social Security card to open a banking account and checking account in a Philadelphia bank under the name of James W. Perry. He had already drawn all of his money out of his bank in New York and was carrying it with him in the form of a cashier's check for over twenty thousand dollars.

On his next and last trip to Philadelphia, he'd have Shana with him. He'd go to the fleabag hotel and pick up his permanent Pennsylvania driver's license certificate. Then he'd shave his beard off and maybe do a few other things to alter his appearance, before he went and had a photo license made. From then on, he'd always call himself James W. Perry. Now that he had a proper license, he'd buy a nice used car with Pennsylvania plates. His old car would have been `sold before he left New York, while he was still Ray Berkshire. The cash from that transaction would be in his pocket.

He and his daughter would start driving west. They'd take a crazy zigzagging, backtracking route, stopping off and holing up for long stretches at several places along the way, just to make it tough for anybody trying to track them.

Jim and Shana Perry's ultimate destination would be Los Angeles. He needed to live in a big city, and if it couldn't be New York it had to be another place where he could feel close to the movie business, even though he couldn't be in it anymore – too risky. He would try his damnedest to make a living as a novelist. Of course, he would use a pen name; nobody would find that unusual. He wouldn't wheel and deal for himself; instead, he'd use an agent – he'd have to be wary of running into any transported New Yorkers who might recognize him.

He'd be home to take care of Shana all the time, because he'd be there writing. He had no intention of enrolling her in kindergarten for another year. She could start when she was five, like any normal kid. And she could go to a public school. The pressure would be off. She wouldn't have to be a Superchild anymore. Wouldn't have to audition for TV commercials anymore either – in fact, she *couldn't* do it, or she might be recognized. He hoped he was right in thinking she wouldn't want to once she saw that she didn't have to. He would re-channel her energies in a loving way. She wouldn't have Linda's ogre eating at her anymore.

Ray's biggest regret was what he had had to do to Foley. He had gone out with her a couple of times after the divorce, and he had seen that they could have something nice together. Apparently, she had been waiting till he was free. He had decided, painfully, that he must turn her off . . . and turn her off hard. He had done it over the phone, to spare himself having to face her so he would run less risk of changing his mind. He had told her he didn't want to see her anymore, didn't want any part of her, or his job or anybody and anything that reminded him of his old life. It was cruel, but it was also kind. It wouldn't have been right to get something started with her that he couldn't finish. She'd be better off falling in love with someone else. Someone who wasn't going to disappear into thin air.

225

CHAPTER 28

David/Augie laid low after the prank that destroyed the Sutter family. He was amused by the details broadcast on radio and TV and printed in the newspapers, blaming the deaths on a psychotic named Charles Stasiak, whom the FBI had apparently been trying to catch for a long time. The fact that he was still on the loose only highlighted their incompetence. But pinning the Sutter murders on him wasn't a bad cover-up, Augie had to admit. It kept people from getting wise to the fact that sweet, innocent Donna had something wrong inside her head. Something that had turned her into a lethal robot.

Two weeks after the Sutters were buried, David Parkhurst graduated from Manhattan University. His parents threw a big bash for him, a posh affair at their country club, and presented him with the graduation present he had asked for, a brand new silver Mercedes. He wished he could pump dear old Mom and Pop and their esteemed colleagues for some straight poop on how the murder investigation was going, but if he acted too interested he might draw suspicion to himself. He didn't like the idea that none of the news reports had mentioned his message: AUGIE WAS HERE. He considered sending a letter to a New York newspaper, the way Son of Sam had done. But he wasn't about to let an ego trip foul him up. He realized that the FBI was actually helping him by suppressing the truth and preserving his anonymity. None of the Receivers would be on the lookout; they couldn't be apprised of the exact nature of the threat against them anyway, since none of them knew how their brains were being controlled. Augie could zero in on them one at a time. But he'd have to be careful, since it wasn't inconceivable that the federal agents would be working some stakeouts.

David's parents had agreed that he deserved a summer of rest and relaxation before starting graduate school. They were so proud that he had graduated magna cum laude that they didn't mind giving him a three-month vacation on a fat allowance. He knew that their pride was not so much in him as in themselves; to them he was not his own person, but an extension of them and a reflection of their radiant glory. To him, it was deliciously ironic that they would be financing his summer campaign against their Ultrachild Project.

During June and July, BAS implantations would be performed on the three- and four-year-olds who would be starting at Tiny Tot Academy at the end of August. Augie had decided that he shouldn't confine his mind invasion to the older Ultrachildren, like Felicia Patterson and Donna Sutter. For the sake of variety and as a test of his own ingenuity, he wanted his next prank to involve one of the fledglings. It would teach his enemies that no part of their domain was sacrosanct.

Thus far, although he was an expert hacker, Augie had not been able to gain complete access to the computer code system of the Fairchild Educational and Psychological Research Institute, which was the hub of the Ultrachild Project. But he had penetrated the security of all the other systems at Fairchild Plaza, including the one used by the hospital. Enough "secret" and "confidential" information

227

was now at his beck and call, able to be siphoned into his personal computer terminal at his Greenwich Village apartment, that he could either find out directly, or piece together, most of what he wasn't supposed to know.

He had learned that two hundred children had been accepted into the first year of classes at Tiny Tot Academy. Of these, only five percent were to become Receivers. Ten children. To figure out which ones, Augie had to keep tabs on who was admitted to Fairchild Hospital, and for what purpose. Any supposed cases of epilepsy, hyperactivity or autism, if they occurred among the future-enrollees of Tiny Tot Academy, were just about a dead giveaway. .

Dr. Marcia Stowe, the trusty, kindhearted pediatrician, had some special "vitamin" pills that could make any normal, healthy child start exhibiting autistic or hyperactive behavior or succumb to violent epileptic seizures. When a "sick" child was brought to her, Dr. Stowe would conduct a thorough examination, including electroencephalograms (EI-LGS), CAT scans, PETT scans and other advanced diagnostic procedures calculated to create the impression that all the most sophisticated resources of modern medical science were being lavished upon one highly valuable little person. Then, with dummied results, the pediatrician would make her diagnosis of epilepsy, autism or hyperactivity. She'd paint a gloomy, frightening picture of the course that the disease might take if left untreated, or if treated by conventional methods, such as drug therapy. She'd recommend the implantation of a brain pacemaker by Dr. Vincent Parkhurst to permanently correct the dysfunction. She'd back the recommendation with glowing case histories of the famous neurophysiologist's past successes. The parents, half crazed with fear and worry, and facing the ultimate horror of having a mentally handicapped child on their hands all of a sudden, instead of the paragon they had believed they were raising, would almost invariably consent to the operation. Then, what would actually be implanted would be a BAS stimoceiver. Another human guinea pig would be created for the Ultraehild Project.

A little over a year ago, David Parkhurst had discovered that he had been the first of the Project's human guinea pigs. His mother and father always were careful not to let him see the combination of the large steel safe in their study. If he happened to be in the room when the dial was being twisted, he'd be asked to turn his head. This angered him and fired his curiosity. Why should his mother and father have any secrets from him? He knew the ostensible reason – they were working on a Top Secret government project – but that didn't cut any ice; it only made him itchier and more determined to find out whatever they were trying to hide. From murmurings and innuendos he had picked up over the years, he had a gut feeling that something inside that safe pertained to him. He became fixated on the possibility of stealing the combination. With his head turned, he listened to the clicks and tried to count them each time he got an opportunity. Over a period of roughly half a year, during which he contrived numerous "chance" occurrences, he was able to piece together the numbers of clicks and the sequence of the numbers. Then, one day when he was home alone, he worked out the twists and direction changes of the dial, by trial and error. Presto! The safe came open.

It was filled with experimental data in the form of charts, graphs, lab journals and computer discs. Like a child who had found a cache of hidden Christmas toys, David

Parkhurst began to delve into this treasure chest of scientific information; He had to do it when his parents weren't around, and he had to be very careful to replace each item exactly as he found it, so no one would discover any disturbance. Bit by bit, he read everything and screened the computerized data at the console that was right there in the study. He learned for the first time about the existence of the Ultrachild Project. He made copies of blueprints showing the designs of ESB and BAS components. And he found out the great secret about himself that his parents had been trying to hide.

They had stolen his personality from him. Perhaps they had stolen his very soul. On the pretense of correcting an autistic dysfunction, they had implanted a BAS stimoceiver in his brain when he was five years old. In their lab treatises they had referred to him as their experimental forerunner of the Ultrachildren they wanted to some day crank out on an assembly line. They had reared him, not as their son, not as a creature of ordinary flesh and blood, but as an electronic puppet under computerized push-button control. When he was eighteen, they had turned off his stimoceiver, putting him in charge of his own "circuits."

Their experiment had been a tremendous success. The puppet was now almost too "psycho-civilized" to be shocked or outraged by anything whatsoever – even the discovery of how he had been mentally and emotionally programmed; in other words, enslaved. He was almost "above" any open display of hatred or of a lust for revenge.

The slightest glimmer of a true and deep feeling of hatred or vengeance would be welcomed by David/Augie. It would be a sign to him that he might be a real person, after all. But at bottom, all his "emotions" – even the ones that drove him to pursue his personal vendetta against the Ultrachild Project – were half-illusory and half-contrived. Freed from the external stimulation that had been piped into him throughout most of his life, he found himself existing in a state of such profound ennui that he had to concoct thrills that were ever more bizarre and perverse to succeed even slightly in turning himself on.

When he thought of the ten Ultrachildren who would be "born" through BAS implantations during this June and July, he forced a chuckle from himself by imagining how pleased Drs. Vincent and Carol Parkhurst would be with their new electronic offspring. And how delighted the genetic parents would be to have their children's supposed brain dysfunctions so miraculously "cured." And how the little darlings would henceforth be so well behaved. And so highly motivated. And so perfectly oriented toward the attainment of all the good things in life that they would gladden the hearts of their mommies and daddies.

CHAPTER 29

Dr. Vincent Parkurst and Dr. Peter Stowe were at work in the operating room, assisted by two nurses and an anesthesiologist. They had the unconscious child's X rays, CAT scans and PETT scans to aid them in making geometrical calculations and arriving at three-dimensional coordinates for the positioning of electrodes. A stereotaxic machine, resembling a metallic skullcap, was fitted to the child's head, providing the doctors with a luminous green reference grid on a calibrated screen so they could pinpoint the exact areas of the brain where they wished to establish contact.

The electrodes were fine platinum wires only a millionth of an inch thick. They would be implanted by a computerized surgical instrument, called a micro-manipulator, capable of such extreme and delicate accuracy that it could place the tip of a platinum filament inside a single, specific nerve cell so that the designated cell could be electronically stimulated to the exclusion of all others. The implantation would leave normal brain function unimpaired and would be entirely painless to the individual, since the brain itself has no sense of "feel."

The nice thing about working with a child under five years old was that the fontanels, or "soft spots," of the skull, which were present at birth in order to facilitate passage through the birth canal, were not yet completely closed. The membranous tissue was gradually hardening and in a few more years would be completely turned to

JOHN A. RUSSO

bone, so that the seams of the skull would resemble a closed zipper. But at age three to five, there was still some space to work with. Very little space, to be sure, but enough so that holes did not have to be bored in the skull. The strong hair-like platinum electrodes could be stereotaxically inserted right through the "mesh" of the "zipper" Then the contacts could be connected to the BAS stimoceiver, the wafer-thin microchip, which would be cemented with dental acrylic and smoothly sculpted to the shape of the outer skull.

The largest fontanel was at the top of the head – at birth, a diamond-shaped opening the size of an elongated quarter. It was always the last one to completely close. So it was perfect for Dr. Parkhurst's purposes.

He waited while one of the nurses drenched the patient's hair and scalp in antiseptic solution. Then he parted the hair in the shape of a crescent, made a small incision precisely curved on the line of the part, and peeled the scalp back and away from the skull bone. If this had been a brain operation that required a portion of skullcap to be removed, he would have been obliged to make a much larger incision, and it would have been necessary to shave away the hair first. But, in this particular ease, he didn't want to do anything that might contribute to an awareness on the part of the child that a brain operation had taken place. The incision would heal in a few days, with plenty of local anesthetic applied daily. During recovery, the child would be kept heavily sedated and would wake up unaware of the passage of time, never knowing that anything had been done except "tests." Parental cooperation was, of course, essential in this regard. Any parents who accepted the scholarship to the Academy and the government-

233

subsidized surgical "cure" for their child's illness had to fully understand and agree to the need for secrecy. They wanted a "normal" child – and that meant one who had no hint of a suspicion that he or she might not be normal. The Fairchild Educational and Psychological Research Institute wanted the same thing – to monitor and evaluate the child's future performance in comparison with other children who had not had the operation. If the parents broke down, they would ruin the experiment to that extent; but all they could tell was what they had been made to believe – a story about epilepsy, autism or hyperactivity. If they got anywhere close to blowing the cover of the Ultrachild Project, there were ways of taking care of them. Dr. Parkhurst shuddered to think of those ways. He hoped they would never have to be used. But sometimes it was a comfort to know that he had cruel, insensitive people like Stephen Brownell constantly guarding his flanks and anxious to spring into action.

He was proud of what he had accomplished, even though he had been compelled to resort to subterfuge. Sometimes the great masses of people were too backward, too intellectually stunted to readily appreciate what was best for them. Somebody had to come along to show the way at key moments in history, or else humanity would still be floundering in the Dark Ages.

Currently, by every measure, the American education system and the American way of life were in deep trouble. Everybody agreed that in order for democracy to work, the masses had to be taught – but they weren't learning anything anymore. The illiteracy rate was shocking. The public schools were turning out hordes of drug-crazed, sex-crazed barbarians. Civilization was sinking backwards into the mire of a primitive anti-intellectualism. The battle lines were being drawn, and Fairchild Academy was in the vanguard, a shining example of a more hopeful future.

The BAS-implanted children had no problems with motivation or with distractions from the learning experience. Each individual stimoceiver was programmed for the specific needs of the particular child. Aspiring artists had their creative imaginations stimulated at the appropriate times. Those with a gift for math received stimulation of the seats of logical and empirical reasoning. Budding musicians were helped toward a strong feeling for rhythm. a perfect sense of pitch. And so on, and so on.

At present, the Receivers were programmed in accordance with the results of aptitude tests and the recommendations of teachers and administrators, but, in the future, when the method was out in the open, the wishes of parents could be taken into careful consideration. Since the Receivers were individually programmed, they were controlled by a centrally located wave generator or Transmitter installed within the Academy. This Transmitter sent out a UHF signal that was picked up by each electrode-implanted child. When the bell rang for the start of the first school period, the Transmitter was turned on, and so were the kids – and they stopped talking and fooling around immediately and gave their full, undivided attention to the teacher. The Transmitter was turned off during recesses, lunch periods and at dismissal time, so that the children's behavior was modified only when necessary.

The intense concentration that each Receiver was capable of, plus the tremendous mental advantages that were bestowed by the Brain Augmentation System, made it inevitable that these special children would be ultra-achievers in today's "laid back" society. Any parent who desired the maximum in happiness and material success for his or her child, ought to realize that the required brain operation was in the child's best interest. If they could be told. If they could only be told . . .

Dr. Parkhurst longed for the day when he would not have to work under a cloud of secrecy. He got sick when he dwelled upon the insidious threats posed by security leaks, foreign agents and nameless, faceless terrorists. He hoped that he would soon be able to stop working covertly and openly proclaim the success of his experiments. He could see that people everywhere were gradually getting used to artificial limbs and organs, spare-parts surgery and organ transplants; the idea of implanting gossamer-thin electric wires in the brain was bound to become less and less "strange" and repugnant, especially once the advantages were well known. It wasn't impossible to envision a time in the near future when BAS implantations would be in demand by parents for every newborn babe, and only the elite would be able to get them. The world was bound to realize that the leaders of tomorrow had to be produced in schools patterned after Fairchild Academy.

CHAPTER 30

Behind Stephen Brownell's highly polished mahogany conference desk, flanking him on either side, were an American flag and a blue-and-gold FBI flag. The flags never got dusty. Their pleats and furls hung straight and true. Once every two weeks, the janitorial service saw to it that they were taken out, cleaned and promptly returned, according to orders from the FBI commander. Brownell had seen too many offices and public buildings displaying grimy, haggard-looking flags that were never taken down and cleaned from the day they were put up, as if they were meant as a metaphor for a tarnished, decrepit two-hundred-year-old Republic in the throes of decline. That sort of decadent symbolism, inadvertent though it might be, sickened Brownell. His flags, like everything else in his office, were spotless and neat. He believed that the Republic, under God, was the free world's last best hope. He considered himself a bastion against the forces of decay and despair, and he comported himself accordingly.

In front of him on his desk was the Berkshire file. On top were the items most recently sent in by the agent in charge of surveillance in Philadelphia. Brownell thoughtfully fingered the itmes – photocopies of the hotel bill, the birth certificate, the driver's license and the bank statements – all in the name of James W. Perry. The file had been started way back in April, when it began to look as though Shana Berkshire would be a prime candidate for the Ultrachild Project. Immediately, full dossiers had been compiled on Raymond and Linda Berkshire, including all the details of their lives – birth certificates, adoption papers, school transcripts, job histories, marriage license, deeds, bankruptcy proceedings, divorce petitions and settlements, etc., etc., etc. The folder was fat and heavy. When Linda had filed for her divorce, surveillance had begun on Ray Berkshire, as a standard precaution at first; but immediately it had begun to look like a necessary measure. He gave in to his wife's demands too easily. He relinquished custody of his child without a whimper. He was a fish who stopped struggling while there was too much life in him. He had to be playing dead. And now Brownell had the proof in front of him. There was only one logical reason for Ray Berkshire to be going through all these monkeyshines of setting up a new ID for himself and arranging for his own disappearance: he had to be figuring on snatching his kid.

Brownell shook his head in dismay over the foibles of the average American citizen. Berkshire, like the vast majority, had no idea how hard it was to pull the wool over the eyes of the United States government. He was being pretty slick, compared to most of the idiots who tried to get away with stuff. But not slick enough. If he could step back and scope the broad picture, he'd realize he was like a mouse creeping toward a piece of cheese, peering just about every which way, left and right and sideways, but not straight up at the sly, lip-licking tomcat perched on the pantry shelf.

Fingering the hard brown mole on his chin, Brownell thumbed slowly backwards through the Berkshire file, as if he were running three people's lives in reverse. There were lots of photos taken by agents with hidden cameras. Photos of Ray Berkshire in Philadelphia – coming out of a shabby hotel, going into the Public Library, standing in line at a Social Security ofìice. Photos of him buying a Greyhound ticket, getting on a bus, coming out of a bank. Deeper in the file, there were shots of Ray and Shana on an outing to the New York zoo and the Museum of Natural History. There were also shots of Linda and Shana – coming out of an ad agency, sitting on a bench in Fairchild Plaza, exercising together at a place called Childplay. Peppered throughout the file were photographs not taken by FBI agents, but gleaned from other sources – like the eight-by-ten glossies from Shana's modeling portfolio. A darned cute kid. Brownell could see from the pictures and her enrollment test scores why the Fairchild people had wanted her.

After looking through the whole file front to back, hc squared the stack and placed it neatly back in the folder. He thought about the photos he had seen of Ray Berkshire with a damned good-looking woman named Foley Ryan. According to her background check, she was a thirty-three-year-old widow with two kids and a high-paying advertising job. Apparently, Berkshire had kicked her out of his bed – probably to leave himself "free" to become a fugitive.

Shaking his head dolefully, Brownell gingerly touched the mole on his chin with the tip of his index finger. It seemed sore. He wondered what chance there might be of its turning to cancer someday. He also wondered vaguely if job pressures might hasten the malignancy.

Why couldn't Ray Berkshire have played it smart? He could have married the Foley Ryan wench, adopted her two children, visited his own kid on weekends and lived happily ever after. But, no. He had to get greedy. It was a good thing, in a way. It would give Brownell the excuse he needed to put Ray Berkshire where he couldn't ever again be any kind of threat to the Ultrachild Project.

Brownell's intercom buzzed and he pressed a button. Over the speakerphone, his secretary informed him that Mr. Trenton was here. "Send him in," Brownell said. Then he closed the Berkshire file and laid it aside, perfectly parallel to the right-hand edge of his clean green desk blotter. He couldn't help wishing that the Augie situation could be so easily "stabilized."

Tom Trenton entered, closed the door and sat in a brown leather armchair in front of the big conference desk. He was very tired, but he tried not to show it, because he didn't want the FBI man to think he couldn't take the grind. He had been up all night chasing down a lead that hadn't panned out. Then he had taken a shower, changed clothes and rushed over here. He didn't expect to be offered coffee, let alone a take-out doughnut or a sweet roll, even though he hadn't had any breakfast. Social amenities were not Brownell's forte. The man was all business, all fastidiousness. To him, having coffee during a serious discussion was like blowing bubble gum in church.

Eyeing Trenton, Stephen Brownell had the same thought he always had: the man was such an unlikely-looking CIA operative. He looked more like one of the TV actors he represented, in his swishy lavender suit with his hair bleached and his teeth capped. But, of course, the fact that he didn't look like what he was enhanced his effectiveness. He hadn't balked at handling some emergency "field work" yesterday that neither man had wanted to detail to any CIA or FBI underlings.

"How'd your trip to Gainesville turn out?" Brownell asked.

"A waste, unless you like seeing Georgia by helicopter. I didn't get back till this morning. Some kind of engine trouble. I was ready to leave by ten last night, but the chopper wasn't. I beat the civilian police to the punch, all right, but . . ."

"But it wasn't Stasiak."

"Not even close. Just a Peeping Tom released a couple of weeks ago from a state mental hospital on an outpatient basis. The neighborhood lady who phoned in the tip *wanted* it to be Stasiak, because she can't stand the thought of having a Peeping Tom living next to her. But there's no resemblance. Besides, the poor sap happened to be in confinement when Stasiak's murders and kidnappings went down. He's never done anything worse than sneak a few peeks at naked ladies."

"Too bad it wasn't Stasiak," said Brownell. "Next time we might not get there ahead of the civilians."

Trenton smiled. "I imagine they're getting there about now, all hot to make an arrest." He chuckled, thinking about the wild goose chase. If the guy in Gainesville had been Charles Stasiak, Trenton would have had to make him "disappear." Otherwise, the cover story that had been invented for the Sutter murders might have been blown.

"I wish we had Stasiak where we want him." said Brownell. "As it stands now, the Bureau could be mightily embarrassed if this situation takes an unfortunate turn."

"The NYPD isn't helping us much," said Trenton. "Unless there's something new?" he added hopefully.

Brownell grimaced and shook his head ruefully. "Nope. So far, they're up a blind alley. No fingerprints except the ones made by the Sutter family. The bloody sneaker tracks were made by a brand sold to more than five million people. None of the neighbors saw or heard anything worth a damn. On top of everything else, it's pretty hard to catch a guy who didn't actually wield the knife himself. And, of course, the New York cops aren't looking at this thing the right way."

"Thanks to us," Trenton said. He watched Brownell gently touching the mole on his chin with the tip of his index finger.

"There are so many things we don't know," Brownell said. "Like, how does Augie zero in on the Ultrachildren? How does he know or guess which ones have had the BAS implantations? If his motive isn't simply to wreck the Ultrachild Project, then what is he really after?"

"Revenge," suggested Trenton.

"On whom?"

"I don't know. Sometimes l wonder if Augie might be a former Ultrachild gone haywire. . .

"Parkhurst claims that isn't possible."

"Still. . . I wonder about it," said Trenton "Don't you?"

"Yes. Of course."

They brainstormed for a while longer, to no avail. They couldn't discern any pattern to Augie`s selection of victims. They were unable to guess where he might strike next.

After Trenton was gone, Stephen Brownell sat behind his desk, fingering his painful brown mole and staring at the closed manila folder of the Berkshire file. Thinking about it gave him a satisfying feeling, instead of the queasy feeling he got when he thought about the Augie file on the opposite side of his desk blotter. Any day now, Ray

Berkshire ought to be making his move. His preparations for changing his identity must seem complete to him. He must be feeling reasonably safe. He probably wouldn't hold off till his daughter started school; he'd be too anxious to spite his wife.

It was odd that Augie hadn't struck in all this time, while school was out. Brownell wondered if it could be a clue to Augie's identity. Did it mean he was somebody who left New York during the summer? An Academy teacher or administrator on vacation? Or did it mean nothing at all? Maybe Augie was simply hanging back, licking his lips and planning his next foray.

Not knowing made Brownell feel unaccustomedly helpless. At least with the Berkshire thing, *he* was in control, set to pounce. With Augie, the shoe was on the other foot.

Tiny Tot Academy would be opening on August twenty-ninth. Two more weeks. In the best of all possible worlds, Brownell thought, the Berkshire situation and the Augie situation would both be stabilized before then, so the new school term could begin with a clean slate.

CHAPTER 31

Ray Berkshire phoned his ex-wife at the Trenton Talent Agency on Monday afternoon to make arrangements for Shana to spend some time with him come Saturday. Linda was polite, but something seemed to be bothering her. Was it Ray`s imagination or did she sound *leery* of him? He couldn't remember getting such negative vibes from her regarding Shana at any other time since the divorce. "Something happen while I was gone?" he said. "I'm sorry I didn't keep in touch." He wished he could rub her nose in it – tell her what in the hell did it matter if his ex-wife didn't know where he was for a couple of months, since, even if some crisis did befall their daughter, his input supposedly wasn't needed or wanted.

"No . . . no, everything's fine." Linda said with what seemed like forced conviction. "When did you say you want to take her?

"Look . . . if she hasn't been feeling well . . ."

"No, she's okay. Nothing to worry about, Ray. She's just getting over a sore throat, so I don't think she should do anything terrifically exerting."

"I just want to be *with* her, Linda. She's still my daughter. I have two tickets to the horse show at Madison Square Garden."

"Oh – she *loves* horses . . ."

"I'd like to spend a full day with her. I'm figuring on taking her to lunch . . . then the horse show and then dinner.

Maybe a movie in the evening, if she's up to it; if not, I'll bring her home early. Will you be in?"

"Yes. I'm not dating anyone. I think it'd be too soon for her to have to deal with that."

If she had divulged the tidbit about her love life in hopes of learning something about his, he wasn't about to give her the satisfaction. "Can I come for her at eleven?" he asked.

"Saturday," she said, with the same touch of reluctance he had detected earlier.

"Yes, Saturday," he told her, steeling himself to listen to some more hemming and hawing.

"Okay. I'll have her ready, all bathed and dressed up for you. Eleven o'clock Saturday morning."

"Thanks. See you then."

He hung up. Stepping out of the phone booth, he was engulfed by the Times Square throng. He walked several blocks on Forty-Second Street and went into a sporting goods store. There he made one of his last important purchases as Raymond Berkshire. He bought a lightweight .32 caliber Colt revolver and a couple of boxes of ammunition. He filled out the prescribed forms and was told by the sales clerk that it would take three days for the firearm permit to clear. Even though he was going to be a fugitive, he didn't feel entirely comfortable with the idea of owning a pistol and had come close to forgetting it. Except, who could tell what kind of nasty situations a man on the run might get into? He didn't want to see the day when he would end up regretting not having the means to protect himself and his daughter.

All the strange things he had been doing over the past few months suddenly took on a hard reality – the phony birth certificate, the bank accounts under a false name and so on. He had been preparing himself to commit the only serious criminal act of his life. But, up till now, it had retained something of an aura of make-believe, as if, in the back of his mind, he had still been clinging to a notion that he could back out. But somehow, buying the gun made it all seem real . . . and irrevocable. Now he knew for certain that he was actually going through with it.

When he saw Ray Berkshire buying a pistol, Augie made up his mind that Ray, not Linda, would be his next target, through Shana. Linda didn't own a gun, as far as Augie knew; it was an exciting new element. It could be very interesting to see what happened after the little girl shot her father. How would the FBI cover *that* up? Would they let her go to Tiny Tot Academy as though nothing had happened? If so, there might be some tricky way to use her again as a "death puppet." At some future date, she could be sent against her mother.

His appearance disguised, Augie had occupied the telephone booth next to the one Ray had used in Times Square. He had gotten a mild kick out of testing his ability not to be recognized as the same debonair young fellow Berkshire had met at the Larsons' hoity-toity dinner party. He looked like a seedy Bohemian – a student or a young professor – with his long hair and beard and his heavy-rimmed eyeglasses; the battered old briefcase he was carrying and the tattered, tweedy jacket with worn patches on the elbows completed the image of "standard seediness" that was not likely to be particularly noticed or remembered by anybody.

The disguise wouldn't have been necessary if he had chosen to go after an Ultrachild whose parents didn't know him. But he liked doing it to people he knew. It helped him visualize their thoughts, feelings and reactions when he scrambled their brains for them. It made the situation more intimate – like masturbating to an image of a pretty girl you had actually sat next to on a subway train, instead of to an unblemished, unattainable center-fold.

He had overheard Ray Berkshire making arrangements to take Shana on an outing this coming Saturday. A horse show in Madison Square Garden. Mobs of people. Augie entertained himself with visions of making the little girl attack her father amid a huge throng of spectators in one of the world's most famous arenas.

Of course, there was probably no way to make sure that Shana would use the gun, or that Ray would even have it with him. Or was there? Augie toyed with the notion of making an anonymous phone call to Berkshire's hotel, warning him not to go to the horse show. Then, if he went, he'd almost certainly take his pistol. But he might also heed the threat and stay away from Madison Square Garden entirely. It might be more practical to try to come up with some scheme to guarantee that Shana could get her hands on the pistol when she and her father were alone. Then Augie could press the right BAS buttons to try to catalyze the desirable reaction. But that way he'd have to give up on the crowds of witnesses he wanted. It was a perplexing problem, and he'd have to think some more on it.

He decided not to follow Ray Berkshire any more that day. It was too risky. Why take a chance of being spotted and recognized? Although that possibility added to the thrill, it would be stupid to push it now that he was zeroing in. Saturday *could* be the big day.

Since he happened to be walking down Broadway, he went into a store that specialized in selling tickets to plays, concerts and other entertainments. He bought tickets to every one of the scheduled events that were part of the horse show in Madison Square Garden on Saturday. He didn't want to find himself stuck without an admission to whichever part of the show Ray Berkshire planned on attending with his daughter.

Moving about Manhattan in disguise made David Parkhurst feel more like "Augie." He liked the spiciness of code names and covert activity, danger and deception. He smirked inwardly over the intricacy of the "counterspy game" he was playing, as he rode a garishly graffitied subway train back to Greenwich Village. At the terminal closest to his apartment, he went into a public men's room.

Inside a stall, while nobody else was around, he took off his cap, his brown wig and beard and put them in his briefcase. He removed his eye glasses, which he had bought in a five-and-dime store and which were of such a weak prescription that they were as good as plain glass; he put them in the case clipped inside his jacket pocket. When he came out of the stall, there was still nobody else in the men's room; unless people were desperate they usually shunned these places out of fear of being mugged or molested. At one of the filthy sinks, Augie washed his face. When he had been working up his disguise, he hadn't been able to do much about his freckles – just soften and blend them with a ruddy shade of pancake makeup. Soap and water took it off, along with the brown coloring he had penciled into his eyebrows.

Coming up out of the subway, he slung his jacket over his arm so its seedy tweed wasn't so noticeable. He wouldn't usually wear such a shabby garment. When he went into his apartment building, he wasn't Augie anymore, but just plain, innocent David Parkhurst.

It was only the third time Ray had been to Linda's apartment. Only the third time he had come to get Shana since the divorce papers were signed over three months ago. He had been too busy making trips to Philadelphia. He knew Linda wouldn't mind if he stayed away forever. She wanted Shana all to herself apparently. She probably thought that the infrequency of his visits proved how little he really cared about his daughter. In *her* mind it would tie right in with his giving up custody without a fight, after he had shot his mouth off about it.

She and Shana were living in a deluxe condo on Park Avenue South. It seemed too much for Linda to afford, and Ray wondered if she could be getting help from someone like maybe Tom Trenton or the Larsons. But he wasn't about to ask. It was one of those buildings with a doorman, a desk man and private parking for tenants and guests. Among the special facilities provided under the leasing agreement were a sauna room, an exercise room and an indoor swimming pool on the first floor. The first time Ray had come here, Linda had shown him around, trying not to act as smug and superior as she must have felt. It was the kind of "class" she had always wanted. The six hundred bucks a month he was giving her for his share of child support might barely cover the fees for maid service and other "extras."

Inside the apartment, all the rugs and furniture were brand new – and expensive. Sitting in the middle of the curve of a huge wraparound sofa, a saucer and a half-empty coffee cup in front of him on a chrome-and-glass table, Ray waited for his ex-wife to bring Shana out to greet him. He hoped he didn't look as tired and haggard as he felt. He had showered, shaved, trimmed his beard and doused himself with pungent, fresh-smelling cologne. Then he had put on some snazzy sports clothes – white trousers, a white silk shirt, and a maroon blazer with shiny silver buttons and a white silk handkerchief in the breast pocket. The idea was to look like a man on a carefree holiday with his daughter, instead of a desperate man "stealing" his daughter from his ex-wife.

All night long, he hadn't been able to sleep. He had tossed and turned, perspiring on a saggy mattress in a run-down, poorly air-conditioned hotel, doubting himself and his motives, tormented by the paradoxical cruelty of divorce and custody laws that could turn a child's father into her "kidnapper." He worried over whether he was doing the right thing, taking Shana away from a new setup that was pretty soft and sane. Could he really give her a better life than Linda was giving her? Of course, it wasn't the first time such thoughts had plagued him – but now they were more immediate, more intense. Was he after what was best for Shana or what was best for himself? Was he hurting his child in order to hurt his ex-wife?

Most people would probably say that he didn't have sufficient moral justification for what he was doing. After all, Linda wasn't a drug addict, an alcoholic or a whore. She was, in the eyes of the world, an ideal mother. A "Supermom." But, damn it, she had swept him out of her life and out of his daughter's life as if she were sweeping away somebody who had never mattered. She had never given him the least bit of the consideration he deserved for being a good and loving husband and father. She wouldn't even have granted the meager "visitation rights" if she could have gotten away with giving him less.

She had so little respect for him that she believed he would hold still for any sort of maltreatment – like a beaten, cowering slave. But now he was going to rudely disabuse her of that notion. Now he was going to teach her that he *would* fight for what was his. Or what ought to be his if the courts and the laws were fair.

He sipped the remainder of his coffee, and it was cold. He shrugged and drank it down anyway. Just then, Linda brought Shana. They both came down the hall, Linda a little behind, ushering Shana forward, as if she was about to meet a stranger and might balk. At the edge of the living room, they halted. Shana was looking her blonde, blue-eyed best, cute as ever, in a bright blue skirt and a white blouse trimmed in matching blue. Linda was in faded designer jeans and a black T-shirt with TRENTON TALENT printed on it in white. It dawned on Ray that this was probably the final impression he would have of her, since he wasn't intending on seeing her again. "Hi, Daddy," Shana said timidly. Then she ran into his arms and kissed him. He hugged her for a long time, despite the odd, disconcerted look he caught on Linda's face when he glanced over Shana's shoulder. He *knew* Linda didn't want him to take Shana today. It was almost as if she subconsciously suspected what he was going to do.

"Maybe Shana should bring along a change of outfit," he said to Linda in a light, pleasant tone. "Some slacks or something. We'll be romping around most of the day. Can't tell what she might get into . . . or step into . . . at a horse show."

He chuckled softly, realizing he had actually had it in him to force a weak joke. Shana giggled delightedly. Linda even managed to smile. For a moment it was disturbingly as if they had recaptured some vestige of their old "family" feeling. A fleeting moment. It evaporated.

"I have slacks and a warmer blouse for her in here," Linda said, holding out a paper bag. "Also a hooded nylon jacket in case it rains."

Ray took the bag. "Doesn't look like rain," he said. "Hot and muggy, but no clouds. It's supposed to be that way all day, according to the weather report."

"Typical August," said Linda. "Come and give Mommy a kiss now Shana. Have a good time and behave yourself, you hear?"

While his daughter and ex-wife were sharing what he imagined would be their last kiss, Ray said, "If we go to a movie after dinner tonight, I don't imagine I can have her back till around ten . . . maybe eleven. Is that okay?"

"Sure. But you know how it is, Ray. Don't get her too worn out."

"Yeah, I know how it is," he said evenly, keeping all trace of irony out of his voice. "Don't worry. I'll take good care of her."

He figured that his last words would at least be something for Linda to cling to, in days to come.

After Ray and Shana left, Linda busied herself with some dusting in Shana's bedroom, taking advantage of the opportunity to move around and wipe off toys, games and doodads while her daughter wouldn't be playing with them. But keeping busy did not chase the bad thoughts from Linda's mind. She couldn't shake an awful dread of what might happen today. What if Shana had another seizure?

Ray wouldn't know how to handle it. He wouldn't recognize the first, relatively mild symptoms. He'd be taken totally unaware. Linda's hands shook and her mouth went dry when she pictured Shana going into convulsions in the midst of the gawking crowds at Madison Square Garden. Unless somebody knew how to help her, she could swallow her own tongue and choke on it. She could fall off the bleachers and break her neck.

Dr. Stowe and Dr. Parkhurst had both given Linda their utmost assurance that after the pacemaker implantation it would be impossible for any more seizures to take place. "The advanced microchip circuitry is impervious to corrosion, immune to failure," Dr. Parkhurst had said with a confident, comforting smile. "It can never wear out. Nobody who has had this operation has ever encountered any sort of problem. No complications. No recurrences. That's why we're able to recommend it so wholeheartedly."

But imprinted indelibly in Linda's mind was the full horror of the attack that Shana had suffered at Brent Strang Associates. The blue face . . . the swollen veins . . . the bloody, protruding tongue . . . the hard, jerky spasms that seemed more than strong enough to break a little child's body in half. The wild, helpless fear that had consumed Linda on that awful day was something she could never forget. She tried to push it from her mind, but she couldn't. It still came to her in nightmares and woke her up crying and cold with sweat, in the middle of the night.

Sometimes she almost wished she still had Ray by her side to share her grief and terror. To help her decide what to do. To stand by her in the face of what she *had* decided. Instead of being part of the faceless, impersonal multitudes who must never be told the secret of how Shana had been healed.

Now that almost three months had passed since the operation, Linda had to admit that Dr. Stowe and Dr. Parkhurst must have recommended the right thing. Shana appeared perfectly normal. She was off medication, even the vitamin supplement that had successfully boosted her red count. There was almost no trace of the small incision that had been made at the top of her head – just a very thin, pink line (not raised enough to be called a scar), that one had to actually hunt for to find under her hair. She had no memory of the hospital stay. Neither did she seem to remember anything about that horror-stricken day at Brent Strang Associates. And nothing remotely like it, not the least hint of a symptom of epilepsy, had been noticed by Linda since then.

Maybe, as time went by, she would become a less worried mother. Maybe she would eventually get used to the idea that a miracle had truly been performed, her daughter permanently cured. But right now it was too soon for her to feel so safe. In spite of the enormous faith and trust she placed in the professional people at Fairchild Plaza, she was still constantly tortured by negative thoughts.

What if something went wrong? Something unforeseen. A quirk. An oddity. God forbid, an error.

What if the brain pacemaker stopped functioning for some unfathomable reason? What if it had a loose element that got jarred or jiggled? What if Shana fell down and bumped it?

Dr. Parkhurst and Dr. Stowe had patiently explained that this kind of thing had never happened and *couldn't* happen, because there were no moving parts . . . nothing in the implantation that could come loose.

Still . . . what if?

Linda couldn't shake the nagging notion that medical science wasn't infallible and omnipotent, and that doctors, even the best ones, sometimes made mistakes.

The hardest part for Ray was deciding how much to tell Shana, and when to tell her. Compared to that issue, all his logistical arrangements – the scheming and the subterfuge – were a piece of cake. If his daughter had been several years younger – a year old, or less – she wouldn't have been able to understand much of what was going on, and telling her about it could have been postponed till she grew up and got so used to living with him that nothing could tear her away. But, at age four, there was no doubt that she was tied very closely to her mother, perhaps closer to her than to him, and he knew it would be difficult to convince her to come with him to another part of the country, where she might never see Linda again.

Shana was an unusually bright, perceptive child. She couldn't simply be dragged off somewhere without an explanation. If she was given a story that sounded too phony, she'd see right through it. And if she wouldn't come with Ray willingly enough not to create a fuss, he might as well not go through with it. It would be too painful for them both. And would be bound to end in disaster.

He'd have to try to get Shana on his side before they left New York. And he didn't want to do it by slandering Linda. He wanted the child to grow up with fond memories of her mother, not ugly ones.

In a taxi, on the way to the hotel on Ninth Avenue where he had been staying, he began subtly paving the way for letting Shana know what was really on his mind. To explain why they had to stop off at the hotel, he had told her he had left the horse show tickets in his room – which was true. If, after talking things over with her, he sensed that there was no way of gaining her cooperation, he'd scrap all his elaborate schemes and take her to Madison Square Garden. He'd ask her not to tell her mother what they had talked about and to try to forget that the conversation had ever happened.

The taxi was one of those with a thick Plexiglas partition between the driver and the passengers. Not that it mattered much anyway. Ray intended to keep the conversation with his daughter general enough that the cabbie wouldn't overhear anything critical.

"How long have you lived with your mother?" he asked in a casual, non-threatening tone.

Slowly, she turned her head from the cab window. "In New York?" she said, looking at him quizzically with her big blue eyes.

"No . . . since East Stanton. From the time I moved away . . . how long have you and Mommy been living together?"

"What month was it when you left?"

He was hurt that she didn't have it down by heart. "May," he said. "The end of May." So far, it didn't seem to bother Shana to talk about it, but he couldn't tell for sure.

He remembered reading somewhere that kids were more resilient than adults, because no matter what happened, they still had so much of their lives to look forward to.

"And what month is this?" Shana said. "No . . . I know – the end of August."

"Almost Yes."

"June . . . July . . . Do I count all of August?"

"Um-hmmm. Because you didn't count any part of May."

"Three months then, Daddy."

"I've missed you," he said, reaching out and touching her face with his fingertips. He was perspiring heavily, and it wasn't solely because of the hot, muggy weather and the non-air-conditioned taxi creeping through Manhattan traffic.

"I miss you, too," Shana confessed. "I wish we were all still living together."

He didn't say anything. After a while, she said, "Why aren't we, Daddy?"

"Because your mommy didn't want it that way. Remember, I told you she stopped being in love with me."

"Did you stop being in love with her?"

"No. Not really." He supposed it wasn't entirely a lie. Not at the time. "I was trying to stay married to her. But it just didn't work out. I hated to leave you both."

"I cried a lot after you left," she said.

They rode in silence for a few minutes. Then he asked her, "Do you think it's fair?"

She looked at him with a questioning kind of sadness.

"What your mommy made happen," he said. "For you to live all the time with her and not with your daddy."

He glanced at the cabbie, who appeared not to be listening. He told himself once again that it didn't matter.

"I don't know," Shana said softly, hanging her head. She started to cry. "I *hate* the divorce," she blurted.

The cabbie didn't flinch. Ray thought that nothing could faze him.

"I don't like it either," Ray said. He leaned toward his daughter and wiped her tears, using the white silk handkerchief from the breast pocket of his maroon blazer. "We're almost at the hotel," he said lamely.

When they got to his room, he was going to make the big pitch, now that he had laid the groundwork. He would bring up once again the three months Shana had lived with his ex-wife and ask her if she didn't think he deserved equal time. He'd then come out and ask her for it. He would even promise that in case she changed her mind in a day, a week, a month, he would bring her right back to her mother. Maybe he was manipulating Shana, playing upon her love and her guilt feelings to some extent – but he didn't believe it was any worse than what Linda had already done to her. And he deserved his chance. He deserved *his* chance.

If he got the three months, he would try to stretch it into forever . . .

Augie couldn't figure out what the hell was going on. He had followed Ray and Shana Berkshire as they walked hand in hand to the corner of Park Avenue and Fifty-Ninth Street. When Ray hailed a taxi, Augie hailed a taxi. He almost told his driver, "Madison Square Garden," because he was so sure that was where his quarry was headed, and it sounded so trite and stupid to say, "Follow that cab."

Luckily he had said it anyway. Because Berkshire and his kid didn't go to the Garden. Nothing wrong with that – at first. It seemed normal enough that they might stop at Ray's dumpy hotel on Ninth Avenue for some reason, so Augie didn't get upset when that's what they did. He told his cabbie to just wait up the block and keep the motor running. The cabbie, a Puerto Rican, didn't bat an eye, didn't ask any questions – either because he didn't give a shit or because he couldn't speak English too well.

The first surprise came when Berkshire and his kid walked out of the dumpy hotel. Augie almost didn't recognize them at first. Both of them had changed clothes. Berkshire was now in blue jeans and a blue denim jacket, and the kid was in a pair of light-green bibbed overalls and a white and green checked blouse. Berkshire was carrying a small leather suitcase. They went to the corner and hailed another taxi.

The second surprise came when they *still* didn't go to Madison Square Garden. Instead they ended up at the Port Authority Terminal on Forty-First and Eighth. Augie paid off his cabbie and followed his prey into the terminal, all his gears churning, trying to figure out what was up – was he going to have to alter his game plan, or would he be forced to scrap it all together?

Berkshire and his daughter went to the Greyhound information desk, and Augie got in line behind them. He wasn't too worried about being recognized – his disguise had passed the acid test the other day, when he had lurked one phone booth away from Berkshire in Times Square. He had to try to overhear something . . . what in the hell was Berkshire up to?

The information clerk was a gray-haired black lady with eye glasses too big and round for her small, bony face. "May I help you, sir?" Augie heard her ask as he turned sideways, pretending not to be interested in anything except watching the crowds of people milling around in the terminal.

"Yes, please," said Berkshire. "I'd like to know if the noon bus to Philadelphia is boarding yet."

"Yes it is, sir. It'll leave on schedule. But we don't have any more tickets for that trip. It's filled up. The next available seats are on the . . ."

"l already have my tickets," said Berkshire.

"All right, sir . . ."

Feeling his prey slipping away from him, Augie eavesdropped while the black lady gave boarding instructions. He began to fit some of the jigsaw pieces together – Berkshire not taking his kid where he told his ex-wife they'd be going . . . Berkshire buying a gun . . . Berkshire and the kid wearing different clothes than what the ex-wife saw and splitting out of the hotel with a suitcase. There was one pretty obvious picture that could be made out of those pieces of information. Now that he could see it, Augie almost giggled. The irony tickled him. Berkshire had never had any intentions of going to Madison Square Garden today. The stuff about the horse show was pure horseshit. He was running away to Philadelphia and probably points beyond, taking his daughter with him. He must not be planning on ever coming back. Goodbye, Ultrachild! Wouldn't the FBI go crazy! Berkshire wasn't the first father to take the outcome of a custody fight into his own hands, but he was most likely the first to inadvertently snatch one of Fairchild Plaza's special darlings.

The idea of topping off what Berkshire already had going began to excite Augie. What a coup it would be against his parents and their stupid G-men! They'd all start to believe he really knew more than they did. He'd show them he wasn't limited to New York, his operations were of a vaster scope. They'd go bananas wondering where he might strike next. They'd figure no Ultrachild would ever be safe anywhere, if he could pull off his next caper in the City of Brotherly Love.

When Ray and Shana Berkshire went to board their bus, Augie stepped up to the information desk. "I need desperately to get on the noon bus to Philadelphia," he told the clerk. "Is there a shot of making it, if I can get on standby?"

She shook her head no, very firmly. "I'm sorry, sir. It's ten minutes to twelve, and we recommend to people to show up a half hour to forty-five minutes ahead of time to buy their tickets. That trip has been booked up since early this morning, and we've had no cancellations. Some kind of big convention going on. Ten or twelve people already are on standby and I'm sure there's no chance of *them* getting seats. They'll have to wait for a later bus. We have buses to Philadelphia every hour on the hour. There are some seats open on the—"

"It has to be the twelve o'clock bus," Augie said.

"We have nothing close to that. I'm sorry, sir."

"What time does the noon bus arrive in Philadelphia?"

"It's scheduled for 2:05. Sometimes it's a bit late, but not usually. Depending on traffic conditions."

"What's the address of your station there?"

"Seventeenth and Market. Downtown Philly. If you like, I can—"

But Augie pivoted and hurried out of the Port Authority Terminal before the clerk could finish her sentence. Outside, he jumped into another taxi and gave the cabbie the address of a parking garage in Greenwich Village, where he kept his car. As the cab zigged through the city streets, Augie couldn't suppress a glimmer of a prankish smile. He figured there was no way a fat, overloaded Greyhound bus couldn't be beaten to Philadelphia by his sleek silver Mercedes.

CHAPTER 32

Shana loved Daddy, but he made her feel funny . . . all sad and hurting and mixed up inside. Wanting so much to please him. Aching to make him feel proud and glad. Mommy made Shana feel the same way. Only worse sometimes. But not now. Now it was Daddy making her feel worse. She just wanted him to be happy. Mommy, too. Why were adults so crazy?

Shana had dreams sometimes that Mommy and Daddy had hold of different parts of her and were pushing and pulling, trying to break her into a million pieces. Actually, it was the same dream over and over. A nightmare. She never told them. Never wanted to make them cry. The way *she* cried in her nightmares.

She hated living without Daddy. He used to be such fun. More fun than now. And she guessed he was probably right. She shouldn't make Mommy her favorite. She should live with Daddy some of the time. But . . .

Were they always going to live in ugly, dumpy places? He said no. He promised they would go to California, where it was always warm and sunny and pretty. And the Pacific Ocean made big, choppy waves. That`s why the movie stars lived there. They only picked the nicest places. On the bus ride, Daddy took a big picture book of California out of his suitcase, and they looked at it together. He sounded so happy and full of fun . . . the way he used to be, but not really. He was pretending to be happier than he felt. Shana could tell. Still, California sure looked like one of the loveliest places in the world.

Not like the smelly, crowded bus.

Not like the rotten hotel Daddy lived in in New York.

Not like this rottener hotel in Philadelphia.

If they were going to have such a wonderful life, why didn't Daddy take her to nicer places? She almost would rather have gone to the horse show at Madison Square Garden.

She bounced up and down on the bed, crossing and uncrossing her legs. The mattress was so saggy and soft she almost couldn't sit up straight without sinking in deep and falling over backwards. She didn't want to lie down on the dirty, yellowish bedspread. It was so yucky. The room smelled yucky, too, like when Mommy sprayed Lysol, but with rottener smells underneath the spray smell. The paint was old and peeling, a funny brown with a pink underneath like dirty bubble gum. It was a worse hotel than the one in New York. Partly, she had agreed to come with Daddy to help him get away from such a sad, ugly place, and now this one was sadder and uglier.

She wished he would come out of the bathroom. He said not to laugh at him when he came out with his whiskers all shaved off. He was going to be a writer from now on. So he wanted to look different – he said it was like shedding his old self. You had to do that sometimes to become rich and famous. Just like movie stars fixed themselves up and had face lifts and stuff, Daddy was going to fix himself up a little. He was going to use a pen name from now on, the way actors and models used stage names and screen names. He talked about old movie stars Shana never heard of. He said John Wayne's real name used to be Marion Morrison. Cary Grant's was Archie Leach.

From now on, Daddy was going to be James W. Perry. And Shana was going to have a stage name, too. She was going to be known as Shana Perry. Neither of them would ever tell anybody their old names – not until they both became rich and famous. Daddy made Shana solemnly promise.

She wished he'd come out of the bathroom. She had already seen how ugly it was in there. Easy to catch germs. The rusty, crusty sink and toilet with curly hairs pasted all over the bowls. *Yick!*

One thing about living with Mommy, it was always sparkling clean. There was a maid, too. And a janitor. You didn't have to worry you'd get sick if you touched something.

Shana felt sick right now.

Her stomach was churning . . . yick, yick, yick. She and Daddy had eaten nothing but some greasy Greyhound station hot dogs. Daddy had joked that the hot dogs must've been made from the Greyhound dogs. They had laughed. But it didn't make the food taste any better.

Why did he bring her here?

It wasn't nice.

Wasn't very nice of him.

Not nice at all.

She kicked her legs and stood up angrily. The suitcase was open on the bed. Her clothes were in there – just a few things Daddy had bought – she'd need lots more, that's for sure. For auditions and stuff. Back home with her mother she had lots of pretty things.

What if she hated California?

Her eyes fell on the book, which was lying on top of the clothes. She picked it up and thumbed through it, hoping she'd like the pictures of the West. Cowboy and Indian land. Movie land.

Something shiny caught her eye, underneath Daddy's other trousers. She rummaged just enough to sneak a peek. A gun! The sight of it made her jump. Her skin crawled. But her heart beat faster and more thrillingly. Mommy was always telling her that guns on the TV were bad, bad, bad.

But here was Daddy with one of his own.

Not nice at all.

Not nice of Daddy.

Her fingers curled around the cold steel-and-plastic handle of the gun.

Not nice at all.

Trying to steal Shana away from Mommy.

How could she get home?

Suddenly she hated him. And loved him. And *hated* him.

Her hand tightened around the butt of the gun.

Augie sat on the edge of the filthy hotel bed, pressing various combinations of buttons on his BAS box.

His silver Mercedes had beaten the Greyhound bus to Philadelphia. He had tailed Ray and Shana Berkshire to the hotel. The place had so few paying guests that he had no trouble checking into the room right next to theirs.

LOVE and HATE. LOVE and HATE. Those were the main buttons to push. ANGER. HATE. LOVE. To turn someone against a person very close to them. Someone they cared deeply about.

A gleeful expression on his face, Augie turned up the juice, anxiously waiting to hear something from the next room – some evidence of the effectiveness of his Transmission.

Perspiration was pouring from him as he worked. The fleabag hotel wasn't air-conditioned. He had ripped off his beard and wig, and they were strewn next to where he was sitting, on the edge of the mattress. He would don his disguise again before going back out into the street.

Shana pointed the gun at the bathroom door and stood waiting for her father to come out. She *hated-loved*-hated him-*hated* to pull the trigger, but knew that she would and that she wanted to. A large part of her couldn't wait to do it. Then she could go home to Mommy. He was *wrong* to try to take her away. He was a *bad* man, even if he was a good daddy most of the time.

She could hardly wait to do it. Was dying to see the look on his face. Would he laugh before the gun went off? He might. *She* might. Her face twisted into a tight scowl, so tight her cheeks hurt. Not to wait any longer, she tugged on the bathroom door knob. The door was locked.

"I'll be out in a minute, honey!" he called out cheerily. "I'm almost done!"

His cheerfulness infuriated her for some reason. But her anger needed no reason. Was beyond reason. Her finger tightened on the trigger. She waited for her father to come out of the bathroom . . .

Actually, Ray thought, he looked much younger without the mustache and beard. And with the gray "rinsed" out of his temples and sideburns and his hair combed a bit forward, making his forehead appear lower. He thought that the changes made him look as much as ten years younger, perhaps.

So far, things were going better than might be expected. He had his driver's certificate . . . all his other papers. When he and Shana checked out of here, he'd go have his photo license made. Then he'd buy a car and they'd start putting more distance between themselves and Linda. By this time tomorrow they'd be maybe a thousand miles from New York. They'd hole up in a motel somewhere. Then keep driving the next day . . . and the day after that . . .

When they actually settled down somewhere, Ray might send for the personal belongings he had stored in a warehouse here in Philadelphia, under the name of James W. Perry. Stuff he hated to part with, but didn't want burdening him right now. Stuff it wasn't yet safe to carry. Like some of his old writings and notes. Baby pictures of Shana. *Dealey Plaza* reviews, clippings and mementoes. Things he might want someday when the smoke cleared.

It occurred to Ray that it might be smart for him to keep a secret diary of this crazy "adventure" he was getting himself into. He wondered if subconsciously a need for adventure might be one of the reasons he was doing all this – a yen to break out of a way of life that for too long had been too tame, too dull, too suffocating. Maybe he needed to plunge into something daring and dangerous in order to get his creative juices flowing again. Out of it might someday come a good novel, a nonfiction book or a screenplay. If he could figure out some way to safeguard a diary so it wouldn't fall into the wrong hands . . .

Shana kept the pistol pointed at the bathroom door, even though her arm was starting to shake from the weight of it and the urge to use it. She was in a helpless rage now. Her big blue eyes flashed and glinted. Her scowl deepened. She glared at the door as if she could melt it. What did she care if it was locked? She'd just shoot right through it . . .

Augie wondered why nothing was happening. Through the wall, he couldn't hear what he was feverishly listening for. No commotion. No gunshots. No sign of a struggle. There should be more noise. Damn it! Why couldn't the girl get her hands on the gun? Maybe she wasn't even trying . . .

Was something wrong with the BAS box? Maybe the FBI had pulled a slick one. Maybe they *knew* Augie had cracked the computer system at Fairchild Hospital. Maybe they had planted false stats on the brain operations.

Maybe Shana wasn't really an Ultrachild.

Angry and frustrated, Augie cranked the juice up almost as high as it would go.

Just then he heard a noise outside in the hall and his head jerked toward the sound. The flimsy door came crashing in on him.

He had the presence of mind to try to hide the BAS box under the bed covers. But a bullet crashed into his chest and he felt himself flying backward against the hard, dingy wall, his arms and legs jerking spastically, as if he was once more a puppet on a string – the way he used to be.

A dead puppet.

Stephen Brownell shot Augie two more times after he came into the room.

Then he picked up the BAS box and put it in his jacket pocket.

Brownell and Trenton had coordinated their assaults. Trenton kicked in "Jim Perry's" door at the same instant that Brownell was barging in on Augie.

Trenton's momentum carried him into the room and his .45 automatic swept the area, looking for a man's chest. Ray Berkshire's chest, to be exact.

All he saw was the child. Naturally, he withheld his fire. By the time he realized she had a weapon, it was too late. His gun barrel had swept on by her. The last thing he saw was the hideously evil look – an unearthly, demonic look – she had on her face before she shot him dead.

Brownell was surprised by the volley of shots coming from the next room. Too many. Not enough noise to be coming from Trenton's .45. A lighter caliber weapon. Bad trouble. He bolted out of Augie's room and dashed for cover across the hall, around the corner, at the top of the stairs. Then he peeked out, squinting in the dim light of a naked bulb in the grimy hallway. He was pointing his gun, ready to fire.

But no rounds were exploding anymore.

All he heard were clicks.

He sneaked across the hall and looked into the Berkshires' room.

Trenton had been shot six times – in the arms, the face, the body. Blood was streaming everywhere, soaking into the dirty, threadbare carpet.

Shana Berkshire was standing over Trenton, shooting him again and again . . . her face a horrid mask of unchildlike dementedness and hatred. Click . . . click . . . click . . . click . . .

Ray Berkshire was standing by the bathroom door, his eyes wide and unfocused, his mouth gaping open. He looked frozen . . . catatonic . . . in utter shock and bewilderment. Then his expression softened . . . and he looked pitiable . . . tears started to roll down his cheeks. "Please . . . please . . ." he mumbled, staring fixedly, pleadingly, at the muzzle of Brownell's .45. Sure. It was a solution of sorts. He was begging for it. But Brownell decided not to shoot him. Instead he took two long, quick strides forward and hammered Ray Berkshire hard across the top of the head with the barrel of the .45. Berkshire sagged and collapsed in the bathroom doorway.

Click . . . click . . . click . . . click . . .

The little girl was still standing over Trenton. Brownell wrenched the still-clicking gun out of her hand, even though she kicked and screamed and fought him to keep pulling the trigger . . .

CHAPTER 33

In the helicopter, on his way back to New York, Stephen Brownell was relaxed and satisfied. Rarely did things work out so well. It had been Augie's well-deserved bad luck to be casing Berkshire while Brownell's agents had surveillance on him. In spite of his corny disguise, Augie had gotten himself spotted and "made" before he even left New York. The registration on the silver Mercedes had been traced to David Parkhurst. He had been followed all the way into Philadelphia. Brownell and Trenton had flown there by chopper to take charge of nailing him.

The cover story Brownell planned to give to the news media was that James W. Perry and David Parkhurst had conspired to kidnap Shana Berkshire and hold her for ransom. When Brownell and "an unnamed FBI agent" (Trenton) broke in on the culprits, Parkhurst shot the unnamed agent to death, then Brownell killed Parkhurst and Perry.

The hotel had been cordoned by FBI agents before Brownell and Trenton had made their assault. In the aftermath, no newsmen had been allowed in. From behind the FBI barricade the radio, TV and newspaper people had watched the child and the dead bodies being taken out. One of the "dead bodies" carried out in a body bag was Ray Berkshire, who wasn't really dead. Brownell had knocked him out to make sure he stayed quiet till he was loaded into the chopper. Once aboard, both he and his daughter were given injections of sodium pentothal.

Brownell didn't want any hassle on the flight back.

He just wanted to bask in the glow of a job well done.

It was too bad Tom Trenton couldn't rejoice with him, but that was the breaks. The CIA man had given his life in a good cause. Once his corpse arrived back in New York, a phony death certificate would be made out by the good Dr. Vincent Parkhurst. Then his body would be cremated. The talent agent's friends and clients would always believe that he had died of a sudden, massive coronary.

Looking out the window of the chopper down at the clean, green fields and forests and white ribbons of highway of the America he worked so hard to protect, Stephen Brownell felt warm and patriotic and totally vindicated for once. He might as well enjoy it to the hilt, till the next time the roof fell in. It wouldn't be long. Too many bad guys down there. This pleasant interlude could not last.

Brownell touched the hard brown mole on his chin with the tip of his right index finger. At the moment, the mole didn't even seem to be hurting.

Life didn't always give you exactly what you wanted, he thought to himself, but boy-oh-boy, when occasionally fortune smiled on you, it was the best of all possible worlds.

EPILOGUE

When Shana came out of her coma, she had no memory of what had happened to her in Philadelphia. She had been luckier than Felicia Patterson. Her RAS (Reticular Activating System) had not been drastically overloaded. The brief, traumatic time Augie had control of her mind was similar to an epileptic fit in one sense, in that such episodes are never remembered. They are like blackout spells. The sufferer does things involuntarily, totally unaware of his actions and not cognitive of his environment.

As she recovered, Shana was given a battery of tests, including X rays, CAT scans, and FETT scans. Her brain waves were quite normal. There was no impairment of function. Her BAS stimoceiver was not damaged in any way.

She was able to attend Tiny Tot Academy on the first day it opened, on schedule with the rest of her classmates, including the nine other Ultrachildren.

Drs. Vincent and Carol Parkhurst were both pleased by how well Shana had come through a potentially devastating experience. It proved beyond question the durability and soundness of their BAS technology. Although they were still grieving over what their son had done to them and the horrible fate he had brought down upon himself, they couldn't allow it to wreck their life's work. They had to find the courage to continue, despite all obstacles. They mustn't halt their efforts to create a much better world, where

274

tragedies such as the ones propagated by their son could never occur.

After a BAS stimoceiver implantation performed by Dr. Vincent Parkhurst, Ray Berkshire became the subject of some wonderful new experiments at the Fairchild Educational and Psychological Research Institute. He was programmed to have very little self-volition, and was, therefore, exceptionally malleable, exceptionally controllable through BAS. The possible applications of this kind of comprehensive brain alteration in an adult interested the Pentagon very much.

Ray Berkshire was given special quarters on the top floor of Fairchild #5 and was never allowed to leave. When he wasn't being scientifically tested and observed, he helped earn his keep by working as a janitor in the building.

His ex-wife and his daughter were told that he was severely mentally ill. The psychiatric staff at Fairchild drummed up a false diagnosis. They said that Ray was an acute schizophrenic, suffering from bouts of suicidal depression coupled with hysterical amnesia brought on by violent emotional stress. They explained that he must have already been on the verge of a nervous breakdown due to his inability to adjust to his divorce, and the fatal blow to his sanity had been the trauma of the kidnapping episode, during which Shana had been snatched from his very arms. According to the psychiatrists, his prognosis was so poor that he would probably never be able to resume a productive role in society.

Every once in a while, Linda and Shana Berkshire came to visit him. He always looked forward to seeing them. He felt close to them in a strange way, even though he couldn't quite remember who they were, due to the special programming of his BAS implant. He hoped that the woman and the child sincerely liked him. But sometimes he caught a glimpse of sadness or even annoyance in their eyes, as if they secretly thought of him as nobody but a peculiar and harmless old man.

ABOUT THE AUTHOR

With twenty books published internationally and nineteen feature movies in worldwide distribution, John Russo has been called a "living legend." He began by co-authoring the screenplay for NIGHT OF THE LIVING DEAD, which has become recognized as a "horror classic." His three books on the art and craft of movie making have become bibles of independent production, and one of them, SCARE TACTICS, won a national award for Superior Nonfiction. Quentin Tarantino and many other noted filmmakers have stated that Russo's books helped them launch their careers.

John Russo wants people to know he's "just a nice guy who likes to scare people" – and he's done it with novels and films such as RETURN OF THE LIVING DEAD, MIDNIGHT, THE MAJORETTES, THE AWAKENING and HEARTSTOPPER. He has had a long, rewarding career, and he shows no signs of slowing down. Recently his screenplay for ESCAPE OF THE LIVING DEAD was made into a five-part comic book released by Avatar to great acclaim; it made the Top Ten of Horror Comics nationally and spawned two graphic novels and ten sequels.

Russo's recent novel is THE HUNGRY DEAD, was published by Kensington Books. He is also slated to direct two movies: a remake of his cult hit, MIDNIGHT, and a brand new take on the "zombie phenomenon" entitled SPAWN OF THE DEAD.

Russo's latest novels DEALEY PLAZA and THE ACADEMY, are published by Burning Bulb Publishing. His short story CHANNEL 666 appears in THE BIG BOOK OF BIZARRO.

His popularity among genre fans remains at a high pitch. He appears at many movie conventions each year as a featured guest, and he considers his appearance at the Orion Festival, hosted by Kirk Hammett and METALLICA, one of the highlights of his career.

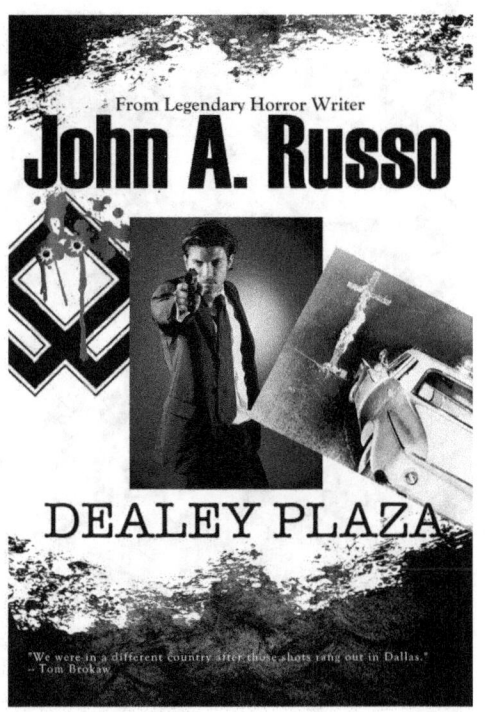

DEALEY PLAZA

From legendary horror and suspense writer JOHN RUSSO comes a harrowing tale where no one is safe!

Dealey Plaza is one of the most notorious places in America, and when youthful conspiracy buffs go there in 1964 to stage their own reenactment of the Kennedy Assassination, four of them are brutally murdered ~ the first victims of a hate-filled legacy that continues for four more decades.

The survivors of that long-ago Dallas trip, each of them now icons of the American way of life, are about to be honored ~ or killed.

Who will live and who will die? Will it be country-western star Lori McCoy? Her loving husband? Her scheming ex-husband? Or the case-hardened FBI agent and longtime friend who risks his life trying to protect them?

www.DealeyPlazaBook.com

Burning Bulb
PUBLISHING

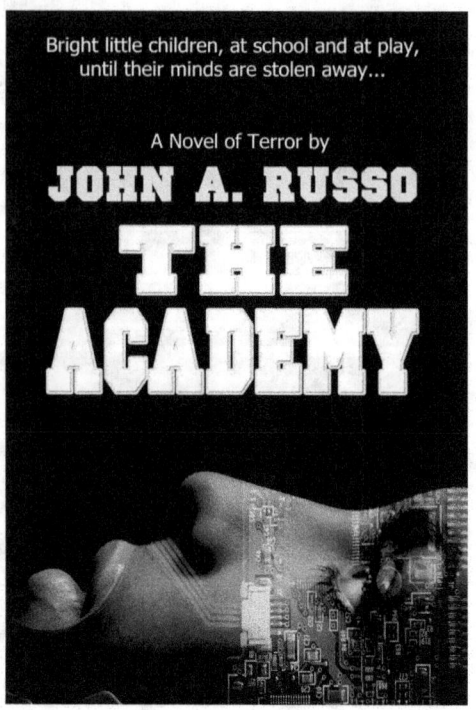

THE ACADEMY

The Academy. It's every parent's dream, turning their little darlings into geniuses, superachievers, perfect little children.

And if there's a problem, the Academy fixes that too. It's a simple operation. Just a little device. Then a teeny pink scar on a tender little skull . . .

One boy knows the secret. Now he wants his mind back. But it's much, much too late. Too late for anything but the ugly feelings. The bad feelings. The messy sexy feelings. The knife-cold hatred, the murderous rage, for total, screaming, blood-drenching revenge . . .

www.TheJohnRusso.com

Burning Bulb
PUBLISHING

OTHER GREAT TITLES FROM

Burning Bulb

PUBLISHING

WWW.BURNINGBULBPUBLISHING.COM

ANTHOLOGIES
BIZARRO AND TRANSGRESSIVE FICTION

THE BIG BOOK OF BIZARRO

The Big Book of Bizarro brings together the peculiar prose of an international cast of the most grotesquely-gonzo, genre-grinding modern writers who ever put pen to paper (or mouse to pad), including:

NIGHT OF THE LIVING DEAD *horror writers John Russo & George Kosana;* HUSTLER MAGAZINE *erotica contributors Eva Hore, Andrée Lachapelle, & J. Troy Seate and established Bizarro genre authors D. Harlan Wilson, William Pauley III, Wol-vriey, Laird Long, Richard Godwin and so many more!*

From Alien abductions to Zombie sex, The Big Book of Bizarro contains OVER FIFTY STORIES of the most outrélandish transgressive fiction that you'll ever lay your capricious and curious hands upon!

WARNING: This book may be one of the most controversial and dangerous books you'll ever read.

WESTWARD HOES

Nine outlaw writers rode into town from obscurity to pen nine tantalizing tales of horror and fantasy, and leaving once they branded their own personal marks on the weird western genre and became living legends of the American Frontier experience.

Like drunken Indian scouts, the writers fervidly tracked down and captured the Western genre, tore off its fashionable veneer and ravished its exposed essence.

So belly up to the bar with your favorite soiled dove and enjoy perusing these thrilling tales of Old West debauchery, danger and desire; compiled by the publisher of The Big Book of Bizarro and featuring the bizarro novella *Big Trouble in Little Ass* by Wol-vriey.

Burning Bulb
PUBLISHING

ANTHOLOGIES

BIZARRO AND TRANSGRESSIVE FICTION

THE BIG BOOK OF BIZARRO SPECIAL KINDLE EDITIONS

Burning Bulb
PUBLISHING

GARY LEE VINCENT'S
DARKENED
THE WEST VIRGINIA VAMPIRE SERIES

DARKENED HILLS

When evil descends on a small West Virginia town, who will survive?

Jonathan did not start out his life to become a rambler, it just worked out that way. William was a troubled youth with something to hide. Both were from Melas, a small town tucked away in the West Virginia hills... a town where disappearances are happening more and more frequently.

After the suicide of a wanted serial killer, the townsfolk thought the nightmare was over. But when a centuries-old vampire is discovered they find out the hard way it's just getting started. Dark secrets can only stay hidden for so long and when the devil comes to collect, there will be hell to pay. Can Jonathan and William find a way to stop the vampire before it's too late? Find out in *Darkened Hills!*

DARKENED HOLLOWS

In the heart-stopping sequel to the award-winning *Darkened Hills*, Jonathan and William must return to West Virginia to face possible criminal charges stemming from their last visit to the damned town of Melas, where both had narrowly escaped the clutches of a vampire seethe.

And as livestock start mysteriously getting murdered with all of their blood drained, worried farmers are searching for answers - leaving the local Sheriff and his deputy racing against time to learn the cause before a more violent crime is committed.

Burning Bulb
PUBLISHING

WWW.DARKENEDHILLS.COM

GARY LEE VINCENT'S
DARKENED
THE WEST VIRGINIA VAMPIRE SERIES

DARKENED WATERS

When the world goes to hell, the chosen must arise!

As Talman Cane orchestrates a flood of epic proportions in this third installment of the *Darkened* series the towns of Melas and Tarklin are caught completely off guard by the deluge. Hell-bent on finishing what they started, the evil brothers return to the lunatic asylum to take care of the witnesses and add to the ever-growing army of the undead.

Aided by Lucifer himself and the insane vampire demon Legion, the stage is set to channel all of the forces of hell to come forth. In an all-out race to survive, Jonathan, William, and Amanda soon discover they are up against impossible odds as Lucifer opens the Gateway to Hell, ushering in the zombie apocalypse and the End Times.

DARKENED SOULS

Melas and the Madison House are about to be rebuilt.
True evil is about to be reborne!

Young ex-priest and vampire-killer William is drawn back to the West Virginian town that almost killed him, where his vampire arch-enemy Victor Rothenstein still stalks the earth.

The town of Melas lies destroyed after the battle of the End of Days. But why is wealthy Jackie Nixon so eager to rebuild it using the bone dust of murdered souls?

Terrible evil has visited before, but the Gateway to Hell is about to be reopened in a horrific climax. And this time – it's personal.

www. DARKENEDHILLS.com

Burning Bulb
PUBLISHING

WEST VIRGINIA-THEMED HUMORROROTICA

BY RICH BOTTLES JR.

HELLHOLE WEST VIRGINIA

From the heights of Mothman's perch high atop the Silver Bridge in Point Pleasant to the depths of Hellhole Cavern in Pendleton County, evil lurks within the shadows as the sun sets upon the haunted hills and hollows of West Virginia.

Bizarro author Rich Bottles Jr. blows the coffin lid off horror genre clichés with this tour de force cast of Eco-friendly vampires, beach-yearning zombies and sex-starved she-devils.

LUMBERJACKED

If you are easily offended or do not possess a truly depraved sense of humor, this story may not be the light summer reading fare you desire. As for the four feisty female freshmen stranded on top of West Virginia's third highest mountain, they have no choice but to experience the sick, twisted debauchery and perverted mayhem described deep inside the tight unbroken bindings of this horrific missive.

Lumberjacked takes the reader to a nightmarish world where character development and aesthetic integrity are prematurely cut short by the swinging axes of maniacal lumberjacks, who are hell bent on death and destruction in the remote forests of Appalachia. And at the climax, when paranoia crosses over to the paranormal, Lumberjacked makes Deliverance look like a family raft trip down the Lower Gauley.

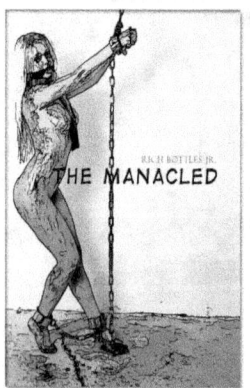

THE MANACLED

What happens when twin brothers lease out the former West Virginia State Penitentiary with the false purpose of filming a documentary on supernatural phenomena, but their true intention is to make a pornographic movie?

Chaos ensues as the disturbed spirits of murdered convicts, along with the reanimated dead from the neighboring Indian Burial Mound, take their vengeance on the unwary and undressed trespassers.

Zombies, ghosts, mobsters and porn collide in this bizarro tale from horror author Rich Bottles Jr.

Burning Bulb
PUBLISHING

WOL-VRIEY
BIZARRO AND TRANSGRESSIVE FICTION

Burning Bulb
PUBLISHING

BOSTON POSH

In 2028 AD, the USA is a nation ravaged by hungry dragons and dinosaurs. In Boston, Massachusetts, private eye Bud Malone is hired to rescue a kidnapped heiress. But nothing is as it seems. Malone works to unravel a tangled web involving Boston China-town, a 200-year-old woman with a 9-year-old body, white robots, a human-liver-eating psychopath, a golem, a porcelain dragon, and a snake goddess with a crush on him. There's also a woman obsessed with chicken sex. Then Malone meets Posh Lane, a gorgeous call girl who's desperate to quit her pimp. Romantic sparks ignite be-tween Posh and Malone, but Posh's past suddenly catches up with her in a BIG way. To save Posh, Malone agrees to run a quest for Earth's new rulers, the Forks. But, Malone has no idea that agree-ing to the Fork's odd request will send him on the weirdest trip he's ever been on in his life.

VEGAN VAMPIRE VAGINAS

The biggest bank heist in US history. And Tom Palmer can't remember pulling it off. And no, this isn't your standard case of amnesia. After a one-night-stand gone horribly wrong, Boston salesman Tom Palmer wakes up with a vagina implanted in his left hand. Then his day gets worse:

Tom is transported across space-time to a nightmare version of Boston, one where the Bizarro virus has transformed half the population into cannibals. Worst of all, Tom discovers that in this new Boston, he's the infamous gangster Pussypalm, wanted for robbing the Federal Reserve Bank of Boston a year ago. He also learns that the vagina in his hand is prophetic, i.e. it talks . . . after sex. With 130 people left dead during his bank heist and six billion dollars missing, Tom knows he's living on borrowed time. It is in his best interests not to remember anything. Because once he does . . .

VEGAN ZOMBIE APOCALYPSE

In the post-apocalypse worlderness, zombies rule the earth. They're allergic to meat, and brains literally make them explode. Zombies now eat blood potatoes, parasitic tubers grown in the flesh of humancows corralled in maximum security farms. Two fugitives meet in the ancient ruins of Texas. The first is Soil 15-f, a womancow who's escaped her farm a week before she's due to be killed and her blood potato crop harvested. The second fugitive is Able Kane, former head necros food technician, now sentenced to death for heresy. But Soil is no ordinary humancow. Unknown to herself, she's the vegan zombie agricultural revolution, and the zombies desperately want her back. And the necros equally desper-ately want Able Kane dead. He's fled with a forbidden discovery which will reshape the world for the worse if used. And Able is just hardheaded/misguided enough to use it.

MINOR CONFESSIONS OF AN ANGEL FALLING UPWARD

by Planner Forthright, as edited by Joey Madia

Confession. Revelation. Rant. *Minor Confessions of an Angel Falling Upward* is all of these... and more. Set in modern times and spiraling back to the swirl of Pre-Creation, this postmodern blend of genre-bending pop-prose and socio-political commentary is a classic tale of the (anti-)hero's quest for Reason and Redemption in a Universe gone mad.

Who is Planner Forthright? A fallen angel made Man. A once-winged evil with un-Divine purpose on this Plane. A cannibal prince chosen to inherit a castled landscape of destruction and despair. An Alchemist of sorts—a mental magician; a mortar-and-pestle wizard converting carbon lies to golden Truth, whose language is his own. A Vampire by nature and condition whose been walking the waters and thorny highways of our planet for over 40 years. And he's seeking a way out...

PASSAGEWAY

by Gary Lee Vincent with illustrations by Andy Hopp

When an archeological dig goes horribly wrong, the team is trapped in an alternate world where evil awaits them at every turn. Find out who will survive the *Passageway!*

From Gary Lee Vincent, the author of supernatural vampire thriller *Darkened Hills*, comes an unforgettable tale that spans four continents and takes the reader to the very realm of Hell itself.

Skeleton warriors, zombies, other undead beings and were-wolves are allvery real inside the *Passageway!* In this Bizarro-genre tribute to H.P. Lovecraft and Indiana Jones, this deadly tale will keep you guessing and leave you breathless to the end!

THE TWELVE STEPS

by Zachary Crabtree

"A Man who Cannot Keep Awake Cannot Keep it Together." There is always something that pulls an alcoholic deeper into his unquenchable thirst – something degenerative to the human spirit. Indeed, there have been incidents in my life that carry tragic significance to me, yet I know they pale in comparison to the tragedies experienced by others.

When the jagged pieces of a disfigured past become a troubled, broken-up, glass-bottled mosaic in one's present life, all the innocent souls affected along the way become entangled in one's conscience; while the depression, pills, manic behavior and soul-searching coalesce in a series of twelve steps.

Alcohol affects the lives of hooligans, stubborn old fools, lovers, and families torn apart by drunk drivers – drunk drivers like me.

Burning Bulb
PUBLISHING

THE FALL OF TOMORROW

Hopelessness... How do you protect your loved ones when Hell itself opens its insidious mouth?

Horror... Nightmarish Creatures invade your world and there is nowhere to hide.

Blood... How long can you hold out before they come for you?

Pain... Where do you run to avoid being eaten alive by monsters with a voracious appetite for your flesh?

Screams... While you selfishly run for your own life.

Questions... Who is to blame? Where did they come from? How many people survived...and how does the human race find the means to fight back?

THE FALL OF TOMORROW is man's last tale of desperation told by those that are striving to salvage some hope against a ravenous bastion of evil beasts bent on ruling our world.

"David Fairhead writes compelling stories that offer very human characters and very inhuman monsters. There is no subtlety in Fairhead's imagination - he is simply dying to scare the hell out of you."
      - Nelson W Pyles - author of DEMONS, DOLLS AND MILKSHAKES

Burning Bulb
PUBLISHING

BLOODLETTING: A TALE OF REVENGE BY ANDY RAUSCH

"Relentless… Addictive… The kind of nightmare you don't want
to wake up from."
—Heywood Gould, screenwriter of *Rolling Thunder*

He was just an average Joe. But when he finds his family held at
gunpoint by merciless thugs, he's told he must murder a Mafia
chieftain if he ever wishes to see his loved ones again.

Against all odds, Joe keeps his end of the bargain, but the criminals
don't. Now at his wits end, Joe is pushed beyond his breaking point
and forced to exact bloody revenge against those who've done him
and his family wrong in this powerful and violent novella by author
Andy Rausch (*Mad World*).

"Andy Rausch has a tight noir style that combines gritty, realistic drama
with a cinematic flair that makes for a powerful, compelling (somewhat
Stephen Kingesque), authentically visual reading experience."
—Stephen Spignesi, author of *Dialogues*

Burning Bulb
PUBLISHING

ELVIS PRESLEY, CIA ASSASSIN BY ANDY RAUSCH

"I can guarantee you. Read this book and you'll never look at Elvis the same way again!"
~ Douglas Brode, author of ELVIS CINEMA AND POPULAR CULTURE

SOON TO BE A MAJOR MOTION PICTURE

In 1970, singer Elvis Presley secretly met with President Richard Nixon. This new comedic novel imagines that Presley became a Central Intelligence Agency operative, eventually moving up through the ranks to become a skilled assassin.

Presented in an oral history fashion, the book tells us about Presley's secret transformation by the people who knew him best.

Did he fake his death in 1977? Was Presley involved with the Watergate scandal? The Iran hostage crisis? Communicating with aliens?

Read this book to find out the answers to these and many more questions.

Burning Bulb
PUBLISHING

MAD WORLD BY ANDY RAUSCH

"*Mad World* is dark, twisted, no-holds-barred fun."
—Jason Starr, author of *Bust, Slide,* and *The Max*

EVERYONE'S PLAYING AN ANGLE IN THE CITY OF ANGELS

Mad World tells the stories of a black hitman who doubles as a university professor, a Catholic priest who longs to be a gangster, a would-be author from Kansas, a gay phone sex operator who claims he's straight, a group of rich twentysomethings playing a deadly game of life and death, a vicious Mafia boss, and a sleazy Hollywood movie director. As each of their stories intersect, the body count piles up and the action comes nonstop in this tense, white-knuckle thriller by first-time author Andy Rausch.

"A wild ride. If you like it gangster, *Mad World* delivers."
—Daniel Birch, author of *Get Some*

Burning Bulb
PUBLISHING